OPENED

S. T. SANCHEZ

Edited by Courtney Johansson

ISBN
978-1-959872-09-2

The Pampered Cat Press

www.thepamperedcatpress.net

BOOKS BY S.T. SANCHEZ

The Keeper Archives Series: The Portal Keeper, The Secret of the Realms, The Keeper's Battalion
The Sunwalker Trilogy: Sunwalker, Nightwalker, Darkwalker

*To my favorite girls
Hadley, Payson, Kennedy, &
Aria
Thanks for your support!*

Sometimes only after passing through darkness can we appreciate the light.

I
CURSED

Most of the time fall is the best season for me. Allergy-wise. This must be the universe playing a joke on me. Today is picture day after all. Who doesn't want red, puffy eyes? I got my braces off over the summer and my acne cleared up. I have been looking forward to having a decent yearbook picture, but this is not going to be the year for it.

I glance up at the clock to see how much time I have to get to first period, but my vision starts to blur. The red digital numbers become unrecognizable. I see those little stars in my peripheral vision, the kind I see when I'm about to pass out. I pause and place my hand against a row of lockers, bracing myself, preparing for the dizziness to hit, but nothing happens.

My vision's getting worse. I turn to head back toward the nurse's office and smack into someone.

"Geez, Emma, watch where you're going," I hear a voice grumble. It sounds familiar; I think it may be my classmate, Dean. I hear him, but my vision is so bad at this point that I can't tell who anyone is—it's all shadows and blurs. I feel panic rising in me.

Uncertain of what to do, I flatten myself against the lockers and wait for the bell to ring. The hallway empties. When the bell dings, I slump to the floor. Tears well up, and I feel them start to slide down my cheeks.

First one, then two, then before I know it, a downpour. My vision now, if you can call it that, is gone. No more shadows. No more blurs. Just utter and complete darkness.

I put my face in my hands and sob openly.

"Are you alright?" I feel a hand touch my shoulder with care. I've heard this voice before but I can't place it. It's feminine. I think maybe she's a cheerleader. She's not in my grade. I know that. I know everyone in my class.

I sniff. I try to pull myself together, not lifting my face.

"I can't see," I bawl.

"Let me help you to the nurse," she suggests, putting her hand under my arm and helping me to my feet.

When I turn toward the direction of her voice, I see light. Not the white light at the end of the tunnel, not the lights in the school, but she is light. I see the silhouette of this girl. A bright beacon in the darkness. No features. It's like I'm seeing her shadow, only it's light instead of darkness.

"You're JJ's sister, right?" she inquires.

I just nod, not in the mood to strike up a conversation while my world is collapsing around me.

We walk down the hallway. I strain to see anything, but it's just black, except for her light shadow. I try to match a face to the voice, but I can't conjure up any image. Before I realize it, we are at the nurse's office.

I hear the girl knock and we wait a moment.

"Francesca, Emma, what can I do for you?" Nurse Hightower asks.

Francesca. That's who's helping me. I don't know her, but she is on the cheer squad. She's not the captain, but I think she's her assistant. Second in command. I don't know the cheer terminology. But at least now I know where I've heard her voice. At the pep rallies.

"I can't see," I say.

"Come in," Nurse Hightower says, "I'll take it from here. Thank you for your assistance," she says to Francesca.

I didn't realize the calming effect the cheerleader had on me until she leaves and I am thrown back into complete and utter darkness.

"Emma, come on in. Sit on the table. Did you get something in your eye?" the nurse questions.

"I can't see," I repeat, unwilling to move. "I can't see anything," I try to clarify. "I can't see you, the table, the lights. Everything is dark."

I hear her step closer.

"You don't see that?"

I have no idea what she is doing. Maybe she's waving her hand in front of my face. Maybe she's holding up fingers for me to count. For all I know, she could be riding on a pink pony in her swimsuit.

"No," I say flatly.

"Umm. Okay. Let's get you on the table and I'll get my light out and um, see what I can see."

Her tone does not inspire a lot of confidence. And for the first time, I wonder if this is how I am going to be for the rest of my life.

I feel her reach for me and I walk with my hand out, trying to feel for the table. It's awkward and frightening, not being able to see. Being dependent on someone else. Putting my trust in someone else.

I feel the table, making sure I am not about to climb up and fall off the edge. When I find what I think is the middle, I pull myself up and sit down, letting my legs dangle over.

"Ok, just stare forward. Try not to blink a lot," Nurse Hightower instructs me.

I stay still, not knowing if she is even doing anything. I hear her in front of me, so I know she is here. I try to keep my eyes open wide, hoping she can see something, but the pain is excruciating. My eyes feel like they are on fire.

She asks me to look to the right, to the left, up and down. I try to do as she requests, but it's a weird sensation. Without being able to see anything, I wonder if I'm even looking in the right direction.

I assume I am since I'm not asked to try again.

"Hmmm," the nurse says. "Well I'm not seeing anything, but I think we should call your mother and have her take you to an eye doctor. They have better equipment than I do and I am sure they'll be able to figure out what's going on."

She hands me something and as I'm feeling it, attempting to decipher what it is, she says, "Better call your mom," at the same time I'm realizing she handed me the phone. I feel the receiver and the cord in my hand.

"Can you dial the number for me?" I ask. Does she think I'm faking? How am I going to use a phone?

"Huh?" she says, before recovering quickly. "Of course."

I tell her the number and I can hear a tone for each digit as she presses it.

It rings several times before my mother picks up.

"Hello?" I hear her voice answer.

"Mom?"

"Emma, aren't you supposed to be in class?" she questions.

"I'm in the nurse's office. I need you to come get me."

"Are you sick? You were fine this morning, and I have a new recipe for bread that just went in the oven."

"I'm not sick. At least, I don't think I am," I say.

"Well then, why are you at the nurse's office? Are you hurt?"

"I can't see," I say.

"Emma, go to class and I'll call Dr. Zimmerman. We'll get you in for an appointment. But it won't happen today. You'll just have to make do with the glasses you have until I can get it scheduled. Just ask to sit in the front of the class for the next couple of days."

"Mom—" I begin. I forget how impatient Mom gets when she's trying out a new recipe. She hates to be interrupted.

"Emma, I have a lot going on today. I'm meeting with a new client in the morning and I need to wow him."

"Mom, I can't see anything," I say, exasperated.

"Emma, I know your eyes are bothering you. I'll work on getting you an appointment. But for now, please go back—"

"Mom!" I yell, trying to get her attention. "I think I'm going blind. This isn't an exaggeration. You're not listening. All I see is blackness. I couldn't walk to the nurse on my own. I couldn't even dial the number. My eyes feel like they're on fire. I can't see anything." My voice cracks. Tears are streaming down my face again.

"I'll be right there," my mom says, and I hear the line go dead.

I feel awkward and embarrassed sitting in Nurse Hightower's office, crying. I can't even see her but I'm sure she's staring at me.

I feel a tissue press into my hand.

"Thanks," I mumble as I blow my nose.

I am surprised at how fast my mom gets to the school. As she helps me to the car, I ask, "Did you get an appointment with Dr. Zimmerman?"

"I didn't call," she says as she helps me into a seat and buckles me in. I feel like an invalid. Will I have to go to a school for the blind? How long will it take to learn how to read braille? Do they have the same selection of books in braille? As frightening as not being able to see is, this might scare me even more. I love reading. How can I survive without books?

"Why didn't you call?" I demand, my tone accusatory. Here I am going blind and she can't even be bothered to call the eye doctor.

"Because he *is* going to see you. And we aren't waiting for an appointment. He will see you now, even if I have to kick someone out of the chair."

Wow, I am impressed. My mom can be a force to be reckoned with, but I only see this side of her when she wants my room clean. And for the record, she never has to ask me twice.

I clench my eyes together as a wave of pain sweeps over me. It is more intense than the burning. This feels like my eyes are being ripped apart. I grit my teeth, trying not to scream out in agony.

The car comes to a stop and I let out a slow deliberate breath, attempting to shift my focus to anything else.

The pain subsides and I almost relish the return of the constant burn.

"We're here," I hear my mom say. She already has my door open. I hadn't even noticed her get out of the car.

I let Mom lead me to a seat as she converses in hushed whispers. I assume she's talking with the receptionist.

My mother comes and sits by me. "He will see us in just a few minutes," she whispers.

I nod, keeping my eyes closed. I don't know if it helps or not, but I imagine the pain isn't quite as intense when they are closed.

In no time at all, I am ushered back. I sit as still as I can while Dr. Zimmerman does his work. I assume he uses lights to look in my eyes, but I have no idea. He asks me if I can see different things and has me move my eyes around like Nurse Hightower did. Then he puts drops in my eyes and makes me wait a while before checking them again.

He brings my mom inside the room once he's finished with his tests.

"I don't understand what's going on," the doctor says.

I feel my body tense. I press my hands against my legs, trying to stay still and strong for the words I know are coming.

"Emma's retinas have deteriorated. She's blind." I hear a sound, as if he has set something on the table. "I've never seen anything like this..."

I try to stay calm, but I can feel my eyes start to tear up again. Mom and the doctor keep talking, but I can't seem to concentrate.

Blind.

Blind.

Blind.

It's all I can focus on.

"I want to go home," I yell. I can't stand it anymore; I need to get out of here.

The doctor and my mom share a few more exchanges but all I can think about is getting out of this office.

I zone out on the ride home. Mom offers to make me lunch, but I just want to be alone.

I lay on my bed and sob. This is my life now. Void of light and color. Dependent on others for everything.

Will my eyes burn for the rest of my life? Is this what it's like for all blind people? It's not like I know anyone I could ask.

I think of Mom and the added stress this will put on her, not to mention the financial burden. I'm going to need special classes; I'll need to learn how to read braille and how to get around without my sight.

I hear the door slam shut and feet thudding on the stairs. It must be around four-thirty. JJ is home from school. I hear Mom call to him, but he bursts into my room.

I sit up on my bed and face the direction I believe the door to be in.

"Why are you home early? Faker. Just wanted to get out of picture day," he teases.

There's silence. I don't know how to tell my brother. He's my best friend, which might sound weird to some. But we've been through a lot together. Ever since his dad and my mom got married about seven years ago, we've been inseparable. We're the same age. He's a nerd, but a cool nerd.

His dad died last year. It has been difficult, but we found a new rhythm. I don't know how I can shatter his world again. Things will never be the same between us now.

"Hey, what's wrong?" he questions. I hear him move closer and sit beside me on the bed. "You've been crying." It's a statement, not a question. "Why won't you look at me?"

I thought I had all my crying out of my system, but the waterworks turn on again. I've never cried this much in my life.

"I can't," I bawl.

I try to tell him but it comes out as an incoherent jumble.

I hear my mom walk into the room.

"What's wrong with her, Mom?" he presses. "What happened?"

"We're not sure. It's her eyes, baby. She has gone blind."

I feel JJ tense. For once I'm glad I can't see. I can't see the sadness in his eyes. The pity.

"People don't just go blind for no reason," he argues. "Take her to the doctor. They've got to be able to do something," he insists.

"We already went."

He doesn't move for a moment, but then he wraps his arms around me. "It's gonna be okay." He tries to sound reassuring and confident, but I can hear the tears behind it.

"It will be okay," Mom echoes. "Dinner will be ready in about a half hour," she adds before I hear her leave.

We sit in silence for a while before JJ speaks.

"I'm sorry, Emma. I don't know what the right thing to say is. What can I do?"

I don't have an answer. What can anyone do? Nothing. I'm about to tell him some lie, like "you just being here helps," when exhaustion comes over me. Not just a tired feeling, but like I've never needed sleep more in my life.

"I think I just need to rest," I say, having a tough time managing the words.

He gets off the bed. "K, I'm here if you need anything."

I feel for my pillow and can barely get my head down fast enough before I am out.

II
HALLUCINATIONS

I feel like I got the best night's sleep ever. I've never felt this refreshed. My eyes aren't burning anymore. I'm kind of afraid to open them, as if the pain will return. Or once I open them, I'll be blind for good. It won't have just been a terrible dream.

I take my time as I open my eyes; it's black...but wait. Though my eyes are blurry, I see a mess of colors and light pouring into my room. I push myself up into a sitting position and blink a few times. I can see. Everything comes into focus a little at a time.

I examine the carpet and I'm disgusted at how dirty it is. I will be vacuuming after school. I look around my room and smile. Just a bad dream. I can't believe how vivid it was. I get out of bed and throw on some jeans and a t-shirt and head downstairs.

My stomach is rumbling. Mom's always making new and interesting breakfasts. She owns her own catering business. I don't even care what she made today. I feel famished.

I kerplunk down the stairs and slide into my chair. JJ is already in his seat across from me, and he freezes when he sees me. Food falls out of his mouth.

He starts coughing.

"Emma?"

Pancakes. Chocolate chip pancakes. My favorite. I pick up my fork and reach for the platter in the center of the table and start loading my plate.

"Bro, did you forget? You're supposed to chew with your mouth closed."

I turn to the kitchen to tell my mother thank you and she has a deer-in-the-headlights look too. She's ladling pancake mix onto the floor.

"Mom, what are you doing? You're spilling everywhere."

I jump up and get a rag and start wiping it up.

"You're o-okay?" Mom stutters.

I look up, confused. "Why wouldn't I be? I'm just hungry. Making sure the batter gets in the pan would be a fantastic start to remedying that," I tease.

"Emma, you can see? Why are you acting like this isn't a big deal?" Mom says, crying as she sets the bowl down and pulls me into an embrace.

"I thought I dreamt that. How can I be blind one day and see fine the next?" I ask, feeling more than a little stunned.

Mom kisses me on the cheek. "It's an answer to prayers. Other than that, I don't care why." She pulls me tighter, not wanting to let me go.

"Can you see just as well as before?" JJ inquires, pushing his chair out and walking around the counter to join our embrace.

Relief washes over me as I think about how close I came to losing so much that I had taken for granted. Action movie marathons with JJ, baking with mom, and my long Saturday morning runs had all almost been a thing of the past.

"I think so," I say, looking around.

"We should get your eyes looked at again, just to be safe," Mom notes as she releases me.

I shake my head. "No, please, I just want to go to school," I insist. "Besides, Dr. Zimmerman was wrong. He said my eyes had deteriorated and nothing could be done. I don't trust what he says now anyway."

Mom doesn't answer for a long minute. "Alright," she agrees. "But if your eyes get the least bit blurry or have any pain, you have to promise to call me immediately."

"I promise." I make an x motion over my heart with my finger. "It was just bad allergies, I'm sure. My eyes were burning and I dumped an entire vial of eye drops in them. I think I just had an adverse reaction."

I can tell my mother isn't certain she agrees with my assessment. "Just for today at least, JJ, I want you to drive."

On a normal day this would bother me. But today I don't care. We each have our own car. JJ's dad had a life insurance policy that made sure we wouldn't want for anything, as long as our tastes didn't become too extravagant. JJ stays after school for chess club three days a week and I wouldn't want to wait on a normal day. But I am looking at life with a new outlook today. The glass is more than half full after what I've just been through.

"Fine with me." I smile.

"Be ready to leave in fifteen minutes," JJ instructs.

"Twenty." I laugh, darting up the stairs before he can protest.

I don't have that much time, so I opt for a ponytail. Then I rush through my makeup and brush my teeth. I don't wear a lot of makeup so it's not too hard. Just some mascara to accentuate my dull blue eyes and a pinkish lip gloss.

My brown hair looks a little greasy, but I don't have time to shower. I spray a little extra body spray just to make sure I don't stink.

Then I rush downstairs. I've just taken two bites of my pancakes when JJ comes in.

"Come on, you're going to make me late. I have a tutoring session this morning."

I almost choke on my pancake.

"You need tutoring?" I cough and cover my mouth with a napkin to keep me from spewing food remnants at him.

"Nice," he says. "I'm tutoring someone. I'm number two in our class. Like I need help. You, on the other hand, could benefit. I charge twenty-five bucks an hour. Think about it." He smirks and heads out the front door.

I look at my plate. I'm starving, but I know JJ being the neat freak he is will not be able to handle me bringing a plate of pancakes lathered in butter and syrup in the car. I glance at my plate longingly, and then grab two more pancakes from the center of the table and rush outside.

"What do you think you're doing?" JJ asks, his eyes wide in astonishment.

"It's either this or I go back inside and grab my plate with the syrup." I raise an eyebrow and wink.

"Fine." He sighs. "But if I see crumbs, you're vacuuming my car the minute we get home."

I open the door and slide in his Honda Civic. I hate vacuuming, so I make a decent effort not to leave any evidence. I look around his car and am appalled. It's filthy.

"I'm not vacuuming this. It's a mess already," I exclaim.

The carpet is grimy. I can see hair and dirt and grass everywhere. There are greasy fingerprints on the doors, steering wheel, and radio. It looks like it has never been cleaned.

"Ha, ha," he says mockingly. "Nice try—my car is spotless."

I wait for him to laugh at his joke, but he looks serious, so I say nothing.

As we drive to school, I am amazed at what I see. I didn't have time to put my contacts in this morning and I haven't had a chance to dig through my bag to find my glasses, but I don't need them anymore. I can see everything. Signs are crystal clear.

We pull up to the school and JJ parks in his space and sprints to the building. He can't stand to be late. I, on the other hand, am a little more laid-back. What's five or ten minutes here or there. The school isn't quite as lax. In fact, they've started turning my tardies into detentions, but it hasn't helped me improve my promptness.

I have an hour to kill. I decide to head to the library. An enjoyable book is just the thing I need. I make my way to the young adult fiction section and start scanning the back of several novels. Ugh, fantasy. The appeal of books about vampires, werewolves, and the like are beyond me. I want a book that has a chance of happening.

I pick up a historical fiction book about World War II and find a chair in the back of the library. I'm just beginning chapter three when I hear voices.

"I hate it here," the girl, whose voice I recognize as Francesca, whispers.

"Me too, but we don't have a choice," says a male voice. "The winter solstice will be here in a couple months. There's nothing we can do but wait."

"But why do we have to do it here? I'm sick of sitting in algebra."

I set my book down and lean to the right, peering around an aisle of books. I see Francesca talking with a senior I've seen around.

He's good-looking to say it mildly. He has dark wavy hair, cut shorter on the sides and longer on the top, and brilliant turquoise blue eyes, more vibrant than any I've ever seen. I wonder if he has colored contacts in. His skin is a golden bronze color and his muscular build is accentuated by his tight-fitting t-shirt. I scan his face; he has sharp chiseled features. I follow the profile of his jaw up and stop when I get to his ear.

I lean forward; my eyes must be playing tricks on me. But I lean too far and tumble out of my chair and splay out on the floor.

Before I can get up, Francesca and her male companion are by my side.

"Eavesdrop much?" the gorgeous teen asks as he reaches his hand out to help me up.

I scoot back and don't reach up to take it. My eyes are glued to his ears that each end in distinct points.

"I came here first," I say, my voice hard as I push myself up. "And I can't help it if you're talking loud enough for me to hear."

He glares at me and opens his mouth to say something but Francesca steps forward.

"Glad to see you're feeling better." She smiles a wide grin, and then pushes her hair back behind her ear.

I almost fall over again but manage to somehow land in my chair. Her ears are pointy too.

"Forgive my brother," she adds. "He forgets his manners." She elbows him in the side. "Well, we'd better get to class. Nice seeing you again."

Nice gene pool, I think.

Although polar opposites, Francesca with her long blonde curls and green eyes, both look as if they just waltzed off the cover of some high-end fashion magazine or off of a runway in Milan.

As I watch them leave, my eyes widen even more. Two wings sprout from Francesca's brother's back. Is the drama club working on a new play? Halloween is still two weeks away. It seems a little early for costumes. He turns and catches me staring. We lock eyes and I can't seem to pull my gaze from his. He gives me an annoyed look and then turns back around. I don't know why but they both move gracefully and elegantly. I don't know how I never noticed it before.

I picture the wings in my head, trying to make a rational excuse for them. But I can't for the life of me think of any material that would have made them appear that translucent, yet at the same time, full of color. Like they are made up of hundreds of prisms.

I don't know how long I sit there lost in thought. The bell wakes me out of my stupor. Another tardy to add to my growing list. Mom will love this. How do I get to school an hour before it begins and still manage to be late to class? I can hear her already.

The first half of my day flies by in a blur. I couldn't recall anything about the movie we watched in science, or one new vocabulary word in Spanish.

I walk into the cafeteria and take my normal seat. I pull out my sack lunch, even though I have no appetite at the moment, and wait for the others to join me.

JJ and Brent arrive first.

"What did Mom make today?" Brent inquires.

That's his favorite question. He loves trying my mom's exotic meals and when they are too adventurous for me, we trade. Good ol' PB&J or turkey and cheese are fine for me anytime.

"Here," I say, shoving my bag towards him. "I'm not hungry."

"Awesome!" He pulls the bag open and removes a rectangular Tupperware. Brent's on the football team. He's not a big guy, but he's always hungry. He plays quarterback, but he's second string, so he doesn't get any star football treatment. His blond hair is looking a little scrufty. He has been trying to grow it out, but right now it's in that awkward in-between stage. He reminds me of a hedgehog, his hair poofing up in all directions.

Leaning forward, JJ whispers, "Are you okay?" He looks concerned. Not that I blame him after the last crazy twenty-four hours.

"Fine. Just ate too many pancakes," I lie.

Jenny and Izza are the last to arrive. Jenny always buys her lunch, and Izza keeps her company. Not surprising, a salad sits on her tray. She has been on a health kick for the past couple of weeks. No carbs, just veggies and a little bit of protein. Jenny is obsessed with making sure she looks great for prom. I wonder if she realizes that prom is still several months away.

"Emma, you missed pictures yesterday. I tried to text you but you didn't answer," Jenny says as she sits down beside me, pushing her red hair behind her shoulder.

"She was sick," JJ explains.

Jenny looks at me and then scoots a couple of feet down on the bench. Izza stares for a second, unsure of what to do, and after a moment sits across from us, next to Brent.

"I'm not contagious. It was just allergies," I clarify. But Jenny doesn't want to take the risk.

It doesn't surprise me when Brent's eyes go straight to Izza's lunch box. Izza's mother is from Mexico, and she always brings amazing food: tamales, pozole, gorditas, quesadillas, ceviche. It's not as experimental as my mom's cooking. I love going to eat at her house, although Izza warns me to stay away on menudo night. Tripe is something I avoid at all costs.

Burritos are on the menu today. I wonder how long Brent will last before asking her if she's going to eat them all.

Izza starts to ask Brent about his weekend, but I get distracted as I notice Francesca and her brother at another table.

"What's Francesca's brother's name?" I ask, interrupting their conversation.

"Why?" Jenny questions me. "He's a senior, and you're a sophomore. Not gonna happen."

I whip my head around. "What? No, I just saw him in the library today and I spoke to him but I didn't want to ask him his name."

"Dante," Brent says. "He's in my computer science class."

Not a bad name. It kind of fits him. He looks like a Dante. Not that I know any other Dantes. I've come across the name once before in my reading, Dante's Inferno. And he has the look down at least.

"What's up with the wings he's wearing? Is he in theater?"

The entire table turns to see what I am talking about.

I lower my head and use my hand to block his view from me.

"Geez!" I whisper yell. "Could you guys make it any more obvious?"

"What wings?" Jenny asks. "I don't see anything."

"Are they on the front of his shirt?" Izza questions.

"No, they're right there, on his back," I hiss, still looking at the table. "Would you guys turn around?"

"Maybe you should pull out your glasses?" JJ suggests.

"Maybe you're still sick," Brent offers.

As everyone turns back around and settles into their lunches, I risk a glance up. Dante turns and stares at me.

This time, with some effort, I look away. Maybe I should go back to the eye doctor. Something is wrong with my eyes. First, they itch and burn for a few days, growing so intense I can't bear it. Then I go blind. Now I can see again, but I'm seeing things others don't see. Am I hallucinating? Is this just a long, crazy drawn-out dream?

The rest of the day I do my best to try to focus. In Algebra II we start a new unit. I take detailed notes, trying to stay attentive. Art is interesting. We are a few days into our unit on clay and it's my turn to try to spin a bowl. Let's just say it's not as easy as it sounds. At the end I have a heap of wet clay.

It is a gorgeous day. The sun is out and it's in the seventies. I sit on the front steps of the school, intent on reading my book and getting some sun while I wait for JJ.

Students stroll past in herds, eager to get to their cars and enjoy the afternoon before we have to repeat this again tomorrow.

Within ten minutes, the school is practically a graveyard. I am immersed in a firefight between Germany and the British when I see something out of the corner of my eye.

Dante.

He's about a half a block away, but I can see him as clear as if he were standing right in front of me. He glances around and then unfolds his wings. Each wing is at least six feet long and several feet across. They are beautiful and sparkle in the sunlight.

He compresses them back down and turns down an alley.

I still can't believe what I am seeing. And although my mind is telling me not to, my curiosity is outweighing my sensibility.

I stuff my book in my bag and sling my backpack over both shoulders before heading in his direction. As I hurry after him, I pull out my phone and text my brother.

Decided to walk. May be home late. Enjoying the sun.

When I get to the alley, I peer down it, but Dante is nowhere in sight. Everything is telling me to turn around and go back. I have a pit in my stomach, the little hairs on the back of my neck are standing up, and I feel like any moment now something horrible is going to happen. I should turn and run, except I can't. I must know. There has to be some rational explanation for what I'm seeing.

I start down the alley with slow, quiet steps, glancing between each house, wondering where he could have gone. I start to feel silly after a few houses. If he has actual wings maybe he flew away. Who do I think I am anyway, 007?

I'm about to turn around when I hear something behind me. I spin around and jerk back when I see Dante there.

"What are you doing?" he demands. "What's your problem? First you listen in on a private conversation, then you stare at me all day, and now you follow me!" He raises his voice, and the muscles in his neck tense.

I step back. A shiver runs down my spine and fear washes over me.

I look at him and wonder if I've made a huge mistake. There is something feral in his eyes. And the more I look at him, the more dangerous he looks. He's at least six inches taller than me, and his entire body is muscle. I can see the outline of his six pack through his fitted black t shirt.

He seems to be able to sense my fear because he takes a step back, then a deep breath. "Look, I'm not going to hurt you. But tell me, why are you following me?"

I am mesmerized by his beauty when he's not sending death stares at me. His voice is even velvety now that he's not yelling.

"Look, I know you've been watching me all day. Emma, right? I just want you to know nothing is going to happen with us. You're too young."

He sounds disgusted by the fact. We can't be more than a year or two apart; that's not that much. I shake my head. As handsome as he is, that has nothing to do with why I had been staring at him...well, almost nothing to do with it.

I regain some of my composure as I hear what I take to be an insult.

"Aren't you cocky," I say. "Wow, someone looks at you, and you think you're God's gift to women."

He laughs in earnest.

"Listen," he says, raising his eyebrows. "Darling, if you *looked* any harder, you'd burn a hole through me."

I feel my cheeks flush, and I jerk away, trying to regain my composure.

"I followed you," I admit. "But not because you're handsome."

He smiles at this, flashing his pearly whites in a blinding grin.

"I know this is going to sound crazy, and I know it's none of my business, but I just have to ask you one question." I look him straight in the eyes, trying to not be intimidated by his looks or confidence.

"Fine." He shrugs. "Ask me your question and then leave me alone."

"What's with the ears and the wings?" I inquire quickly, my words slurring together. Tomorrow I'll be known as that crazy Hawkins girl.

His eyes widen and his face pales for a split second but I see it.

"I beg your pardon?" Dante asks. "You spoke fast; I must have misheard you."

I take a deep breath and square my shoulders. I already look like a lunatic—I might as well make sure he never doubts it.

"Your ears, they're pointy." I lean closer. "And you have wings..." I reach forward, almost touching them. "And they don't appear fake. They look more real to me than anything I've ever seen." Just as my fingers are about to brush against them, he slams me up against the fence.

"Hey!" I cry out.

He shoves up against me hard, his arm under my neck. He's applying too much pressure; I can't breathe and I struggle to fight against it.

"Listen up, Emma," he hisses and says my name with so much disdain I'd have run for it if I could have moved. "Don't ever mention this again. Not to me. Not to anyone."

I'm choking. I try to nod. Tears are welling up in my eyes.

"If I even see you glance my way again, things will end badly." He pushes me one more time for good measure and then releases me.

I crumple to the ground, coughing and gasping for air. When I peer up, I'm alone. Dante has vanished.

I wrap my head around our conversation. He didn't deny anything. Could his wings be real? What if there is no rational explanation to what I've been seeing except that it's reality?

And if the wings and ears are real, why have I never noticed them before? Why can no one else see them? And what is he? An angel? Or from his temperament, maybe a demon? I watched all those *Lord of the Rings* movies. Could elves be real?

One thing is for sure. Dante doesn't need to worry; I have no desire to ever see him again.

III
BIZARRE

The next morning, Mom lets me drive myself to school. I pull up just a few minutes before the bell. I glance around, hoping not to run into any psycho mythical creatures. When I don't see any sign of Dante, I get out of my vehicle and head straight to class.

As I enter the school, I see Dante standing in the hallway talking to a teacher. He glimpses my way, his face expressionless, and I turn and go the other direction. I don't care that it's longer, it's better than the alternative.

I make it to lunch without seeing him again. I'm about to sit down in my usual spot when I hear my name being called.

I turn and I am shocked to see Francesca waving me over. I don't move. Why is she calling me over? Why is she even talking to me? We run in completely opposite circles.

Her incessant waving and smiling make me relent. Dante isn't here yet. Maybe if I hurry, I can see what she wants and be back before her brother arrives to the cafeteria.

I try not to stare at her ears as I approach. Why doesn't she have wings like her brother? What are they?

"Emma." She smiles. "Sit with me today."

My eyes widen. Is she crazy? Does she not know that her brother almost killed me yesterday and threatened to finish the job should I even breathe in his direction?

"Um, I sit with my brother," I say lamely, trying to find any excuse to get away.

"Come now, he can survive a lunch without you." She waves at someone over my shoulder and I turn to see her smiling at JJ.

"My brother's not at lunch today. He left early. I thought this would be a great chance for us to get to know each other better."

Why? I wonder.

I relax a little, now that I know Dante isn't going to appear out of nowhere.

I sit down and Francesca beams like we are best friends.

I feel out of place next to her with my greasy hair pulled up into a ponytail, wearing jeans and a t-shirt, while she has beautiful bouncing curls, perfect complexion, and is wearing a cute white off-the-shoulder blouse (that I'd never dream of wearing) and a black pencil skirt.

"You know," she says, sitting beside me, "the other day when I walked you to the nurse, I thought, 'I don't know Emma that well.' Here we are." She giggles. "What do you enjoy doing, Emma? I see you with your stepbrother often. Do you guys do a lot together?"

I open my backpack and pull out my lunch.

"Brother," I correct her. We are family. We love each other, we are there for each other. Blood doesn't define family. I hate the term step. We've never used it.

She gives me a confused look so I just let it go.

"Yeah, I guess," I continue, trying to answer her question. "We're close. Like you and Dante—you guys are together most of the time."

She shakes her head.

"Dante is the overprotective brother who takes his job way too seriously. He never lets me have any fun." She turns and looks at JJ. "I bet your brother is different."

"I guess," I say, uncertain of what she wants to hear from me. "I mean, we enjoy each other's company. We like the same movies and have the same friends."

I open the Tupperware my mom packed and just about gag. She made escargot for my lunch. I don't even think Brent would touch this. Francesca doesn't have a lunch at all, just a Styrofoam cup that I imagine has some fancy latte in it.

She turns back to me, the epitome of attentive. It's a little creepy the way her eyes bore into me. Her eyes are like Dante's, deep and endless, except where his are blue, hers are green. They don't look human; there's something wild about them. I don't know why, but I'm getting this vibe. She is a lot more pleasant than her brother.

"Movies. I love movies. We should have a movie night!" Francesca claps her hands together excitedly. "At my house. You can bring your brother. And we can all hang out."

The idea of going to her house sends a cold wave through my body. But she's excited. Maybe Dante doesn't let her have any friends. He seems the controlling type.

"Will your brother be there?" I inquire as I shut the Tupperware and pull out the tangerine she packed. At least there's something edible.

She eyes me as if we are sharing a secret. "Ah," she says, then straightens her face, "no, he works on the weekends."

For some reason, picturing Dante working is incomprehensible. I can't imagine him doing something as mundane as making burgers or working in a retail store.

"Look at the time," she says as her eyes flick up to the clock. "I have to go to my locker before class starts. See you Saturday night, my house. I'll text you the address." She starts to leave and then looks back over her shoulder and adds, "Don't forget to bring your brother."

Funny, I don't remember ever agreeing to movie night, nor did we exchange phone numbers. Even if Dante weren't there, if he found out that I hung out with his sister, it wouldn't sit well. The entire encounter was bizarre to say the least.

There's still ten minutes until lunch ends, so I grab my half-peeled tangerine and return to my normal table. I'm greeted with four sets of curious eyes.

When I don't say anything, Jenny is the first to speak up.

"Well, what was that all about?" she asks. "Cheerleaders don't give us the time of day."

"Umm." I shrug. "I'm not sure. She invited me over to her house, I think. JJ too. She wants to do a movie night."

Apparently, I'm not alone in thinking my conversation and "lunch" with Francesca was odd.

Izza leans forward. "Well, when you become popular, don't forget about us little people."

"We're not going to go," I say. "She didn't even get my number. I don't even know where she lives."

"Oh, we're going," JJ counters. "Francesca is hot, if you hadn't noticed."

Brent lifts his hand up to give JJ a high five. "She's a 15."

JJ gives him a half-hearted high five.

"You guys are disgusting. Numbering us." I shake my head in revulsion.

"Hey, that's not the only reason," he explains. "She's in a few of my classes and believe it or not, Francesca is pretty smart."

JJ is in a couple of junior classes and even a senior class. He has the brains in our family, although I start to doubt them now that he is acting like a neanderthal.

"Yeah sure, you have a crush on her brain," Jenny teases, rolling her eyes.

"There has to be some attraction too. I'm just saying, she might just have it all. And she invited me too. Maybe there's reciprocation going on."

"I think she just has brother issues, and wishes she had the kind of relationship we have," I say.

"We'll see who's right this weekend," JJ insists.

"Sure, if I somehow get a text with the time and address, we'll go. But I find the chances of that happening slim to none since she forgot to get my number." I smirk.

"Promise," he asks.

I notice a sandwich in front of him. "Fine," I promise, before adding "if you give me your PB&J." He slides it towards me. "How did you get this anyway?" I ask before taking my first glorious bite.

"I saw Mom cooking this morning and figured I'd better pack a backup lunch."

"Smart," I concede.

The rest of the school day is pleasant. I hadn't realized how tense I had been until Francesca told me Dante left school early. I feel free. It is nice, until I wonder if I'll feel tense and stressed every other day for the rest of the school year. At least Dante is a senior. He'll be graduating soon.

I have never considered JJ annoying until this evening. Every five minutes he comes in and interrogates me, wondering if Francesca has texted yet, when do I think she'll text me, and what movie we'll watch.

The fifth time he asks, I throw my pillow at him and get up and lock my door.

"She doesn't even have my number." I remind him as I yell at him through the door.

I turn my lights off and put in my AirPods. Maybe if he thinks I am asleep I can get a break from his incessant pestering. I log into Netflix on my phone and scroll through the top picks. I choose an old musical, not in the mood for anything scary after the week I've had.

I fall asleep sometime after midnight.

Light creeps through my window as the sun peeks over the horizon. I pick up my phone, still half asleep, to glance at the time. I have a new text message. It's from a number not in my contacts and I cringe. It can't be Francesca, right? Maybe it's another dumb car warranty message.

I dread reading the text, but I promised JJ. I take a deep breath and swipe.

    Hey Emma! So excited about our movie night tonight.

    2354 Nightcourt Lane
    8pm
    Chesa

Chesa? Am I supposed to call her that now? I wonder how she got my number. JJ is going to be thrilled. After tonight, I am going to have to find some excuse not to hang out with her anymore. Maybe I'll get a job. Anything to avoid Dante finding out that I hung out with his sister. And what about JJ? If Francesca's brother is such a psycho, could she be too? She has been so nice, but even if she's not a psycho, is it safe for JJ to hang out with her? Probably not with her brother lurking around.

It's still early, but I don't ever sleep this long. On Saturday mornings, I'm up on the trail before the sun shows its face. But the last few days I've been exhausted. I don't know if it's the blindness or something else, but the past two nights I've slept better than I ever have.

I spray on some deodorant and throw on a pair of turquoise running shorts with a matching t-shirt. I lace up shoes and slide my phone in the arm band, cranking up my running jam.

Mom is in the kitchen as I jog down the stairs. I don't have to wonder where my early bird side comes from. I give her a wave, but she is too preoccupied to notice. Whatever she is experimenting with today does not smell appetizing, and I don't think the black smoke trailing out of the oven is part of the recipe.

I have a couple of runs that I alternate through on Saturdays. I feel like I need to clear my head. I decide to run the longer one, up around the gorge and then down through Turtle Creek. It's about ten miles all together.

I run the couple of blocks through our neighborhood and enter the trail. There are tall pine trees all around me. The smell is amazing. I don't think I'll ever take it for granted. When I was younger, we lived in Chicago. A big city, lots of traffic, pollution. But I love living here in a small town. There's a bigger metropolis about forty-five minutes south of here, so we don't do without anything. But really, I could do without it all as long as I had this.

The trail is long and shaded. It has just the right number of inclines to make it challenging enough without killing me. The first couple of miles wind through a thick pine forest which then opens to a six-mile loop around a gorge. It's not nearly as big as the Grand Canyon, but it's just as breathtaking to me. Then it slopes back downhill and the last two miles crisscross back and forth over cute wooden bridges that connect the two sides of Turtle Creek. I love that most days I can run without seeing another person. It's my own personal oasis.

Just as I crest the top of the gorge, I see movement off to the side of the trail. I turn to glance in that direction and see Dante standing at the very edge of a cliff. There's no question it's him. His muscles gleam under the rays of the sun as his wings glimmer, stretched out wide and beautiful. They're almost translucent, but they have a hint of color. Every color. I'm so caught off guard that I don't see a root. My foot catches and I start to fall. I throw my hands out to brace myself but still I fall hard. There are a few rocks on this trail and one cuts into my knee while another one scrapes across my hand.

I try to scramble to my feet. My hand stings but the pain in my knee is worse. I look up and see Dante walking towards me.

I stagger back, gasping in pain, a rock wall barring my path.

"I wasn't following you," I say with as much grit as I can muster. "I run this path on Saturdays," I add.

He continues stalking towards me. It's a little unnerving to see him walking shirtless, in just a pair of khaki pants. His graceful strides bringing him ever closer.

"Well, not every Saturday, but at least once or twice a month," I blurt out, trying to think of anything to say to convince him that I'm telling the truth.

"You're hurt," he replies, catching me off guard. He doesn't look as angry as he did the other afternoon. His face is more neutral.

"It's nothing. I'm fine," I assure him.

"I've seen you here before," he admits. Now just a foot or two separate us. My heart beats like a drum in my chest; he must be able to hear it. "You're the only human that ventures this far up the gorge on a Saturday morning. But most weekends you've already passed this area by this time." He stares at me expectantly, waiting for an explanation.

He knows my schedule. I'm not sure how I feel about that revelation. "I overslept," I say. "If I'd known you were here, I'd have run a different route."

He nods approvingly. "It's not good for you to be around us."

"What are you?" I demand. The question comes out of my mouth before I have time to think. I brace myself for his wrath.

"Nothing you need to concern yourself with," he answers.

Blood is dripping down my leg. I take a step forward and wobble. "Well, I'll leave you to it," I say, but as I take the next step, my knee gives out and I collapse. Before I realize what happened, I am in Dante's arms.

I freeze. I don't even breathe, uncertain of what might set him off.

"You'll never make it home like this." He sighs and runs a hand through his dark waves, holding me up with his other hand. He is strong but still gentle with his grip. "Well, I guess there's just one thing to be done."

I tense and close my eyes. This is it. I wait for my life to flash before my eyes, but nothing happens. Then I feel him kneel beside me.

"Since you've already seen the real me, I guess this won't matter too much." He waves his hand over my knee. Faster than a heartbeat, the pain stops, and my injured knee is healed.

I take a tentative step and am stunned when I can put pressure on it. I rub my hand that's stinging from where I landed on it and he looks up.

"Here." He reaches for my hand and turns it over in his, then he waves his other hand over my injury and it heals too.

"Thank you," I say. I don't understand what's happening. Does Dante have an evil twin? Because this is not the Dante I encountered in the alley.

He shrugs as if healing me is nothing. "Same rules apply. Don't mention this to anyone." He glares at me, the feral beast returning.

I nod, but for some reason, I'm not as terrified as I should be. If he wanted me dead, he could have just killed me, right? Thrown me down into the gorge. It would be easy. No one would expect foul play. They would just think I tripped getting too close to the edge.

I watch as he turns and sprints towards the cliff. I gasp as he jumps off.

"Dante!" I yell, running forward, but before I can reach the edge, he soars upwards, gives me a parting look, and then flies away.

I sit for a while, trying to catch my breath and take in all that has happened. Once I can breathe again and I'm not feeling as shaken I begin my run home. It takes a lot longer than normal. I can't get my mind off Francesca's brother and his Jekyll-Hyde mood swings.

By the time I get home, the smoke has cleared from the kitchen, leaving a burnt smell in the air. JJ's at the table eating a bowl of cereal.

He looks up and tries to finish chewing the food in his mouth as fast as he can.

Before he can finish, I shrug. "You win," is all I say as I head to my room to shower.

It feels good to be clean again, my hair washed, no longer greasy.

For a second, I think about what I should wear tonight. Think about Dante. But then I remember he's working tonight. It's for the best anyway. I don't know why I'm drawn to him. I should have my head examined. Threatening my life one minute, healing me the next. It has all the makings for the perfect red-flag relationship that psychiatrists would have a field day examining.

I wrap my hair in a towel and sit on my bed, pulling my laptop from off the nightstand. I type "mythical, healing, winged creature" into my search engine.

I sigh as I scroll through the results. I don't know what I expected. But images of unicorns, dragons, and griffins was not it.

I swap creature for humanoid and still get nothing. Isn't the internet supposed to be the end-all when it comes to finding information?

Maybe if I give it less information. Human creature with wings. Of course, Chesa doesn't have wings but I've got to put in something.

At last, a list that sounds plausible. I laugh out loud. Two weeks ago, if I had seen a list like this and someone told me it was plausible, I'd have had them institutionalized. I make a mental note to myself to not share these insane theories with anyone and to delete my internet search history.

I don't live with a family of snoopers, but it's better to be safe than sorry. I don't need anyone to start questioning my sanity. I'm not sure that I could pass those tests right now.

Mothmen

Um, eww. Those just sound gross and the image looks nothing like Dante. I cross it off the realm of possibilities.

Seraphim

I don't know what those are. I look it up, and after reading the definition I don't understand how they differ from the next suggestion on the list, other than the number of wings, so I skip it. Dante definitely does not have six wings.

Angels

These sound the most realistic thus far. I mean, Dante has wings. But he does not have an angelic disposition. Then I pause for a moment. Can there be angels from the other direction too? Because that might fit a little better. Then again, wouldn't that fall under demon?

Valkyries

Not sure about these, although the name strikes a chord somewhere in the back of my memory. I search for specifics about these creatures. Female. Well, that knocks Dante out of the running. Then I remember why they sound familiar. The Avengers.

Elves

It doesn't pull up on my list, but with the pointy ears, I think I have to add them. I'm not sure about the wings though. Do elves have wings? I think back to stories with elves. The elves and the shoemaker...no wings. My mind goes blank and I can't for the life of me remember any other stories with elves. So, I keep it on the list.

Fairies

Like Tinker Bell? They are a little big to be fairies. But fairies do have pointy ears, I think...and wings. I can't believe I am debating this.

At the end I am left with three possibilities: angels, elves, or fairies. I can't envision an angel with pointy ears. I cross that off.

Elves or fairies. I'm leaning towards elves, but I'm not certain. I decide to get some advice from the fantasy expert. I go downstairs to find JJ.

He's done eating and I don't see him anywhere. I trounce back upstairs and knock on his door.

"Enter," he calls.

He's in his bathroom. He has on a pair of gray sweats and shaving cream all over his face.

He lifts his chin as he scrapes the razor down his cheek.

"Did you need something?"

"I was wondering…" I say, not sure how to ask without drawing suspicion. Fantasy is not my thing.

"Yes?" he asks.

"Well, I heard two guys arguing in the library and you know I'm not much into fantasy…I just thought I'd pick your brain." I hear the nervousness in my voice. And I wonder if I'm even making sense. My excuse sounds lame even to me.

JJ brings the razor to his chin, making slow deliberate movements.

"They were arguing about which one is better: an elf or a fairy."

My brother freezes, puts down his razor, and looks at me like I'm the creature from the black lagoon.

"You want to know which is better?" He turns around and looks behind him, then steps into his room and opens the closet door.

"What are you doing?" I inquire.

Stopping, he points to himself. "Me?" he questions. "Why, I'm looking for the hidden camera. This must be for some TV show, right?"

"Ha. Ha," I say. "I don't want to know which one's better. I mean, they're fictional. Who cares?"

He picks up a towel off the counter and wipes the remnants of shaving cream off his face.

"Then what are you asking me?"

"I just wondered what the difference is." I shrug, attempting to act nonchalant. "I mean, just so I have a basic understanding, should the need arise…" I have no idea what I'm saying.

"Like you're in a life-or-death situation and to save the world you have to guess what creature is standing in front of you?" he teases, then laughs and throws the towel at me.

I'm about to leave or go die of embarrassment when JJ decides to be serious.

"I don't know exactly. It's fiction, and each story is a little different. I think elves are immortal. Skilled at fighting. May or may not have magic.

Fairies can fly. They definitely have magic. I'm not sure about the immortality. I guess it kind of depends on if you're thinking Cinderella fairies—"

"Sleeping Beauty," I correct.

He just shrugs. "Sleeping Beauty or the kind that come from the Fey."

I lift an eyebrow, "What's the Fey?"

He sighs. "The fairy realm, where fiercer fairies and creatures dwell. The kind that would make Sleeping Beauty want to stay asleep."

The bed starts to vibrate and JJ reaches for his phone. "Oh man, I gotta get dressed. Me and Brent are going shopping. I need a wicked new shirt for tonight."

I give him a mock salute. "Thanks."

The Fey. Just thinking the word fills me with mystery and dread. Could another realm exist? Fierce could fit Dante.

I go back to my room and lay down on my bed. I've got to stop thinking about this or I'm going to go crazy. How will I ever know if I'm correct anyway? I close my eyes and the image of Dante haunts me until I drift asleep.

I'm in a grassy courtyard. There are shadows scattered throughout the area. It's hazy out, and I can't see that far in front of me. The fog has a pinkish tint. I step towards a shadow and realize that it's a stone sculpture.

The image is of a warrior wielding a sword in one hand and a shield in the other. The details are exquisite and I notice the man has pointed ears like Dante. I move towards another shadow but as I step, I am no longer on grass. I look at the ground and see a stone path. I look to the right and then to the left, unsure which direction I should take. But then I see the haze almost part and at the end of one of the paths is a palace. It's gray and tall and bigger than any building I've ever seen. There are several spires that skyrocket up towards the heavens, each one containing a flag of a distinct color. The palace seems to be beckoning me forward. But in the back of my mind I can hear Dante's voice, furious and filled with rage.

"Get out of here!" he screams. "Go, before it's too late!"

I hear a trumpet sound and voices calling, searching for someone. I hear animals howl and something or someone is fast approaching. I scan the area, frozen, in terror. I have no idea which direction I should run.

Something hot grabs my arm, burns it.

I shoot up in bed. My heart's pounding, sweat is dripping down my face. My shirt is plastered to my skin. My breathing is ragged and rushed. And even though I had been asleep, I feel physically and emotionally drained.

I try to tell myself it was just a dream. I need to calm down. I just worked myself up reading about all those mythical creatures. JJ's comments didn't help either.

I look at the digital clock on my bedside table and can't believe it's already seven-thirty.

"Ems," I hear JJ call. "Be ready to leave in ten. I'm driving."

I go into my bathroom and splash water on my face. My skin is a splotchy red-and-white mess. So much for looking nice.

I pull out a nicer blouse from my closet and throw my sweat-soaked t-shirt into the hamper. As I start to slide my arm into a sleeve, I see a red mark on my arm. I prod it with my finger and it stings. I can make out what looks like the imprint of fingers that wrap around my bicep. I hear JJ calling me again. I can't process this right now. I put the blouse on, taking extra care, being cautious not to scrape it across the mark. Then I spritz on a gallon of my body spray and reapply deodorant. I have just enough time to brush my teeth and drag a brush through my hair before JJ is knocking.

"Let's go. I don't want to be late."

I open the door and his mouth drops. He is gawking at me. "You look...nice," he finishes lamely.

"Shut up," I retort. "Let's just get this night over with."

I know I'm a mess. JJ, on the other hand, looks great. He has on his favorite jeans and I can tell his shirt is new. It's a vibrant green with some band's name plastered on it. They are uber popular right now but I don't keep up with that. JJ loads most of the music on my phone. He knows what I like. I just don't know who sings anything.

He keeps his dark hair short, almost buzzed, and he has on his glasses. They're black and a little thick-rimmed. But they look good on him. That's one reason I call him the cool nerd. Not everyone can pull off glasses. His brown eyes are the same chocolate shade as his skin. He's gone a little heavy on the cologne. Hopefully it will have time to fade before we arrive.

We pull up to Francesca's at seven fifty-eight.

JJ reaches into a compartment in his door and pulls out a Listerine square. He chews it up and swishes it in his mouth before swallowing. Then he offers me one. I decline.

"Obvious much?" I say.

"What? I just don't want to be the guy with the bad breath."

Dante and Francesca's residence is enough to make me stop dead in my tracks. I gaze in awe at this home that seems more fit for a story book.

The outside of the house is made of a polished white stone with granite columns lining the front. I can see three levels. Two large balconies overlook the front of the house, both covered in bright flowers cascading down the front of the rails.

Two marble griffins guard the entrance. I stifle a laugh. Earlier today I wouldn't have even known what a griffin looked like.

We approach a large metal door with a design etched into its surface. I raise my hand to touch one of the markings when the door opens with a loud creaking sound and Francesca pops out from behind. "Welcome." She flourishes her arm and invites us in.

"I hope you guys like horror movies. I thought with Halloween just over a week away, we'd do a themed movie night."

I'm not in the mood for horror. I still feel a little off after my nightmare.

"Great," JJ says, pulling out a bouquet of flowers he had hidden behind his back. I hadn't even noticed them. "These are just a thank you for inviting us over." He smiles an easy smile. "From both of us," he adds.

We step into the foyer and face a grand staircase. It's marble with creatures carved into each spindle. Many I don't recognize. The staircase ascends for a dozen steps and then splits off into two separate staircases.

The residence is much larger on the inside than it appears on the outside. Looking up, I see more levels inside.

I'm about to comment on the staircase when Francesca says, "If you'll follow me."

She leads us to a private media room. There are two white leather couches, each on a separate level. Each seat reclines. I take a seat on the back couch, but JJ motions for me to move to the other one.

Even though I don't know why he cares where I sit, I move.

JJ sits where I sat and I glare at him. He just winks at me.

"JJ, do you mind if I sit with you?" Francesca inquires in an innocent voice. "Sometimes these movies can be too much for me, but it helps if I'm sitting by someone strong." She caresses his muscle. "You must work out a lot."

I turn, looking for a barf bag. I can imagine JJ's face is as red as a strawberry. He isn't used to this kind of flattery. Heck, I'm not used to it. She might as well just plant one on him now for how subtle she's being.

"Of course," he says and scoots over to make room for her.

We're halfway through the first movie when the lights flick on.

"Chessy, are you in here?"

I try to squeeze myself into the back of the chair as I hear Dante's voice. Maybe he won't see me.

"Who are you?" he demands. "Chesa, what are you doing?"

I hear JJ stand. "I'm JJ. We were just—"

"I know what you were doing," he spits the words. "I think it's time you leave."

"Dante, stop being so dramatic. It was just a kiss." I can hear Francesca yawn. "What are you doing home anyway?" she asks. "I thought you had a shift."

I peer between the tops of the cushions. Watching him, praying he won't notice me.

"Some drunk hit an electrical box. The entire block lost power so they sent us home."

"Well, take a load off. Why don't you just come enjoy the movie?" Francesca offers. "I mean, I did invite them over to atone for your rude behavior."

"Them?" he questions, locking eyes with me right then.

"Yes, remember how rude you were to Emma? Now's the perfect opportunity to make it up to her."

For a moment I think he's going to debate her. But then his expression changes. "You know what, you're right," he agrees.

"Of course I am." Chesa nods to herself.

"But I've been stuck inside all night. Emma, how would you like to get some fresh air?"

Honestly, I didn't know what I wanted. Who would I be walking with, Dr. Jekyll or Mr. Hyde? I must have taken too long debating in my head how to answer because JJ speaks up.

"She'd love to. Right, sis?"

The feral look returns to Dante's eyes. "Perfect," he purrs, offering me his arm when I stand.

I glance back at JJ and Francesca, who make no pretense of returning to the movie. I wonder how long it will take before my brother notices I never came back.

IV
WARNINGS

We wander down a long white hallway. There are several doors on each wall, each of them closed. The walls are bare, no photographs or paintings, just blank space. An unusual-looking door lies at the end of the corridor. It's not a typical rectangular frame—instead it's curved at the top. It is also alive. Not alive in the sense that it can move and talk, but it's made up of green vibrant living vines and branches with bright purple flowers sprouting out of it. I open my mouth to ask him about it, but he holds a finger up to his lips, silencing me.

"Not here," he whispers.

He places his hand on the door and pushes it open. The backyard is breathtaking. It's like I'm stepping into another world. For all I know I am, if the Fey is an actual place. Floating globes of pinks, purples, and oranges light the garden. It looks wild and tame all at the same time. Some of the plants move, and not because of a breeze. Fireflies flit between bushes. The aroma is amazing, and I can imagine exploring here for hours and I still wouldn't see every species of plant. A shimmering path leads through the garden. It's like a million baby stars have come down to earth just to make this walkway.

Dante wordlessly takes my arm and maneuvers me back through a canopy of exotic brightly colored vine flowers. There's a bench in a tucked-away corner of the garden, looking much like the door we entered through.

He gestures for me to take a seat.

I feel a little more at ease now, sitting in these beautiful surroundings. I don't know why, maybe I'm just being naive, but I don't think he'd kill me somewhere this utopian.

Dante turns to me and his eyes take on an animal likeness. They don't look wild and savage as I've seen them before. Instead, they glow out here in the darkness. Like they've changed to night mode or something.

"I didn't know how to say no to your sister," I say. "She seems like she's used to getting her way."

He laughs. "You have no idea. And she has her sights set on your brother."

"Is she dangerous?" I press, then add, "Like you?" I swallow hard, waiting.

I swear his eyes flash with sadness but when he looks at me, they turn serious.

"Yes," he says, taking a seat on the bench beside me, "and no."

I wait for him to expound but he doesn't.

His eyes bore into me so intently that I swear he can see into me, see my every desire, every secret, every fault. It's unnerving. I shudder.

"I tried to keep you away from us." He sighs, his eyes looking tired and defeated. "Just remember that."

Riddles. He must like talking in riddles. I have too many questions, but he wouldn't answer any at our last encounter. I debate trying again, but then I decide against it. He's acting more like Dr. Jekyll for the moment. I don't want to risk bringing out Mr. Hyde.

"I need to tell you some things. Things I didn't want to. But now that Chesa has her eyes fixated on your brother, I don't feel like I have a choice."

I look in the direction of the house. "Is JJ safe with her?" I question.

"Yes and—"

Anger swells inside me and I stand up and face him.

"Look, this isn't a game to me. You can do what you want to me but leave JJ alone."

He tries but fails to stifle his smile.

"You're brave," he says. "Or stupid."

I turn to leave, but he grips my wrist. It's like a vice. A gentle one, but I can't budge his hold.

"I forget how impatient and rash humans are. I try not to spend too much time with them. Forgive me."

He releases me and motions back to the bench. I take a seat.

He's standing now, hovering over me, his dark hair taking on an iridescent quality in the shadows.

"Yes, physically, your brother is safe with Chessy. But she'll become bored with him and emotionally, well, I can't say. How does JJ fend after getting his heart broken?"

"Maybe she likes him. Francesca is at least nice," I say. It's not like she has tried to kill me.

"Listen up mortal, Francesca may be *nice*, but remember this. She is selfish. She thinks of herself first and foremost. And she is the most dangerous thing in this world to you."

I shift on the bench, my legs tense, ready to sprint back to JJ, but I stop. "You said JJ is safe with her."

"He is, but you're not. You will never be safe," he pauses, then adds, "unless you listen to me."

He steps towards me, placing his hands on my shoulders, and stares straight at me. A shiver runs through me, whether out of fear or because he's touching me, I don't know.

"If you want to stay safe, if you want to stay *alive*," he hisses the last word, "you can never tell Francesca that you have second sight." He leans his face forward until I can feel his breath on my cheek. A low guttural growl emanates from within him. "I am the tamest of my kind," he whispers. "Remember that."

He drops his hands from my shoulders and I miss their warmth. Which is crazy since I think he just threatened me again. Although now I'm also starting to think that maybe he's just trying to scare me. But that's wishful thinking, that he wouldn't tear my throat out.

"I don't even know what that is," I explain. "How can I tell her?" I straighten up as I realize I have crouched down some. My mind may not want to fear him, but my body is smarter.

"It's the ability to see us in our true forms. To see past the glamour. It is a rare gift and you would be sought after by my kind and *not* in a good way."

Glamour. JJ mentioned that in one of his geek rants about a book he'd read. But I can't recall if it had been an elf or fairy thing?

"Chessy's obsession with your brother complicates things. It's not easy to pretend you don't see things that are glamoured if you don't know what is and isn't glamoured."

"Huh?" I'm confused.

"Now you see things how they exist sans glamour." He expands his wings and touches one of his ears. "But you know that no one else can see them, so it's easy for you to pretend."

I nod to let him know that I'm following him thus far.

"However, everything else you see that is unglamoured, you don't realize that it appears glamoured to others."

He must be able to tell by my expression that he lost me.

"Take the house for instance. When you walked in the entryway, what did you see?"

"Marble flooring and an enormous staircase." I shrug, trying to think back.

"Exactly. Did you comment on any of it?" he inquires, leaning forward, his eyes looking a little apprehensive.

"Almost, but your sister started walking off, so I followed."

He closes his eyes for a second and breathes, looking more relaxed. "Good."

"Why? What's the big deal about saying, 'Hey, nice staircase'?"

"Because JJ can't see it. So, Chessy would know that you have second sight." I look around. "What else am I not supposed to see?"

"Everything!" Dante exclaims, turning around and gesturing to the garden. "This is just a small backyard with grass and a picnic table. That's the point. You won't know. Anything you say could put you in mortal danger."

"What are you?" I ask, exasperated. Maybe if I knew what he was, this would make more sense.

"I am part of the Fey. A fairy."

"Part of the Fey? I thought the Fey was a place."

He turns and picks a flower off a nearby branch and rolls it between his fingers.

"Humans have everything wrong. Don't believe the movies and novels. The Fey is more akin to humanity. It encompasses all the beings in our world. Fairies are just one."

"Are there many more of you?" He's more willing to answer questions, so I press my advantage.

"Of course. We spread out; some stay in our realm, others travel back and forth, and some prefer the human world." He says the words "human world" like it's a disease.

"You don't like it here. Then why do you stay?"

The flower drops from his hand and he looks angry again, although I can tell it's not directed at me.

"I have a task to complete. When I finish, I will return to my realm and never bother with this place again. If you'd ever seen my world, you'd understand. It's beautiful and it's home. We don't have traffic, pollution, crime. I don't have to hide who I am there. It's paradise. All my kin are there. I'd have never left if I didn't have...obligations."

I take a step forward. "What task?"

He opens his mouth as if he is about to answer but shuts it quickly, glaring at me. "I've told you enough. More than enough." He rolls his eyes. "Just remember, Francesca is selfish and dangerous. If you can do that, you should be fine," he repeats. Although I'm not sure Dante even believes what he is saying.

The flowers follow us as we walk back to the house. Dante doesn't speak to me again. We head back into the media room where Dante announces that I'm not feeling well and I'm ready to go home.

If looks could kill, Dante isn't the only one who could have murdered me tonight. JJ looks like he'd like to wring my neck.

We get in the car and JJ turns off the music as he drives us home.

"What's wrong with you anyway?" he asks, his tone thick with hostility.

"Headache," I answer, saying the first thing that pops into my mind.

"Seriously!" he exclaims, his voice raised. "And you couldn't take an aspirin?" He points at the clock. "It's just ten o'clock."

"I'm sorry," I apologize, although I'm not. "And you might want to wipe off your face before Mom sees you. And good luck with that, red isn't an easy color to get off." I smirk and then turn back and face the passenger-side window, but as I do I see JJ looking in the mirror, attempting to rub away the red smears around his mouth.

I smile smugly. He has no idea what I've been through tonight, or even what he's kissing. And yet he has the nerve to be upset with me. I'm the one who stood up to a fairy tonight, for HIM!

I can't stay mad for long. I know JJ has no idea what's going on. I wish I could tell him. I need to talk to someone else about this, if only to cement in my brain that I'm not crazy and that this is happening.

My brother doesn't look up from his phone the entire way to his room. I imagine he is texting Francesca.

I throw myself on my bed, reflecting on the last hour.

My curiosity hasn't been slaked. Even with all the knowledge I now possess, all the answers Dante did give, I didn't find peace. All I am left with is more questions.

What is Dante's task? How long will it take for him to complete it before he's gone forever? Who ordered the task? Why is Francesca dangerous? Why would the Fey care if I can see them? It's not like I'm singing this information from the rooftops.

It's dark and cold, the kind of cold that gets deep in your bones. I see a faint blue light at the end of a long, winding staircase. I take the first step onto the stone steps and look behind me, checking to make sure I'm not being followed. My steps echo down the stairwell and I wonder how long it took to build something this endless. I can't even see the bottom, just a faint bluish glow that I assume marks the end. I can't explain why, but I feel like something important lies at the bottom of the stairwell. I make my way down the stairs, trailing my hand against the wall on my right. To the left is just a sheer drop off. Down and down I go. Torches mounted on the wall every fifteen feet offer me the only source of light.

I wonder if the stairs will ever end, but the light becomes brighter the deeper I plunge. After what feels like thousands of steps I arrive at a door. Brilliant blue light pours out from the outline of it. The door reminds me of the one I saw at Dante's except this one is cold and frozen; the flowers are limp and would have fallen off already were they not glued in position by a thick layer of ice.

A chill runs through me as I reach for the door. It doesn't open easily. I shove on it, digging my feet in the ground, trying to find some traction and heave with everything I have. When my last bit of strength fails, I feel the door give way and it swings open.

I jolt up in bed. I'm shivering this time. My hands and feet are frozen and it's almost impossible for me to move. I rub my hands together but can't get warm. I tiptoe downstairs. The clock shines in the dark kitchen; it's just past three in the morning. I microwave a cup of water. I planned to make tea or hot chocolate. But as soon as the warm cup touches my hand, I feel a little better.

I sip on the hot water as I make my way back to my room. The warmth envelops me in an instant and I feel the shivering subside. After I finish, I feel normal again, albeit still shaken from the dream.

I worry what will happen to me next time I fall asleep.

I turn the TV on low and watch reruns until I doze off.

I wake up to the smell of something amazing.

Sundays are family days. Mom doesn't take catering events on Sundays and we try to take a break from friends and school to spend time with her.

I throw on a pair of fuzzy slippers and go knock on JJ's door.

"I'm up," he calls, although I swear I heard him yawn through the door.

I hop on the railing and then slide it down the stairs, jumping off at the end.

Laughter comes from the kitchen and I turn to see my mother shaking her head. "I haven't seen you do that in a few years."

I shrug. "It just felt right today." I inhale deeply. "Whatever you're making, if it tastes as wonderful as it smells, then I don't want you to make anything else ever again."

"It's just a new recipe I'm trying out for fall. Pumpkin spice waffles, homemade whipped cream, and a chocolate ganache syrup."

I move over to the plate of waffles and lean down over it, inhaling the aroma. "Well, I think you nailed it."

Heavy steps come down the stairs and I hear JJ. "My mouth is already watering. What is that?"

"I know, right?" I agree.

Mom places the last waffle on the serving tray and we all find our seats around the table.

It's a little sad that we are so busy with all our comings and goings that we only have breakfast together one day a week. I look at Mom and JJ as they pour chocolate sauce and heave mounds of whipped cream on top of their waffles. I hope I never take this for granted.

I fill my plate and have barely taken three bites before JJ is already helping himself to seconds.

"Hungry?" I laugh.

"This is delicious, Mom." His compliment is redundant. One look at his plate says it all. This time, instead of a single waffle, he piles three on his plate. "Besides, I'm carbo-loading. Brent and I are going to start going to the gym three days a week. His cousin got a job there and gets three free memberships for friends."

"I hope you're going to the gym. If you keep eating like that, you'll need it," I tease as I take another bite of bliss on a fork.

"So, I was thinking," Mom says, "how about an afternoon movie? We haven't been to the theater in a long time."

"I'm game," I say while waiting for JJ to respond. He's got his phone out, texting rapidly. If he keeps this up, he'll have carpal tunnel in no time.

"JJ." I wave my hand in front of his face.

He looks up briefly. "Umm, movie. Yeah, sure. Just text me the time." He finishes his last bite. And by bite, I mean half a waffle stuffed in his mouth. He mumbles what might be a thank you, and doesn't look up from his phone again as he heads to his room.

"Girl?" Mom asks.

"Yeah," I say without enthusiasm.

"You don't like her?" she asks as she starts to clear the table.

"She's fine, I guess. I don't know her that well. I don't think she's JJ's type."

"Well, shouldn't that be his decision?"

If my mother knew everything I knew, I don't think she would be saying anything. I just give the answer I know she wants to hear.

"You're right, I should give her a chance." I take the dishes from my mother's hands. "You cooked. I'll clean up."

She looks surprised. "Well, isn't that a treat."

I make a mental note to help more. Mom does everything for us. I don't even make my bed most days. I've been so focused on everything going on with me that I haven't paid that much attention to my mother as of late. But as I watch her leave, I notice things I should have picked up on sooner. She got a new haircut in the past few weeks and put highlights in her hair, covering up all her gray. Mom has also been getting regular mani-pedis, and now that I think about it, her teeth are whiter as well. I wonder if she is seeing someone again.

It has been so long since Mom has dated, but I do remember she always tried to keep it hidden until things got serious. She never wanted me to get too attached to someone. JJ's dad has been gone a year.

I wonder how JJ will react to the news. Hopefully he will be happy for her. In a couple of years, we'll be away at college, and I don't want Mom to be alone. She deserves to find someone great in her life. I mean, my father deserted us when I was two and then her second husband died. Mom hasn't had the greatest luck.

I'm halfway through the dishes when there's a knock on the door. I turn the water off and dry my hands on a dishtowel. But before I can get to the door, JJ beats me to it.

Giggles reach my ears before I see Francesca skip into the house.

"Hey Emma!" She smiles and waves at me.

I'm still in my pajamas and I am certain I have bed head, and here she comes dressed to the nines. Now that she's here, am I going to have to get dressed? Sundays are my t-shirt and yoga pants day. The day I just get to relax and I don't have to try to impress anyone.

"You weren't lying when you told me that JJ loves movies." She rubs her hand on his arm. "I mean, movie night last night and now we're going to the theater today."

Sundays are supposed to be the one day we spend with Mom. I can't believe that JJ did this. And with Francesca. I feel my face redden as I am consumed by anger. My brother must be able to tell because he sends her upstairs to his room.

"The second door on the left. I'll be right there," he calls after her. Then he spins back towards me, putting his hands up, palms out, in a placating gesture.

"Look, I didn't invite her." His voice is soft and low. I can tell JJ doesn't want Francesca to overhear him. "I said we were going to the movies and somehow she misunderstood." He turns back, looking up towards his room. "But Chesa has been nothing but nice to us. I didn't want to be rude and I thought I might hurt her feelings if I tried to straighten it out."

"Whatever," I say with more volume than I need. "You're just a big chicken. I can't believe you did this on Sunday."

I push past him, hitting my shoulder against him hard as I pass and almost take my first step up the stairs. However, I remember that I still have half the dishes to finish, so I walk back into the kitchen, my dramatic exit not making quite the impact I had hoped.

As I finish scrubbing the silverware, I think back to JJ whispering. I wonder if it even did any good. I mean with fairy ears being much larger than ours, it makes sense that they would hear better. If Dante speaks to me again, I'll have to ask him.

It's a tight fit, the four of us driving in Mom's mustang. The weather is starting to get colder though, making this the last time this year to drive with the top down. I take shotgun. JJ and Francesca squeeze into the back. They don't seem to mind the cramped quarters in the backseat.

If it bothers mom that Chesa has joined us during family time, she does an excellent job of not showing it. There's a subtitled flick that I know Mom would rather see but she picks the action movie for us. Chesa insists on buying the popcorn and sits in between JJ and my mother.

She talks my mom's ear off. Sucking up to the umpteenth degree. I am relieved by the time the movie begins.

The movie ends in a spectacular fighting scene with lots of special effects. JJ and I start clapping at the end. We're the only ones in the theater applauding, but it doesn't bother us. This is what we do.

"So, I don't get it," Francesca says as we make our way to the car. "How did the humans win?"

"Did you not see that last scene where they go back in time and blow up the factory?" JJ inquires.

"No, I did. I just mean how is that realistic? How could puny little humans ever win in a real fight over artificial intelligence that can heal itself, shift shapes, and has many other advantages? I just don't see how anyone could buy an ending where the weak humans win."

I bite my lip, wondering how JJ will react. Is that how she sees us humans? Tiny and brittle?

"Puny?" JJ flexes his muscles. "Does this look weak? That's why we'll never be taken over by AI, aliens, or magical creatures. They all underestimate us. We are survivors."

Francesca laughs. "Well at least you are," she agrees, then slips her arm through his.

As we drive home, I am counting down the seconds until JJ's new *friend* leaves. I take a sip from a water bottle and almost spew it all over Mom's dash when she asks, "Francesca, would you like to stay for dinner?"

"I'd love to." She beams.

"I guess I should tell you first what we are having. I'm quite adventurous in the kitchen and I'm attempting something new today. It might be a little too exotic for some people."

"I'm game for anything," she responds.

"I'm making rotolo di coniglio," my mother adds.

"I love rabbit. It's my absolute favorite type of meat. We have it quite a bit where I'm from."

"Fantastic." My mother's smile widens as I slump further down in my seat. Rabbit. I think that might be a little too strange for me. Most days Mom doesn't tell me what's in her exotic dishes until I've already tried them. I have a weak stomach, but I do better if I like something before I know what it is. I'm not sure I can eat Thumper.

V
SKETCHING

It's hard to concentrate or do anything in my room. I can hear constant laughing and giggling from the other side of the wall. I never realized how paper-thin these walls are.

I try reading and streaming a show but I can't get into anything. I open my nightstand drawer to toss my book back in and something catches my eye. Underneath the clutter of pens, a calculator, and extra charging cords, I see a notebook.

I dig it out and flip it open. It's filled with sketches. Drawings Dad and I did together. JJ's father was an artist. He taught classes at the local college. He had been teaching me to sketch.

After the funeral, I had thrown it in a drawer to forget about it. At the time it had been too painful to think about Dad at all, especially the one thing that was just ours. But something about sketching is appealing to me at this moment. I dig deeper through my drawer until I feel a case. It contains my drawing pencils. We had never progressed past black and white. But in some ways, I liked the images better using that approach.

I take out a pencil and start to draw. My strokes are slow at first as I build my confidence back up, line by line. The image starts to take form and I begin to add different shades of gray like Dad taught me. I don't even realize what I am drawing until I finish.

It's an image of the statue I saw in my dream. It's so detailed. I didn't think I remembered even noticing everything in my drawing. The etchings on the sword remind me of an ancient language. There's an image on the shield, a square with eight swords lying across it to form the shape of a star.

The eyes of the fairy look familiar to me. I've seen the same look in Dante's eyes. Maybe that's why I dreamed it. Just a twisted manifestation of real life in a dream.

I turn the page, and this time I know what I am sketching even before I make the first line. It never ceases to amaze me that some lines, curves, and smudges can make a 2D paper appear to look 3D.

This image depicts the stairwell I descended in my second dream. I wonder what lurked behind the door. That is how dreams are though, you never get the full picture.

By the time I've finished with the second picture, my hands are smudged and dirty. I start to head to my bathroom to scrub them when the doorbell rings.

Twice in one day, and on a Sunday. It's unusual for us to have this much activity and I wonder who it could be.

I can hear my mom talking to someone, but then the voices stop. Maybe someone trying to sell pest control or get us to switch electricity companies had stopped by.

My door bursts open and Dante stands in the doorway. He's wearing blue jeans and a white button-down dress shirt. If not for his angry expression, I'd think he could have just walked off the page of a magazine or a movie set.

"My apologies," he says, looking embarrassed. "I thought this was the room your mother said Chessy was in. She has been here too long and overstayed her welcome."

He looks at my hands. "You're filthy, you know."

"I've been working," I say, pointing to the notebook. I hop off the bed and start towards the bathroom sink. "Francesca is in the next room."

He looks startled and swipes the notebook off my bed.

"That's private," I stammer.

Holding the notebook up, the image facing me, he demands, "What is this?"

Before I can answer, he turns the page, but he flips it to a blank page in the wrong direction. Then he goes backward, and when he sees the image, he drops my notebook.

"I thought we had more time," he whispers as his face pales.

"More time for what?" I press.

He shushes me. Actually shushes me. This is my house and he dares to come in and treat me like a child? I don't care if he's a fairy. This is crossing a line.

He can sense my anger; or at least, I assume he can because he apologizes again.

Then he points to his ears and motions towards JJ's room. I knew it, they must have superhuman hearing.

"Do you have time for a walk before dinner?" he asks as he kneels and picks up the notebook, shutting it before returning it to my bed.

I turn on the faucet and scrub my hands. "I guess." I try acting nonchalant, but the truth is I'd still go whether I had time or not. A pang of guilt sweeps over me as I remember how harsh I've been judging JJ for acting the same way, putting others ahead of our Sunday tradition. But in my defense, Dante seems like he wants to share more information with me. Maybe he knows why I'm having these vivid, lifelike dreams. That's why I'd be willing to miss Sunday dinner. I try rationalizing my behavior to myself. But the reasons are flimsy even to me. Of course, if I'm being realistic, I'd still go with him even if he didn't hold answers I can't get from anyone else.

I dry my hands on a towel and sit on my bed. His eyes stay on me, intent and focused as I lace up my shoes.

"K, I'm ready."

As we head downstairs, I call to my mother in the kitchen. "I'll be back in a bit."

"Dinner won't be ready for at least an hour." My mom winks at me.

She winked! In front of Dante! I can feel my face redden. I want to sink in a hole and die, but then I'd miss my walk with him.

"And Dante, don't try to disappear on me. I hold people to their word, and you already accepted my dinner invitation."

"I wouldn't dream of it, Mrs. Harper." He offers a slight bow with his head and then holds the door open for me.

Once it's closed, he says, "Your mother might rival Chessy on getting her way. I came here to take my sister home. To try to limit her exposure around your family. But your mother wouldn't take no for an answer."

I follow his lead through the neighborhood and we end up in the forest. We stray from the path and walk for a few more minutes.

"Man, how far can you guys hear?" I ask as I think about all the precautions Dante is taking before speaking to me.

His eyes are intense; there is no humor in them. "A ways, but not this far."

I wait for more and he offers nothing.

"Can you not tell when I want something explained?" I widen my arms and point to the trees and the secluded nature of our position. "Or are you just trying to annoy me on purpose?"

"I had hoped that if I kept not answering maybe you'd show some sense and realize more knowledge isn't always a good thing." He brushes his hair back with a hand. "You're a frustratingly annoying human."

"Well, I think that goes for you too, fairy." I try to say the word with as much disregard for him as he shows for me.

"Touché." He gives a half-hearted laugh. "I try to share what I deem necessary with you. But there hasn't been someone with second sight in over a century," he says.

"You're over a hundred years old?" I ask, my eyes widening to the size of saucers.

He lets out a genuine laugh this time. "No. I'm not close to being that old. But we keep records and we hear stories. The records are not as accurate as I thought. When you're blessed with second sight," he says, pausing for a moment.

I bite my tongue and don't interrupt him because thus far, I haven't seen the blessing part of this entire situation.

"There is more to it than just seeing through the glamour. That is a small part of it. You're also blessed with the ability to see the past and future.

"I believed based on accounts I have read that it takes time to develop these talents and that they don't appear right away. But based on the drawings I saw in your room, I know that's not the case. You've seen things from my realm."

"Those are real?" I ask, astounded.

"The statue is of my distant relative; I don't recall how many great grandfathers back. And that stairwell leads to one of our most sacred places."

"But how is that even possible?" I lean forward, waiting in earnest for an answer.

"Magic has always existed. But over the course of many millennia, we acquired some knowledge about magic and its uses. We don't understand it completely. We do know it's living and changing. We have learned how to harness it, how to place it in objects to make them magical. But even some of that has been forgotten. I'm not sure how the gift of second sight was bestowed upon humans or why it manifests in some and not others. There are some Fey who study this sort of thing, but alas, I am not one." He breaks off a branch and begins spinning it in his hand. "But there is one thing I should warn you of. Each member of the Fey is blessed with a magical gift. Most fairies start to manifest their power for the first time during adolescence, sometimes earlier if the gift is immensely powerful. Mine is healing." He pauses for a moment. "Some gifts are not...not as pleasant. I've even heard of some being able to enter dreams. I don't believe they can hurt you, but now that the visions have started, some of my people will have sensed it." I think he sees the concern on my face because he continues in a rush. "They don't have a GPS signal to track you, but if you have any control during these dreams, don't let anyone see you and perhaps the most important piece of advice I can give you is don't tell anyone your name or where you're from."

I start shaking, remembering the mark on my arm. Could that have been from another Fey in my dream? Would it be possible for them to capture me in a dream and bring me to their realm?

"Don't worry, you'll be safe," he promises.

"You. Are. Wrong." I speak each word clearly and deliberately. I'm still shaking. I hate this. I wish I could make myself stop. Suck it up. But my body is not listening.

I take my time rolling up my sleeve and then hold my arm out. The marks aren't quite as red as they were a couple of nights ago. But if I look closely, I can make out the imprint of a hand wrapped around my arm.

"Who did that to you?" he demands as he looks around the woods, panicked, as if someone might jump out at any second.

"A dream," I whisper. I feel faint and I halfway collapse on the ground, only being able to slow myself a little before I fall to the ground. How can I ever go to sleep again? I don't know what I had thought. It has been a crazy couple of days. I haven't had the time to process it all. But knowing I could be hurt in my dreams? How does someone protect themselves from that?

"No," he argues. "It can't be." He's saying the words but there is no confidence in them. "I'm sorry," he says as he kneels beside me, placing a hand on my shoulder consolingly.

A tear runs down my cheek and he brushes it away with a gentle caress.

"We'll figure this out," he promises.

I look up. "We? You aren't going to threaten to kill me anymore?" I bite down on my lip as I wait for him to answer.

"I would have never hurt you." His eyes have softened and they look the closest to human I've ever seen them. "I just wanted to scare you. Really scare you. Away from all this. But I didn't realize that wasn't possible. Things are far different than I ever imagined."

"What do we do now? I'm scared to shut my eyes. Can they kill me while I'm dreaming?" I ask.

He offers me his hand and pulls me to my feet.

"We should get back. I'm sorry I don't have more answers. I don't want to offer you false comfort," he explains as I follow him out of the forest. "We don't have a lot of magic but there are spells and herbs which might help. I'll have to search through some of our ancient texts. See if I can find anything."

He stops and takes my hand in his. It's calloused and strong, and butterflies fill my stomach, almost making me forget that my life is falling apart. Almost.

"I can tell you with a fair amount of certainty that no one from the Fey will try to kill you. They want to control you. Use your gift to find the missing artifacts and open the borders of our realm."

"If I can help you I will. Can't we just tell them that? If I have a vision of where a magical item is hiding, I promise I'll tell you Dante."

He pulls me forward and we step back out onto the sidewalk. It feels like years have passed and not just an hour.

"It's not just that. There are fairies who, just like some humans, are consumed with becoming more powerful. They would imprison you. Make you their slave and use your gift of sight for their benefit. Once someone claims you, there is a bond. Your freewill is gone unless they allow it. You can't escape it. The bond is forever. It's very intimate. No fairy would ever relinquish the bond. You'd be their prized toy."

"Why don't you just claim me? Then no one can. You'd let me have my free will, right?" I question.

"To claim someone is a very public event. There is a ceremony, and it must be done in my realm. I don't want to risk bringing you there. A jealous Fey can still kill you, either to spite me so that I wouldn't have access to your power, or just out of their pure hatred of humans."

We walk the rest of the way in silence. I want to go to my room, shut myself off from everyone and just try to figure out a way through this. There must be a way. Maybe there is a way to get rid of second sight.

My mom is setting the table when we walk in.

"I wondered if you were going to make it." She nods to me and asks, "Will you go get JJ and Chesa?"

She is already calling her Chesa. I don't know why it bothers me but it does. As I head up the stairs, I hear Dante ask if there is anything he can do to help.

I knock on JJ's door. "Dinner," I call.

"K, thanks," he answers back.

We gather around the table and Mom places the rabbit dish in the center, then takes the seat at the head of the table. JJ and Francesca take the seats to her right and I take my seat on the left where Dante joins me.

The dish doesn't look weird. It just looks like a roast with stuffing inside. I try to tell my stomach that it's just a pork roast. Good ol' ordinary pig meat.

We've never had a clean-your-plate rule in our house. Mom doesn't parent like that. But she has insisted we try everything. Three hearty bites. She says you need three to be certain. That sometimes food just tastes different than you're used to and you need a couple of bites to become accustomed to it before you can make up your mind.

"This looks wonderful," Dante praises.

We pass dishes around the table and prepare our plates. I wonder if with the added company Mom will notice if I don't put any of the rabbit on my plate. It's worth a try. I pile on an oversized helping of salad, then add mashed potatoes, green beans, and a roll to my plate.

It doesn't look like anything is missing to me. I let out a relieved sigh when everyone starts to dig in and Mom doesn't notice.

I've taken about two bites of my salad when Francesca decides to open her big fat mouth, making me dislike her even more.

"This is amazing," she exclaims. "It just melts in your mouth, and the seasonings are spot on."

Dante, mid-chew, nods his head in agreement.

"Emma, aren't you going to try some?" Chesa smiles at me.

Mom's eyes fixate on my plate. "Emma, you know the rules. You need to at least taste it."

"There just wasn't space on my plate," I lie. But I place my roll on a napkin and begrudgingly spear the smallest piece.

I continue with my salad, trying to prepare myself for three bites. With how my stomach is churning, I can't imagine that I'll be able to keep it down. If I throw up on Dante, I'll never be able to show my face again.

Mom makes small talk with Dante and Francesca about school and their home life as our plates get barer and barer.

Why don't we have a dog? I whine to myself.

"That's a beautiful painting," Dante comments, pointing behind my mother. She turns and beams.

It's a landscape from one of the overlooks that hikers like to stop at when they're climbing the gorge trail I run.

While Mom is turned, going on about how JJ's father painted it and how much talent he had, Dante uses his fork and in a stealth move stabs my slice of rabbit, shifting it onto his plate.

He gives me a conspiratorial wink.

By the time she turns away, he gives her a polite nod and is halfway through my piece of rabbit.

I give him a look that I hope shows my thanks and finish off my mashed potatoes by scooping them up with a piece of my roll.

"Well, thank you for the beautiful day, but as my brother hasn't been shy in pointing out, we've, or at least I have outstayed my welcome." Francesca pushes her chair away from the table and stands up.

"You're both welcome here anytime," my mother insists.

"We couldn't even consider leaving until we clean up," Dante says, eyeing his sister. "After all, you made us a delicious meal. I insist."

If they teach sucking up to the Fey, then Dante must have scored high marks.

"Thank you," my mother says. "I actually have a few chapters of a book I am just dying to finish."

Francesca offers a pleasant smile to my mother as Mother leaves and then glares at Dante.

"Come on, sis," Dante says as he stacks dishes and brings them to the sink where he instructs Francesca to wash.

Chesa crashing our Sunday was worth it just for this moment. I can tell she has never had to clean a plate or scrub a dish in her life, as if it's beneath her.

After Dante has finished clearing, while JJ and I put the food away, he takes over for Francesca, who looks like she's about to faint.

"Are you okay?" JJ asks her.

"I'm feeling a little tired. Why don't you walk me to my car? Dante can finish in here."

I can't contain myself, and a giggle escapes my lips. JJ looks at me, horrified by my bad manners, but Dante starts laughing too and soon we are both almost rolling on the floor.

After they leave and we both have contained ourselves, I help Dante finish the dishes.

"Is she always like that? Do fairies," I whisper the word, "not work?"

"There's a hierarchy," he says as he dries his hands on a dish towel. "It just depends on where you rank in it. As you can see from Chessy's behavior, she's not used to doing menial tasks."

"But you're siblings. Wouldn't your rank be the same?"

He shrugs. "I told you before, I'm not like the rest of my kind, even my sister."

After glancing up at the clock, Dante turns to me. "I'd better go. I have research to do." He gives me a slight bow and departs.

His exit must have wrapped up whatever was going on with JJ and Francesca because my brother scurries inside just moments after Dante's departure.

He glances at me in the kitchen and then takes the stairs two at a time with his long legs until he is out of sight.

Tomorrow is a school day. After my discussions with Dante, it feels surreal to be focusing on such trivial things as homework. But since I don't think my teachers would buy my excuse even if I had permission to tell them, I decide to try to work on some schoolwork.

I start to work on my English assignment first. I have three chapters of Macbeth to get through. My eyes start to get droopy midway through chapter two, and I toss the novel aside.

There is no way I'm falling asleep. At least not until Dante can figure something out.

I switch to math. I have to move around to do algebra, well at least my hand. We just started a new unit on rational exponents and radicals. It's a little confusing but I think I figure it out as I watch the videos working out a few example problems.

It's close to midnight by the time I finish all my homework. I'm still determined not to fall asleep. I flip on my television and scan for something to watch. I settle on a comedy. If I'm laughing then it will be harder for me to drift off. Or that's my theory anyway.

I'm standing in the largest room I've ever been in. Crystal chandeliers hang from the ceiling. Too many for me to count. The room is adorned with gold and silver. The floor shines brightly, the tile looking like it's made from gold. There are countless stained-glass windows lining the room on either side. The images are etched in gold and silver as well.

There is a long processional leading up to a fairy. This fairy is different from the others, more regal somehow, but also more ancient. He wears long shimmering robes, while the other fairies are dressed in tunics and fitted pants.

I step forward tentatively, not wanting to draw attention to myself. I can somehow recall Dante's warning, triggering me to realize I am in a dream. But this time it feels different somehow.

A creature with the torso and head of a man and the body of a goat rushes right past me and I let out a startled cry. I cover my mouth and don't move, but no one appears to have noticed.

I make my way forward to the end of the line and stand beside the goat man. It's as if I'm invisible.

I wave my hand in front of his face and still nothing. I continue down the line of creatures. Some of them I've seen in movies or books and others are a complete mystery. Every one of them ignores me.

As I come to the front of the line, there are eight fairies at the head.

The ancient one speaks and I stand motionless.

"There has been discussion among the houses that I have lost touch with the will of the people. There are those who wish we were cut off completely from the mortal realm and those who think we should rule it. After centuries of ruling, I tire of these debates. As no one has come forward as a clear successor with the support of the people behind them, I have deemed it appropriate to divide the power of the Fey that flows through me as the ruler of our people. A king has been selected from each of the houses to rule together in my stead.

"After these proceedings I will retire to isolation. I yearn for silence and peace. To keep our world secret and protected, I have infused these eight swords with the power of the Fey. For now, each house will have the same amount of power. Together the swords will keep our world hidden, yet open to the human world. However, to make certain that not one member of the Fey can take control of all the power and become unstoppable, I have spelled one for each of the royal families. Only a member of that bloodline can wield their sword."

The ancient-looking fairy takes a step forward and looks into each of the representative's eyes.

"The swords will offer the most protection when they are together. Therefore, I have created a special location to contain them. It will be up to each king whether to place their swords there or not. I offer only my counsel in the form of a warning. The magic in our realm has been placed in these swords. If one sword is removed, then the barrier will no longer remain open all year. With the removal of more swords, the time the barrier remains open would lessen. But if all these swords are taken from our world into the human realm, our power will be diminished and the gateway between worlds would close permanently."

The old fairy turns and a long table appears out of nowhere. As he reaches forward, a beautiful sword materializes. Long and straight, with etchings on the blade. In the center of the golden hilt is a red gem.

"For the red house."

One of the eight fairies steps forward and claims the sword. His tunic matches the color of the stone. The fairy offers a small bow and returns to his place.

The ancient one turns back to the table and a second sword appears. He repeats the process eight times total. The colors of the stones must have some significance to the royal houses because the stones always coincide with the color of the tunic each fairy is wearing.

The colors of the eight houses are red, green, yellow, purple, orange, pink, white, and blue.

The last house to claim their sword is the blue house. I gasp as I see the fairy step forward. The fairy who claims the sword for blue is the same as the image of the statue I saw.

This is Dante's ancestor. This is a vision of the past.

Dante warned me I'd be able to see visions of the past and the future.

Once the last sword is presented to its representative, the fairies file out through an open passage. I start to follow them, wondering what more I can find out when I wake up.

I take a second to make sure I am intact. No burns this time, nor am I half frozen. Seeing into the past isn't bad.

I pull my notebook from my nightstand, eager to transcribe some of what I just saw. But before I try to sketch the vision, I jot down the basics because I don't want to forget.

8 swords given to 8 houses:

Red

Green

Yellow

Purple

Orange

Pink

White

Blue

Once I've jotted down the pertinent information, I start to work on the sketch. Drawing each individual member of the Fey takes time, but I don't have any trouble recalling their individual features. I start with the fairy who presented the swords. I try to capture the look of wisdom in his eyes, and the way he comported himself. His beard hung long with lots of tiny braids, while his hair had been trimmed much shorter and close-cropped at the sides.

As I make my way down the line of creatures, I pause and try to identify them. Then I add them to my list under the names of the eight royal families.

Satyrs

The name of the half goat creature I saw.

I see four female-looking creatures, each one looking unique. One dressed in a blue flowing dress that reminds me of water. Another in red. Her skin is blackened in some areas, her hair a reddish orange. She reminds me of fire. The next dressed in green. She had actual flowers sprouting from her dress and woven through her auburn hair. She just reminds me of life and growth, of nature. The last had almost translucent hair, which waved back and forth. She wore a silvery dress that also moved, as if caught in a breeze. I thought of the wind when I looked at her. I have no idea what kind of creatures they were.

There were smaller creatures that had much in common with the fairies. Their ears were pointed and they had wings, but were much smaller in size, about two feet tall. Perhaps even a little shorter. I think I had seen them in children's books. Pixies.

Pixies

There were several animal-like creatures. One resembled a worm but was much larger and furry. It had pink eyes and purple fur. I have no idea what it is.

Another resembled a fish about the size of a middle schooler. It walked upright, shuffling forward with its tail, and carried a saber at its side. The lack of water didn't appear to be a hindrance.

I wish I had scrutinized them more as I passed by. But once I realized they couldn't see me, I didn't pay most of them any attention. I just draw a vague shadowy outline in those spots.

I am just closing my sketch book when my alarm buzzes.

It is time for school already.

VI
DANGER

The past two weeks have been uneventful. JJ and Francesca are practically glued to each other. I try to avoid them as much as possible. First, because they are nauseating, and second, because I am afraid of seeing something I am not supposed to and slipping up. It has been frustrating too because as much as she is around, I still haven't figured out what magical talent she was blessed with.

Dante has been MIA most of the time. He's either doing research or working on his mysterious task. At least he still believes it is a mystery to me. From what I've pieced together from conversations with him and my dreams, I am confident he is looking for the blue sword. Although I am curious to know how it came to our world.

My dreams continue each night. Although as of late, the images I see are random. Some of them look like they come from their world and others like they might be from mine. They had been milder until last night.

The dream is unlike anything I have yet experienced. I stand in a forest, different than any I have ever seen. Some of the plants are familiar, ones I saw in Dante's garden. I'm sitting by a beautiful pond. It looks like a watercolor painting, deep turquoise with ripples of pink and white on the surface. A small waterfall empties into the pond. Rocks build a natural barrier around half the pond, providing seclusion for any who wish to enjoy the beauty of this little oasis.

I'm sitting on a grassy knoll, overlooking the landscape. I'm dressed in boots, black pants, and an aqua tunic with white lace trim. The sun is out and its rays are bathing over me. I close my eyes to enjoy the warmth when a chill rushes over me. I stand quickly, glancing around my surroundings. I hear whispers, harsh and cold.

"Who are you?"

"Where are you from?"

"What are you doing here?"

The voices hiss innocent questions, but it sounds like they come from the devil himself.

I remember Dante's warning, but even with it I struggle against an overwhelming desire to answer them.

I start to open my mouth when an image of Dante comes to my mind. I exert all my power and turn to run. But as I turn, a handsome young fairy appears before me. He looks younger than Dante, closer to my age. His tunic is gray. I can't tell which royal family he aligns himself with. His hair is white and tied back in a braid. His eyes are silver and bore into mine. His wings look the same as Dante's.

"Hello." He nods, offering me a shy smile. "I didn't realize anyone else would be here. My apologies for intruding. Shall I leave?" he asks, staying back and not approaching.

My mind feels muddled and confused. Something warns me to tell him to go, but he's polite, and he's offering to depart if I want. Besides, this isn't my pond. It would be selfish to deny others its beauty.

"No, please stay." I beckon him forward so that he can get a better view.

He walks toward me, his graceful demeanor a mirror of Dante's. The fairy does not stop until he is beside me. "Where are my manners?" he chides himself before offering an introduction. "I'm Griffin."

I revert to the manners my mother has taught me. "It's a pleasure to meet you. I'm Em—" I force my mouth shut. He's trying to trick me.

"Em—" he prompts, his smile easy, friendly.

I turn to leave, realizing this had been a terrible idea. But the moment I try, he seizes me. All pretenses of friendliness gone.

His grip is tight, rough, nothing like Dante's strong but gentle force.

"I tried being nice."

I attempt to pull away, but his hand is like an ever-tightening vice on my arm. White hot pain sears into my arm where he's holding it.

I scream and writhe in agony.

"Just tell me your name and this stops." He sneers, and I wonder how I could have ever thought him handsome.

"No," I manage as tears stream down my face.

The pain worsens and travels down my arm towards my wrist.

I continue to scream as I fall to my knees. "Please," I beg. All I want to do is wake up. As the sizzling continues, darkness creeps in around me. When I pass out in the dream, I wake up in reality.

Blisters and burns cover my arm from my wrist up to my bicep where Griffin held me. My arm looks bad, like movie effects bad. He was ruthless. It's difficult and painful, but I manage to pull on a long-sleeved flannel shirt over my t-shirt. The pain is excruciating. But I can't let anyone see it. Not my family, not my friends, Brent, Jenny, and Izza, and above all, not Francesca.

Jenny and Izza have become close friends with Chesa and we now all eat lunch together. I almost don't make it to lunch. I take two hydrocodone under the guise that it's aspirin for a headache. I have some leftover from getting my wisdom teeth out, but they are dwindling quicker than I'd like.

"Halloween's tonight. We're still all meeting for Fright Night, right?" Izza asks excitedly.

Fright Night is an event the school puts on every year. It's like a zombie apocalypse. The staff and even some parents dress like zombies and attack the students. Attack meaning they have to grab a ribbon off your waist, like in flag football. Students can dress up or just come as they are. Whoever is left standing at the end of the night, meaning they still have their flag, gets their name put in a drawing for a hundred-dollar gift card to this swanky restaurant in town, Bisque.

Or if you can find the cure, a little vial of green gel that the science teachers cook up, you win. You save humanity and get a five-hundred-dollar Visa gift card, plus your choice of parking spaces and free food at the school cafeteria. This last option might seem more like a punishment than a perk to some, but our cafeteria workers are the best. They are always offering free samples, taking suggestions, and upping their game on a regular basis. It's like the lines are each their own mini restaurant. This would be my favorite perk. Then I wouldn't be subject to Mom's exotic or weird creations.

But the chances of anyone winning are slim to none. I think the last kid that won claimed the title a decade ago.

"Yes, let's meet up here at seven-thirty and plan our strategy," Francesca answers as she intwines her hand with my brother's.

"And then we're going back to your place for dessert?" Brent confirmed.

Leave it to a guy to want to make sure the food is covered.

"I think I'm going to pass tonight," I comment. It will be nice to be in a JJ-Chesa free zone for a few hours. Dante works on the weekends too, so there's no draw on that front.

Chesa leans forward, "You must come. I even made Dante take off. He needs to live a little."

I turn to face him. "You're going?" I ask, thinking if he went, I might be willing to change my mind. Plus, we haven't had much time to talk as of late. But with the entire campus free reign, we could just find a secluded spot and slip away from the group. And just maybe he might be willing to heal my arm.

"Apparently," he responds with no enthusiasm in his tone.

"Great!" Jenny exclaims. "The entire gang."

When did we become a gang? Maybe Francesca's power is the ability to make everyone adore her. It doesn't work on me because of my superpower. However, after a moment I remember that Dante's healing still worked on me. I guess that's another idea I can scratch off my list.

I can't decide on costume or no costume. JJ is dressed like a soldier in fatigues with dark lines painted under his eyes. I am certain Francesca will be dressed as something fabulous, but I don't see Dante as the dress-up type. Plus, I'm not eager to try to change out of shirts with my arm throbbing nonstop. I've taken two more hydrocodone for the pain, even though they barely put a dent in it.

After searching through my closet, I decide to half dress up. I throw on my Doc Martens with jeans and stay in my button-up flannel. Then I pull an old army jacket I found at a thrift store out of my closet. Either I could just be dressed retro, or maybe I'm some kind of off-the-grid soldier. It's too painful to wear the jacket now, so I just carry it, hoping Dante will heal me.

"You two have fun tonight." My mother waves as we get into JJ's car. "Wake me when you get home if I've fallen asleep."

Mom says she can't sleep unless she knows we are home. Which makes zero sense to me. If that were true, why do I always have to wake her up?

It's just starting to get dark when we pull into the school parking lot. It's kind of amazing how much the teachers and parents have gotten done in a few hours. I almost don't recognize the school. It looks different, like we've stepped into an apocalypse.

There are flipped-over cars and debris. There are signs that are bent in unnatural positions, and bodies spread throughout the campus. True, the debris, cars, signs, and most of the props are just cardboard or Styrofoam, but it's still amazing. We have a great drama department.

The game doesn't start for another half hour so we head to the gym to meet up with everyone.

"Hold up!"

I turn to see Brent jogging towards us. He is dressed just like JJ. They must have coordinated.

"Hey, ready for a zombie apocalypse?" I ask.

"Nice costume," JJ comments. "It almost looks as good on you as it does on me."

Brent rolls his eyes. "Get a girlfriend and your head swells three sizes too big." He glances around as he centers his belt on his waist. "Anyone else here yet?"

"Not that we've seen," JJ answers.

"Wow, you sure pulled out all the stops, costume-wise," Brent teases, and then hits me in my arm.

I jerk away, biting my lip, as my eyes well up in tears. Sharp pain shoots up and down my arm and the throbbing that had been just a low roar is now uncontrollable. I'm not sure how I haven't screamed yet, but I continue trying with all my might to keep my jaw clenched and keep myself upright.

The school hallways are as crowded as during passing periods, except instead of a flowing stream, there are groups on each side of the hallways. Friends meeting up, picking teams, and strategizing the best ways to stay alive tonight. The hallways are dimmer; there is some trash strewn in them and the lightbulbs have been changed to blue and green making it look more eerie.

I make a quick scan of the students. A fair amount are costumed—I'd guess more than half but there are still many who chose not to dress up. I think I'd feel more relieved if I weren't dying in agony. I hate standing out.

JJ participated in zombiegeddon last year, but this is the first year I've attended.

The bleachers are pulled out in the gymnasium. There are groups of students spread thinly throughout the two sides. A long rectangular folding table is along the back wall, underneath the scoreboard, where three teachers sit. A white posterboard has the words "sign in" scrawled across it in black Sharpie. This is the only room not decorated.

Most of the teachers love this event. Any room is fair game, as long as it is unlocked.

We must sign in individually. JJ, Brent, and I make our way to the table.

"Hello Emma," Mr. Brenton, my English teacher, greets me. He's in the middle seat at the table. I recognize him from his voice. His makeup is very thorough. He looks as good as one of those TV zombies, but it shouldn't shock me that much. After holding this event for many years, they are bound to have become experts at zombie makeup. "I didn't think zombies were your thing."

I shrug. "They coerced me," I say as I sign my name and nod towards Brent and JJ.

Mr. Brenton hands me a belt with two ribbons. "Remember, if either of your ribbons gets pulled by a zombie then you're out of the game."

"Got it." I say, stepping to the side, allowing JJ and Brent to sign in.

As JJ turns, Francesca jumps into his arms. Jenny and Izza are trailing behind her. They wave to me. The three of them are in matching costumes. I stifle a laugh, as they are dressed as the three fairies from Sleeping Beauty. I can't remember the fairies' names, but one of them is blue, one of them is red, and one green. The costumes look expensive and cute. But I wouldn't be caught dead in one. Too much gossamer and lace for me.

I crane my neck, trying to see past the girls. The gym is getting more crowded as everyone is eager to sign in before the event begins. I don't see Dante. I can't deny my disappointment.

As I turn back towards my group, I step back, startled. Dante is standing straight in front of me. He is dressed up, in a sense. My eyes go wide and I almost gasp. But he grabs me and turns me from the others. Luckily, he grabs my uninjured arm or I don't think I'd be conscious.

"Remember, you can't see me like that," he whispers, close to my ear.

It is a little difficult to pretend. He is dressed like the way I'd seen members of the Fey dress in my visions.

He looks striking in a blue tunic, as is his family's color. It has a v-neck with golden lace embroidered around the collar and sleeves. He wears tan fitted pants tucked into black leather boots. He also dons a belt made up of hundreds of tiny gold interlacing rings, which join in the center with an oval clasp engraved with the word blue.

If all of this is not striking enough, Dante has his wings extended. They are amazing. It's almost like looking into a waterfall that is covered in rainbows, but even more stunning. No description can do it justice.

"Are your clothes glamoured?" I whisper back.

"No." He laughs. "Today's the one day I can be myself."

I motioned around the room. "I'm not the only one staring. The look suits you." I reach forward, feeling the edge of his tunic between my fingers. The fabric is thicker than it looks, but softer than any fabric I've ever felt.

"Two minutes," a teacher calls.

I start to ask him if we can talk privately, not knowing how much longer I can survive the pain in my arm.

Dante offers me a low bow. "I'd better sign in or Chessy will never forgive me."

I watch as he signs his name. His handwriting is impeccable. Then he gets his belt and Chessy is calling us all over for a quick strategy session.

"I think when the bell rings we should all separate in different directions. That way we have a better chance of surviving."

JJ told me that when the bell dings to start the event, we have ten minutes to leave the gym and find a decent spot to either hide or have room to run.

If pain didn't continue to sear down my arm, I'd pick a wide-open space. I'm certain I could outrun any of the teachers at my school.

"Let's get in groups of twos and three," JJ suggests.

Just then, the bell goes off.

"Great, I'll go with Dante," I call, grabbing him and pulling him from the gym before anyone can argue.

He doesn't ask where we are going, but I hurry towards a storage area that I know has access to the roof.

"Darn," I say when I realize the doors are locked. "Any ideas on how we can get to the roof?"

The roof is off limits, making it the last place anyone would look for us.

He cocks his eyebrow up and offers a mischievous grin. "I may have an idea."

I follow him behind the cafeteria, out by the dumpsters. It's dark outside, but I know any moment the lights will be turned on.

He extends his wings. We are well concealed in our present location. Most of the kids opt to stay inside, preferring to hide rather than run.

"Wrap your arms around my neck," he says.

I lift my arms with as much care as I can muster, grimacing as I wrap my arms around his neck. I'd like to say that the pain vanishes when I hold him, and when he then grabs my waist. But that would be a lie. My arm presses against his shoulder and neck and the pain is so great as we rise that by the time we land on the roof, waterfalls are pouring from my eyes.

"Emma, what's wrong?" he inquires, releasing me and taking a step back.

I'm shaking now, the pain too intense.

"My arm," I gasp. "Can you…heal it?" I try to speak between the sharp stabs of pain.

"I have to see it," he says, his eyes full of sympathy.

I start to try to unbutton my shirt but fail at it with my one hand.

Without saying a word, Dante unbuttons my flannel shirt. Luckily, I left my t-shirt on from last night, not daring to take it off before putting the flannel on.

He doesn't even ask which arm is injured. I must be doing a poor job at concealing it.

I bite back the screams as he pulls my arm out of the sleeve, even though he tries to be as gentle as he can be. At first, it's impossible, but after sliding my good arm out of the other sleeve, it becomes doable.

I can see the shock and fear in his eyes. "I'm sorry. When did this happen, this evening?" he questions, setting the shirt on an empty milk crate as he maneuvers me to another one to take a seat.

"Last night," I whisper.

The outdoor lighting flashes on, and its reflectiveness almost makes it look like Dante is about to cry.

"Emma, why didn't you say anything earlier?" he demands, almost angry.

"There was never a moment."

"Then TEXT ME!" he says, raising his voice. "I'm sorry. I just feel horrible you went through this."

He kneels in front of me. "This healing isn't as simple as a skinned knee. It may take some time."

I try not to look at my arm; it's pink and brown and black and charred all over.

Dante starts near my wrist and moves his hand up my arm little by little. His eyes are closed, brow furrowed, an intense look of concentration on his face.

It takes a while but every second my pain lessens, and I breathe a little easier.

Finally, Dante finishes and he sits beside me looking exhausted.

I extend my arm back and forth and twist it, not believing what I am seeing. I can see a faint pink shadow where Griffin burned me, but I don't think I'd notice it if I weren't looking for it.

"Thank you," I exclaim, grateful that my arm no longer stings. "You're amazing."

I touch his shoulder tentatively.

"Are you alright?" I ask, my voice laced with concern.

He waves a dismissive hand. "Just a little tired. The more intense the healing, the more it takes out of me."

I had no idea that healing could hurt him. Dante must notice my worry because he winks at me and offers a small smile. "I'll recover soon. Let's just sit here for a bit. Tell me about your dream," he suggests.

I recap all that has happened in my dreams, and he tenses when I say Griffin's name. His hands ball into fists and his knuckles turn white.

"I'm sorry," I apologize as I notice his reaction. "I tried."

"It's not your fault, it's my kind. I'll kill him. Griffin. For what he did to you," he responds angry and cold. "And you did well, fairies all have an intense power of persuasion. It shows you have a strong mind since you were able to fight it so well." He runs a finger down the arm he healed as if checking his work.

His cool touch sends shivers down my spine, and I wish he wouldn't stop.

"When you're feeling up to it, I'd love to see your drawings of the places you saw. Maybe I can help you piece them together."

"That's your task, right? The secret one. You're looking for the lost swords?"

"I should have known you'd guess. Yes. There's something you don't know. You know the swords will restore all the magic back to our world, that much you got from your dream, but they've been missing for some time. Well, at least six of them have. Two remain in the Fey and have never been removed. That's why we can still travel between realms. However, because there are only two, the doorway can only stay open for short amounts of time." He pauses, searching for the right words. "In order to hasten the search, the eight ruling families came to a decision. Instead of sharing rule over our realm, if any house finds the majority of the missing swords, that fairy's house will rule.

"Long ago we had a high king who abdicated the throne and divided the power among the eight houses. Each sword contains a portion of the original high king's power. But the high king knew it would be easy to just take a sword and claim another house's power, so he put a spell on them. Each sword matches to a particular house and only a member of that house can use the sword. But the king of the house can pass control of the sword to another house.

"So when all the swords are found, there will be a new high king instated, and his say will be final." He shakes his head. "That's why Griffin is desperate. He wants to be high king." Dante reaches into his pocket and pulls out an unusual-looking flower.

The petals are dark orange with black swirls which connect to a black stem with matching leaves.

"I'm sorry I didn't figure this out sooner," Dante says, placing the flower in my hand.

"This is called Tiger's Dream. It's a flower from my world. Based on my research, it should...should," he looks pained as he repeats the word, "keep anyone from harming or touching you in the dream state if you keep it under your pillow," he cautions.

"Thank you." Before I realize what I'm doing, I throw my arms around him and kiss him on the cheek. "Thank you," I repeat it slower as I realize what I've done and start to cautiously release him.

As I pull away, he stops me, locking eyes with mine. It's night now, so his eyes are more animal-like, a glowing yellow. He pushes a strand of my hair back, caressing my face in a gentle manner. "I'm sorry it wasn't sooner," he apologizes again. I can't move. The world stops as he leans forward.

The earth around me shakes and the butterflies in my stomach intensify.

Dante releases me and pulls me to my feet. "Earthquake," is all I hear as he wraps his wings around me, protecting me.

I'm glad he can't see me. My face is red, embarrassed. I can feel it. I thought the tension between us made it feel like the earth shook but it was an actual earthquake.

I'm glad for the distraction because Dante doesn't notice my cheeks flush from embarrassment.

It's loud. I can hear things breaking and shaking, but I don't feel it. I realize Dante is hovering just over the roof. There's screaming and crying and the earthquake seems to last forever.

When the shaking stops, Dante sets us back on the roof.

"Careful," he warns.

I look down and see that just a few feet away is a huge crack jutting across most of the roof. It's a good foot across.

I gape as I scan across the campus and see the damage and devastation.

"We need to get down there to help," I insist. Then I mentally kick myself for not thinking of him sooner. "JJ!"

VII
INDIFFERENT

In the chaos, Dante takes us down from the roof in a different spot than where we went up. Walls have collapsed, water is spraying from random places, and I see sparks out of the corner of my eye, likely from downed power lines if I had to guess.

I start to run. I have no idea where to go. Which direction did JJ go in? Why didn't I just wait a few seconds until Francesca had mapped the night out?

The gymnasium. That's the last place I saw him. I'll start there. Maybe someone has seen him. Dante says nothing but follows my lead. I try not to think about the hurt and injured people I am running past. Some are crying for help. I can't think about them. Not until my brother is safe.

I slide to a halt and then turn into the gym. The basketball goals have fallen from the ceiling. One blocks the entrance. Glass is everywhere.

"JJ," I yell.

"Let's start down this hallway," Dante suggests, pointing to our right. "I'll check the rooms on the right and you check the rooms on the left."

Chaos is all around us. Lockers have toppled over in the hallways, many lights have fallen, while some are half hanging from the ceilings, and water is flowing down the corridor. It's not deep, but it's coating the already waxy floors.

I take a cautious step, which is maddening because all I want to do is run. People shove past me trying to get outside. Most are crying out of terror, but some have shirts held to injuries. I see two students helping a teacher through the wreckage. His arm is twisted at an unnatural angle. He screams as they try to shift him over debris.

I could help. But I can't think about that.

I wrench the first door open. It's a science room. It is empty. However, I think I smell gas, which makes me want to hurry. One spark and this whole place could come down.

I climb over some lockers, my wet boots slipping on the slick surface. It takes a minute, but I make my way over with sheer determination. The next room has two students, one I recognize, huddled in a corner. They don't appear to be injured.

"Dean, you guys need to get out of here," I yell, not waiting to see if they respond.

I don't even know if JJ is inside the school. I start to panic that I'm wasting my time searching in the wrong location.

I fling open the next door and enter the room. Jenny, Izza, and Brent are inside. Brent has a leg stuck under a large metal filing cabinet.

"Help!" Jenny calls. Izza is sitting down, leaning against a wall. She has a wad of paper towels, which has turned red, pressed to her head.

I hurry forward and help Jenny lift the filing cabinet.

We groan as we heave with all our might. Where is the adrenaline rush that people talk about getting during a crisis?

I feel like we only lift it a smidgen, but it's enough for Brent to slide his leg out. He screams in agony but can move it.

"Where's JJ?" I ask, panting from exertion.

"I don't know," Jenny cries.

Brent's leg has a gash in it and it's bleeding some. I take off my belt.

"Tighten this around Brent's leg to stop the bleeding," I command. "I must find JJ. I'll be back."

Jenny hesitates.

"You can do this," I reassure her and shove the belt in her hand.

This jars her into action.

"I think," Brent manages in a gasping breath, "I heard JJ," he winces in pain as Jenny tries to get the belt under his leg, "mention the robotics department," he finishes, breathless.

I almost barrel into Dante as I exit the room.

"Robotics."

He must have heard Brent. We turn around and head for the opposite end of the school. Dante easily maneuvers through the wreckage, turning and assisting me when needed.

When we reach the stairwell that leads to the robotics wing, I pause. It's impassable. Half the ceiling has collapsed.

Dante glances around and then picks up a massive section of the ceiling and pushes it to the side, making a small opening.

I hunch down and halfway crawl to get through. Dante's right behind me.

As I finish sprinting up the second half of the stairway, I see Francesca. I can't believe my eyes.

She is leaning against one of the few intact walls and filing her nails. Francesca is indifferent to all the chaos surrounding us.

"Where's JJ?" I ask, panting.

"In there." She waves to the room behind her. "But it's too late," she adds, sounding like a robot.

I run inside and see my brother's body crumpled on the floor. A light fixture is hanging down, blood dripping from its corner.

I slide to his side.

His eyes are open, rolled back into his head, and he's making a gurgling sound.

A deep gash is on the side of his head and I swear I can see brains; blood is pooled around him. I see more blood on the corner of a metal work table.

Dante is by my side then.

"Emma, I'm so sorry," Dante says.

"He's still alive. Help him," I plead, trying to be strong. Feeling an overwhelming sense of nausea but not wanting to vomit.

He doesn't move. "Emma, I can't."

By now Francesca comes in. "Dante, can we leave now?" She looks down at me like I'm a little child who lost their ball. "Sorry about JJ," she says with no emotion.

I throw myself at Dante's feet. "Please," I beg him, pushing everything aside, only thinking about my brother having minutes to live.

He looks at Francesca, and I understand his hesitation.

"I don't care!" I yell. "I release you from any guilt or obligation for what may happen to me. Please, just help him!"

He looks at me and something softens. He takes a deep breath and kneels beside my brother. "It may be too late, but I'll try," he whispers.

He places his hand over the wound and uses his magic. I'm not sure if it's because of the complexity of the injury or if it's due to the fact that Dante has performed two significant healings in one evening, but by the time he finishes, Dante, as pale as a sheet, collapses against the table.

"Did it work?" I ask.

He shrugs. "I don't know."

Francesca glances back and forth between the two of us, and I can tell the moment she pieces it all together.

"You broke fairy law for a human," she mutters. "A human that would have to see you to know that."

I ignore her. I'll deal with the repercussions of Chesa knowing after I find out if my brother survived.

I use the edge of my shirt to clean some of the blood off his face.

"JJ," I call softly as I nudge him on the shoulder.

I see him shift slightly, and then he opens his eyes, blinking a few times. "Ems, what happened?" he asks as he slowly sits up. He looks dizzy. "My head is killing me."

Francesca starts to laugh at his last statement. Little does JJ know how close that came to happening.

"Chesa?" He angles his head around me and his eyes widen. "Did you change costumes?" he inquires, looking confused. Then he notices Dante, resting in the corner.

"What's going on?" JJ scoots away from them, closer to me. "What's with the ears? And why does Dante have wings?"

"You can see them?" I ask, stunned.

"Of course I can," my brother answers, looking at me like I'm crazy.

"JJ, I'm glad you're alright." Francesca leans forward, reaching her hand out to help him up.

"Stay away from him," I growl. "Don't ever come near my brother again."

JJ looks back and forth between the two of us.

"What is going on?" he presses as he starts to stand up. I get up as fast as I can and help him.

"Chessy, go home," Dante orders, his voice firm and cold.

She huffs and storms off.

"How is this possible?" I wonder.

"Maybe it's some aftereffect of my…" Dante stops and looks at JJ.

I step away and speak to Dante in hushed tones. "I'm going to have to tell him now. He can see everything."

Dante places his hand on my shoulder. "I'm not sure that's wise," he whispers. "But I don't know what to do now that he can see. I guess it's up to you."

"Hello!" JJ says. "I'm right here." He must have looked around the room for the first time. "What happened?" he asks, pointing to broken robots and debris.

"We should go help people," I respond, looking at Dante, ignoring JJ.

"No, you should get your brother home. I'll do what any human would do and help get people to safety.

His eyes linger on me for a long moment before he leaves.

I turn back to JJ. "Let's get you home. You've had a long day."

"But why can't I remember, and why are you acting strange?" he demands, and then he must have remembered my conversation with Francesca. "And why were you so rude to Chesa?"

I sigh. "Look, I'll explain all this tonight. Right now, just know we had an earthquake. MOM! We need to go check on her."

I am the worst daughter in history. How could I have not thought of Mom once during this entire catastrophe?

"Just keep your mouth shut. Don't mention the ears or wings or anything strange you may see. Not until I can explain everything."

JJ's eyes widen. "Earthquake?" he asks. "Hurry, let's go home."

I bar his path.

"Emma, come on, this isn't the time for jokes."

"I need you to promise me. You won't say a word. TO ANYONE."

He sighs and shrugs his shoulders. "Fine. Can we go please?" he asks, his tone impatient.

Instead of answering I just grab his hand and start running. He's a little slow. I forget that he hasn't seen the damage as I have. He pauses and gawks from time to time, and I must keep urging him forward.

By now there are fire engines, ambulances, and police on scene aiding the injured.

One stops us as we try to leave the building.

"Hold up, let me check you out," he calls to JJ.

My brother starts to slow down, but I grab his arm and keep running. "It's not his blood. We are fine." It's not entirely a lie.

We find the car. Although it's undamaged, downed light poles create too many barriers.

"We're going to have to run," I tell JJ.

He scoffs. "Are you crazy? It's like five miles from here." He takes a few deep breaths; he's already panting from the small run we've just done. "I'm not a runner like you."

"Fine, walk. But come straight home. I'll run ahead."

"I'll try to keep up, but don't wait for me if I can't," he adds.

I wonder how big the earthquake was. As I run the familiar streets to my house, they look unrecognizable. A few houses are undamaged but most took a major hit.

My normal pace is too fast for this obstacle course I am running. It's also darker than normal. Many of the street posts have fallen and shattered. So, I must make my way more carefully.

JJ falls behind after about the first mile, grabbing his side and panting.

As I continue, cries come from quite a few of the houses, and some from outside, as families survey the damage of their properties.

My heart races as I turn onto my street, and not from the exertion of my run. A tree has fallen over and some of the branches have broken through our family room window. Part of the chimney has broken off and scattered remnants slope down the roof. A gutter has fallen off into the lawn, but for the most part, the outside looks unaffected.

Before I even get the door open, I'm already calling to her.

"Mom! Mom! Where are you?"

It's dark inside the house. The power must be off.

"Emma?" I hear crying and follow the sound.

I bump into furniture as my eyes try to adjust to the darkness. A beam of light flashes in my direction.

"Oh my gosh, Emma," my mother exclaims. "You're okay." She runs toward me and crushes me in an embrace. "Where's JJ? Is he—" she begins, but I interrupt.

"He's fine. He just couldn't handle all the running. We couldn't get the car out of the parking lot. He's coming."

I can feel her relief as the tension leaves her body.

"I'd have come for you, but I worried that if I left and you came here, we'd miss each other."

"A smart idea," I agree.

She sobs. "It has been agony. The waiting. Not knowing."

"We are all okay. That's what's important." I glance around and can't see much. "Let's see if we can find some more flashlights or candles," I suggest.

"I've just been getting stuff together." Mom sniffs. "Lying everything on my bed. I even dug out our camping lanterns."

"Good thinking."

We head into her room. As Mom lights some candles, I switch out the batteries in the lanterns. By the time JJ runs through the door, we are seated at the kitchen table with a dim glow shining through the house.

"Mom!" JJ cries as he rushes over to her before she can even get out of her chair.

"JJ. I'm glad you're alright."

They hug for a minute and when Mom releases him, I offer to make JJ a mug of hot chocolate, like we are sipping on. It's a lucky thing we have a gas stove, because with the whole city a mess, it may be a while before power gets turned back on for everyone.

As I'm stirring in the chocolate packet, I hear Mom gasp.

"JJ, is that blood?" she inquires as she reaches a tentative hand to his forehead and touches the dried blood.

"It's not his," I give a quick holler from the kitchen. I hastily finish the chocolate and almost splash it all over him as I rush back, shoving it into his hand.

"Geeze, Emma. Careful," he complains.

"Sorry," I say. "At least it looks like the house is pretty much intact." I try to change the subject as fast as I can.

"I think so," Mom agrees, taking a sip of her hot chocolate. "But we will be able to tell better in the light of day."

I guzzle down the remains of my mug. "Well, I'm exhausted. I think I'll call it a night." I pick up a flashlight. "Aren't you exhausted too?" I ask JJ.

He's annoyed but can't miss my meaning. "Yeah, me too."

"Okay," Mom says. "It has been an eventful day."

I give her a quick kiss on the cheek and then flick the flashlight on so we can make our way upstairs.

"Night, Mom," JJ says. He kisses her and takes his mug of chocolate off the table, following me.

Once we are alone in my room, I shut the door.

"You could have given me a few minutes with Mom," he complains.

"We need to talk. And I am exhausted. I've been running around frantic for the last couple of hours."

I pick up a lamp that has fallen over on my bed and make room for us to both sit. The mirror above my dresser has fallen and shattered along with everything hanging on the walls, but I'll deal with that later.

He sits down beside me. "Okay, spill," he orders as he takes a sip from his mug.

"First, just realize that this is hard to believe but I am telling you the truth."

He nods.

"There isn't an easy way to say this, but Dante and Francesca are fairies."

"Yeah, right," JJ says. "You're so funny. What's going on?"

"JJ, I'm serious. It all started when I went blind," I say. I tell him about the process of me acquiring second sight. How, once the blindness passed and I could see again, that I am now able to see through glamour.

I tell him how I followed Dante, about our meeting at the gorge, about the house and the garden. I spill everything. Flying on the roof, my visions, burns, and at last JJ's injury and the healing that Dante performed.

He sits there watching me the entire time. I can tell he's just waiting for me to say "just kidding."

When I finish, I wait for him to speak first. Instead, he takes the flashlight and goes into the bathroom. The mirror must have broken because I can hear broken glass.

After a few minutes he comes back and sits beside me.

"My mind is telling me this is impossible. I keep looking for logical reasons to explain all this. I don't like not remembering." He touches his matted hair. "But there is a lot of blood here." He doesn't say anything for a moment, then asks, "I was dying, like for real?"

Tears well up in my eyes as I remember how he looked, lying there on the cold floor, blood pooling around his head. "Yes." I sniff.

"Why were you mean to Francesca? I mean, they seem good. Him healing me and all."

"Dante told me she was selfish. I didn't believe him at first but the more I'm around her, I see it." I lean forward and grab his shoulders. "JJ, you were inside that room dying, and she sat outside filing her nails. She could have been by your side comforting you or begging Dante to heal you."

"Maybe she was in shock?" JJ argues. "Did you think of that? And how great can Dante be if you had to beg him to heal me?"

I huff and jump off the bed. "I can't believe you're defending her. He saved you. It's against fairy law, and no wonder. This must be why because now you can see through the glamour. That's why you could see their ears and Dante's wings. He has always had them...And now Francesca knows about me. That's dangerous."

JJ shakes his head. "Dante just doesn't have a good relationship with Chessy. She's always telling me how controlling he is. It's him you should be worried about. Chesa cares about me, and I care about her. She'd never do anything to hurt either of us. She's only ever been kind."

I wonder briefly if brainwashing is her gift.

"You're so stubborn, JJ Harper."

He gets off the bed. "Look, I'm not going to say anything to anyone. I promise. For one, who would even believe me? I'm still not certain I believe it all myself. Maybe I'm concussed. Or having a crazy vivid dream I'm about to wake up from. Besides, I wouldn't do that to Chesa. Don't worry about me. But if you want things to be good with us, you'll apologize to Francesca, and you'll be nice to her because she's important to me."

Not waiting for an answer, JJ opens the door and I assume he goes to his room.

I can't believe he doesn't believe me about Francesca, nor can I believe how he tried to turn everything around on Dante, even after Dante saved his life.

Maybe Dante had been right. Maybe I shouldn't have shared that much with JJ. But he's my brother. We always tell each other everything. And I hated having so much of my life hidden from him.

I throw myself on my bed and growl into the pillow. As I'm lying there, I remember the Tiger's Dream plant that Dante gave me. I pull it out of my jacket pocket, taking care not to break the flower and set it under my pillow. At least I have one less thing to worry about. If it works, that is. The records from Dante's people haven't exactly been spot on about things in the past.

VIII
BEAR

The next few weeks pass in a blur. The school closes due to the numerous repairs. The city is all but shut down. The focus for the time being is to repair the utilities and clear the roads.

Mom keeps JJ and I busy though. The morning after the earthquake, when light floods the house, we get a proper look at things and realize we have more damage than we thought.

With everyone in need of a contractor, mom has us do as much as we can do ourselves. Which is difficult at first but becomes more bearable once the internet and electricity are restored and we can watch how-to videos.

Our house has not sustained tremendous damage like many others, however there are cracks in the walls and ceilings. Furniture has been damaged, some beyond repair. There is a lot of inside cleaning to do, mainly glass and broken jars. I don't think a single mirror survived in our house.

We learn how to spackle and seal cracks and how to texture, and read up on the differences between indoor paints. I never knew how many options existed. Or that if your choice isn't the exact shade as what is currently on the wall or ceiling then you have big mismatched spots when the paint dries. We end up repainting all the ceilings and walls in our home.

Mom doesn't want us tackling the window or chimney. Instead, we just clear the debris away and put a tarp over the window as Mom gets her name added to the list of a recommended general contractor. I think March is our estimated time frame. It's going to be a cold winter.

We reach out to our friends by text because everyone is preoccupied with their own repairs. Izza sustained a mild concussion and had to get a few stitches. Jenny is a little worried about aftershocks or more earthquakes, but is otherwise in good health, and Brent must have surgery on his leg. His shin is fractured badly, and a few pins have to be placed. He is looking at a minimum of three to six months to recover. However, his spirit is improving now that the electricity is back on and his Xbox works again.

I don't see much of Dante, or thankfully Francesca. I think Dante has kept her at bay. I text back and forth with him, letting him know that the Tiger's Dream is working. I have no new burns. The dreams also slow down. I'm not having them every night anymore. And since I've had the exotic plant, all my dreams have been flashes. No more unwanted visitors.

With school still canceled until further notice, I don't keep track of what day it is. I glance at my wall calendar and I'm shocked that tomorrow is Thanksgiving.

I head downstairs to scrounge up something for breakfast. Mom hasn't been in much of a mood for cooking as of late. She's not depressed or anything, it's just that most of the grocery stores have had a smaller selection of items. A few have closed due to the extensiveness of damage from the quake. The other three that remain open all need some repairs and have had to make do with smaller sections of their stores being open.

The first week, everything was gone, nothing but empty shelves anywhere you looked. It was a little strange to say the least. People began to panic.

But by the second week, the roads were all cleared and trucks came back to town again. A lot of people started to hoard things, worrying that the empty shelves would return. But the hoarding ceased as the trucks continued to come.

I'm alone in the kitchen. I open the fridge and stare. We have eggs and bacon, but I don't feel like cooking. Instead, I just pull out the milk and then move on to the pantry. Cereal pickings are slim. It's either Cheerios or Frosted Flakes.

I know JJ loves the sweeter cereals, so I pick up the Cheerios and pour a significant amount in my bowl. I feel famished, like I've run ten miles, which I haven't. In fact, I haven't run at all since the earthquake, and I am determined to rectify that today. I'm certain today will not be quite as enjoyable; having been on such a long hiatus, my run will take a little more effort than normal.

JJ comes bounding down the stairs just as I sit down.

"Gross," he says, looking at my bowl.

"They're greeaatt!" I wink at him as he pulls out a box of sugar-coated corn flakes.

He laughs. "That was pretty good," he says, pouring his bowl and joining me.

"Did you know it's Thanksgiving tomorrow?" I inquire, and then continue before he can answer. "It feels like we just celebrated Halloween."

"I know. It has been a crazy month. Mom invited Francesca and Dante over for dinner tomorrow."

I'm careful to keep my face blank. My relationship with my brother has been tense as of late. Especially when it has anything to do with Francesca. I've been trying to keep my opinions to myself.

I sense his eyes on me as if waiting for me to react. When I don't, he picks up a spoon and digs into his breakfast.

"Where's Mom?" I ask between mouthfuls.

"She went to the store to see if there's been any new deliveries. Don't say anything tomorrow—Mom didn't find a turkey, so we're having chicken."

I look at him. "Why would I? Besides chicken, turkey, there isn't a big difference." I shrug.

He chokes on a mouthful of cereal. "Don't let Mom hear you say that."

I know better than that.

After a second, JJ sets down his spoon and looks like he's going to say something but stops.

"What?" I ask.

It takes him a moment, but he finally says, "I didn't dream it, did I? That conversation..."

He can't bring himself to say the word fairies.

"No," I say simply.

"It's like I'm actually a part of T*he Hobbit*." He shrugs. "I guess that's kind of cool."

"Weren't those elves?" I ask.

"Close enough," he says.

I finish my cereal, wash my bowl, and set it in the dishwasher. JJ, on the other hand, sets his in the sink and starts to walk away.

"Um, don't you think you could at least clean up after yourself?" I ask as I put my box of cereal away.

He rolls his eyes. "It's a bowl, oh no," he gasps.

I point to the table. "And your cereal and the milk."

"You used the milk too," he counters.

"Before you," I respond. "What are you, like two?" I swipe the gallon of milk off the table and put it in the fridge. "I'm going to go running. Let Mom know where I am if she comes home before I get back."

"Are you sure it's safe?" JJ questions me, sounding concerned.

I shrug. "It's not like there's downed power lines or glass in the forest. Maybe a tree or two. If the trail's unpassable I can just turn around."

"Okay." He nods.

I run upstairs and throw on a pair of sweats and my shoes. The significant drop in temperature the last few weeks has made it frigid. I hate being cold.

I grab my AirPods and pop one in each ear, then find the playlist I'm in the mood for and turn the volume up.

The frigid air bites into me when I step outside, making me want to run back inside, jump on the bed, and throw the covers over me. But having run as much as I have, I know I'll warm up if I just get moving.

I have no desire to be reminded of broken homes and a city in ruins. I run the couple of blocks to the forest. As I ascend the mountain trail, I see some frost on the tree trunks, and frozen dew droplets on grass that's starting to brown. It has gotten colder than I thought.

The path is empty. Everyone else is too busy trying to repair damage from the earthquake. I have to climb over a few logs and one ginormous fallen tree that I struggle to scale.

It's gray and overcast; clouds fill the sky and I miss the sun and its golden rays. As I crest the last hill before I hit the flatter trail around the gorge, I slide to a stop.

Less than ten feet off the trail is an enormous brown bear, his head down. He's chewing on something. By the antlers sticking up, I guess a deer.

I'm in real danger. A bear will defend his food as intensely as it will a cub. This time of year, as food becomes scarce and bears try to thicken up to survive hibernation, they can be even more on edge.

Luck must be on my side today. The bear hasn't sensed me yet. But I'm afraid to move and cause any sounds.

I push pause on my music. It's much too dangerous to continue forward. If I proceed, I'll be in the bear's line of sight in just a few more steps.

My options are to either stay still and hope he doesn't turn around after he finishes his meal, which I feel is unlikely, or to retreat on the trail as slowly and quietly as I can manage.

Retreating sounds like my safest option, but it still carries risk. I don't want to turn around; then I won't be able to see if the bear notices me. However, stepping backward on a downhill slope that has rocks and branches sporadically doesn't sound like the brightest idea either.

I go with option two. Nothing is a perfect solution, but the longer I wait, the sooner the bear could finish eating and the less likely he is to be distracted.

I rustle up my courage and I'm about to take my first step back when a gust of wind blows past me.

I freeze as the bear halts his eating, putting his nose in the air. He sniffs and turns his attention towards me.

He looks at me and belts out a loud growl.

Too many thoughts crowd my mind in that second. How fast can a bear run? Will running cause the bear to chase me? Do loud noises scare bears away? Does playing dead help?

I try to think of everything I know about bears, or what I think I know.

He turns towards me, rises on his haunches, and growls a second time.

I make a split-second decision. Make as much noise as I can and hope it scares him off and then run like the dickens.

I wave my arms frantically and scream. I think I remember reading that I should make myself appear as big as I can.

The screaming makes the bear more upset. He leans forward, falling down onto all fours, and bounds towards me.

I spin around clumsily, frantically, and step forward, my ankle sliding awkwardly. I fall to the ground as my ankle painfully twists and I roll a few feet.

When I look up, the bear is just a few feet in front of me. His jaw is open, his razor-sharp teeth coming straight at me. I duck my head and shield myself with my arms, offering up a silent prayer.

As I'm sitting there wondering why my life isn't flashing before my eyes and how it is going to feel to be eaten alive, a second roar, even bigger than this bear's, comes from behind me.

I twist to see the new bear emerging from the forest. He's even bigger than the first, but this one is colored black.

I cringe as he bolts towards me, growling ferociously, but just as he's about to attack, he lunges over me and plunges into the other bear. I scoot back off the path, hiding behind a tree as the two bears wrestle, rolling into trees and smashing the smaller plant life. At last, the brown bear runs off, and the black bear turns to my previous position. Obviously, he's wondering where his lunch went.

I brace myself against the tree and try to calm my breathing. As my respirations become quieter, I can hear him approaching me, his paws crunching on twigs and fallen leaves.

I'm too terrified to look. I scrunch my eyes closed and hold my breath.

He brushes against me and I scream bloody murder.

"NOOOOOOOOOOOOOOOOO!" I jerk away, opening my eyes as I fall back, trying to scramble away, and stop.

"It's okay. You're safe," Dante says, kneeling and healing my sprain. He's like an angel wearing a brilliant white button-down shirt with intricate embroidery down the sleeves, dark pants, and with his leather boots.

This is the second time he's had to heal a running injury for me.

"But there were bears. They might come back," I argue.

"That brown bear is long gone," he assures me.

"But there was another one—" I begin, but the look in his eyes stop me. "You were the bear?" I ask. "You can change into animals?" I press, not certain why anything surprises me anymore.

He laughs. "Not any animal. We can each shift into one. We are blessed with a specific animal bond when we are born. Mine's a bear." A sheepish grin spreads across his face.

"Well, I'm just happy your animal isn't a squirrel."

He laughs a second time, even louder. "Yes, that would have proved to be a little more challenging." He reaches his hand up and helps me to my feet. "I've been wondering if you were ever going to run again."

He's been watching for me. I feel butterflies attacking my stomach.

"Thank you," I say. "We've been busy with repairs and I haven't had time to get out. I bet you've had a lot to do in that mansion of yours."

He brushes a thick section of his dark hair from his eyes. "No, our home remains undisturbed."

I brush the leaves off my backside, hoping I don't look too disheveled. "That's a lucky break," I respond, but he grins.

"Not really, our magic protects it. A small area like a home doesn't take much. Not to change the subject, but I wondered—" he doesn't finish but takes a step closer to me. I can feel his breath on my face as his eyes lock onto mine.

I swallow hard. "What are you wondering?" It's hard for me to even form the words, to make my mind think clearly enough to make sense.

"How were you ever able to complete a run before I met you?" His voice is teasing, but I still look away, embarrassed by my clumsiness and my constant need for rescuing.

Then before I even know what's happening, he turns my head back towards him, caresses my face in his hand, and leans forward and kisses me.

Our lips brush against each other, a light touch at first, and little electric shocks go through me. He leans in with more pressure and I pull him forward, my lips parting. His lips are soft and warm and he tastes like spearmint and something I don't recognize. For the first time in my life, I know what bliss feels like and I never want to let go.

But too soon for my liking he pulls away.

"So that's what it's like to kiss a human." He smiles, his brilliant white teeth in a perfect row.

I pull away, taken aback.

"This was what, an experiment? A game?" I demand, anger seething through me. I can't believe I let him in. Of course he wouldn't want a relationship with a human girl. He's just like Francesca.

His face goes serious. "No, Emma."

I turn and stomp away, tears welling in my eyes. I'm not about to let him see.

"Please. I didn't mean it like that." He reaches out, grabbing my shoulder, but doesn't try to make me face him. "Wait, please don't go. Let me explain." He sighs. "All my life I've been taught that humans are the weaker, lesser species."

My shoulders slump and I wonder why I am standing here listening to him degrade me.

"But," he continues, "I've never really believed that. I always knew humans were different, but I didn't think less of them. After kissing you, I can't imagine anything better."

I wipe at my eyes with the sleeve of my sweatshirt, trying to hide my tears.

He turns me until I'm facing him again. "I'm sorry that I made you feel like it was just a game. I never intended that. I spoke without thinking how that would sound to you." He reaches up and brushes a tear off my cheek.

I sniff and feel stupid.

"I'm sorry, I overreacted. It's just I feel inadequate next to you and all your abilities."

"Inadequate? I don't know any fairy that could have lasted an entire day with that kind of burn on their arm." He pulls me close and wraps his arms around me. "Emma Harper, you have your own kind of intensity. It's very impressive." He winks and leans down, kissing the top of my head.

"Thank you," I whisper, not trusting my voice not to crack.

He holds me for a long minute. After I feel like I've pulled myself halfway together, I lean back. "So, I hear my mother invited you over for Thanksgiving dinner. You never mentioned it."

"So, it wasn't your idea?" he teases.

"I wish I had thought of it, but if I'm being honest, I didn't even realize that it was a holiday until this morning."

"You've been gone a while. We don't want them to send a search party out for you. How about I walk you home?"

I'm relieved he wants to escort me for reasons more than just to protect me from the bears.

He reaches his hand out towards mine and interlaces his fingers with mine.

"This will be my first Thanksgiving. I mean, I've been in the human realm on the day, but I've never celebrated it before. I'd like to bring something to thank your mother. What would you suggest? What's a typical Thanksgiving specialty?"

"Pumpkin pie and pecan pie are two staples. My mom loves both, but you remember she's a chef, so her expectations are quite high," I remind him.

He chuckles. "It will be a challenge. That'll make it even more exciting."

When we turn around the next bend, we run into the ginormous tree.

"You climbed that?" Dante asks, astounded.

"Barely," I answer honestly.

"See," he says, looking me up and down, "impressive." Then he unfolds his wings. "But if you don't mind," he pulls me in towards him.

I wrap my arms around Dante's neck and we magically lift over the log. It's amazing, the feeling of floating, even more now that I'm not having excruciating pain shooting through my arm.

I wish the tree were even bigger.

Dante's strong arms hold me up with ease, but the ride is over much too soon.

"That felt amazing. Could we go higher sometime?" I inquire as we continue down the path.

He cocks an eyebrow up. "You're not scared of heights?" he asks.

"The girl who runs the gorge path? No." I laugh. "Heights don't bother me at all."

"What exactly were you envisioning?"

I blush and turn from him.

"Come on," he prods, nudging me with his elbow.

What am I envisioning? A scene I saw in a Superman show, where Superman takes Lois up into the night sky with stars all around them. I can't imagine saying that. It's too embarrassing.

"Just a nighttime flight," I answer, and then add, "so no one sees you."

He stares at me. I can tell he knows I'm holding something back, but he doesn't press me.

As we approach my house, he notices the tree in the front yard along with the broken window.

JJ had managed to cut the branches back. They no longer stick into the house.

"Isn't your home cold with the window broken?" he asks as he walks over and examines it.

"A little." I nod. "The contractors are all booked up."

"Of course, that makes sense." He turns back towards me and leans forward, kissing me on the cheek. "I should go."

"Ok-kay," I stutter awkwardly, wishing he'd never leave.

I make my way inside and wave to my mom in the kitchen. She's baking away and doesn't notice me.

I head upstairs and shower, then throw on a pair of clean sweats and a t-shirt. I have a small space heater in my room, making it nice and toasty, even if the rest of the house has a chill.

I relax on my bed, binge-watching holiday movies. I've just started my second movie when I hear banging sounds.

Mom can be loud when baking, but I've never heard her make this much noise. I poke my head out of my door and see JJ doing the same thing.

"What's that noise?" he asks at the same time I say, "What is that?"

I skip down the stairs and almost trip. The tarp over the broken window is down, and Dante is on the other side prying the old window out with a crowbar.

I look to my mom and back to Dante. "What's going on?"

Mom walks over to me and rubs my shoulder. "He just showed up with a window and asked if I would mind if he installed it." Then she leans closer. "He's a keeper," she whispers.

I feel my face flush, knowing he can hear my mom's hushed words, and Dante smiles.

Mom returns to her baking and I go back upstairs. I can't believe he came back to fix my window. I put on a jacket and slide on a pair of snow boots, just because it's quicker than lacing up my tennis shoes.

I bound out the door just as Dante is removing the old window.

"Careful," he cautions as he carries the broken pieces to the back of a pickup truck I've never seen.

"I don't know what to say. You didn't need to do this," I insist.

"I don't want to hear Chessy complaining tomorrow night. I'm doing this for purely selfish reasons, and everything else is just a bonus." He winks as he pulls a new window from the bed of the truck.

"Well, that makes sense," I agree, leaning back against the house beside the gaping hole in the wall. "Well, I guess that answers one question," I continue.

"What's that?" he inquires as he removes the wrapping from the window.

"I've never seen you wear a jacket. I thought maybe you don't get cold. Guess I need to work on my detective skills," I explain.

He shifts the window into position. "Would you mind holding it here for a minute?" he asks.

I move forward, placing my hands on the window frame as Dante grabs a hammer and nails.

"Okay." He sighs with a grin. "I lied, which is unlike me. I will have to be careful; you notice more than I'd have thought. We don't get cold. I just knew that humans feel the temperatures more easily than we do. I couldn't let you guys freeze."

He finishes nailing the window in and sends me inside.

I want to stay out there with him, but the temperature is dropping and I can't keep my teeth from chattering, so he banishes me.

He finishes the window without another word and then waves at me through the window as he hops in the truck.

I feel my heart drop as he drives off. I tell myself it's silly. I'll see him tomorrow, after all.

IX
THANKSGIVING

I am underwater. The water is clear and aqua blue. Beneath me are rocks and stones, many worn smooth from the rushing water. The current here is strong, and I realize I'm in a river. I see a few fish swim past me as I kick to the surface, my lungs warning me I am almost out of air. Just before I breach the top of the water, I see a glimmer with a hint of blue. I push through the water and take in a lungful of air, then dive back down and swim towards the location of the glimmer.

The waters are rough here, and I'm not making any headway. My eyes are sharper now, and as I focus on the location, I can see the hilt of a sword.

I struggle uselessly, kicking and stroking my arms forward. The sword is close, yet so far. My muscles ache and turn to jelly. I take another breath and give one last effort, using all my strength. It's to no avail and I resign myself to letting the current take me away.

I wake up wet and cold. My hair is dripping and I smell like river water. I roll out of my bed wide awake and jump into a hot shower. As I let the water warm me up, I replay the dream in my mind. I know I saw a flash of blue. This vision must be showing me the location of the blue sword. I wish I'd thought to look around more above water. Maybe then I'd have a better idea of a location.

Rivers can extend for miles and miles. The Mississippi River alone cuts through the entire length of the United States. Even if I could narrow it down to a specific river, it would still be like finding a needle in a haystack.

After I shower, I throw on my flannel pajamas and open my laptop. I do a quick search of rivers and find there are one hundred and sixty-five major rivers in the world. Who knows how many minor ones? Without some other geographical marker, I don't know how we'd ever find it.

Still, it's a little exciting to have seen it. I can't wait to tell Dante. Maybe his research will help us narrow things down.

It takes me a while to fall back to sleep, but once I do, I'm pulled into another dream. I'm back at the waterfall and Griffin is there. His wings are outstretched and they shine in the light.

"Hello again." His smile is too wide to be friendly. His eyes are playful, his expression taunting, like he knows something I don't. "Ready to play again." He fingers the hilt of a silver sword sticking out of a scabbard that hangs around his waist.

"Stay away from me," I yell. I step back but the water is behind me and I'm on the edge now, unable to go any further.

"You could make this easy. Tell me your name. Then I can come find you." His eyes widen wickedly as he stalks towards me. He no longer touches the blade; his hands are deadly enough.

"I won't ever tell you anything," I spit the words at him.

"You will." He shrugs nonchalantly. "In the meantime, more fun for me." He dashes forward and grabs for my arm.

I cringe, trying to brace myself for the agony that is about to come my way. Grateful that at least I know whatever this psycho does to me, Dante will be able to heal.

But nothing happens. I watch as he steps closer and tries to get a hold of me, but his hand just passes through me. It's like one of us is a ghost.

He swipes frantically, frustration and anger evident on not only his face, but every inch of him. He groans and stomps his foot.

I'm about to say something smug but his next look stops me dead in my tracks.

A slow eerie smile creeps across his lips. Then he starts laughing. He grabs his stomach he's laughing so hard.

I stare, not understanding what's happening, but my sense of uneasiness grows.

At last, he regains his composure. "Clever, you found help. This is going to make it too easy. Less fun, for sure, but way too easy." He gives me one last disappointed shrug and then disappears.

I wake up shaking. Not from cold, but fear. I'm not certain what Griffin thinks he just discovered. I never shared my name or location, but whatever it is, I know it's nothing good for me.

I think of sending an immediate text to Dante. But it's still too early, and I'll see him later today. Besides, Dante said that I'd be safe if I didn't tell him my name or where I lived. I hadn't. I knew that for certain.

Maybe Griffin thought he could bluff. Attempt to scare me since he can no longer inflict torture upon me. And if he bluffed, it worked, because that psychotic fairy terrified me.

The desire for sleep has long escaped me. I pull out my notebook and start sketching the underwater scene I saw. I need any distraction to take my focus off my last vision. I am still shaken to the core.

Even though the sketching helps and starts to ease my mind, every creak or sound the house makes brings the fear back in full. Could he know where I live? If he does find me, what can I even do? I am powerless to do anything to the likes of him.

I get bored with my sketch pad and toss it to the side. It's six in the morning. I can hear Mom up downstairs, starting our traditional Thanksgiving pumpkin chocolate chip cinnamon rolls. She makes everything by hand which means the pastry won't be ready for at least two hours.

I think about going downstairs and offering to help, but I am certain Mom would know something was wrong. The sun still isn't up. I'm never awake this early unless I'm going for a run. And after my encounter with the bear yesterday, I think it will take me a while to build my confidence back up. Even though I am sure the odds of running into a bear twice are astronomical.

I chicken out on both accounts and hide up in my room, opting to listen to music instead.

Sometime later I'm lying on my bed, lost in one of my favorite songs and the door flies open, I see a flash from the corner of my eye and a loud voice says something. I can't distinguish the words with my music playing.

I jump out of my bed screaming. My first thought is that Griffin has found me.

JJ jumps back. "Whoa, Emma, chill. Can't you take a joke? Breakfast."

I pick up one of my throw pillows and chuck it at his head as hard as I can. "Jerk."

He catches it with ease.

"Um, I hope you chill out before our guests come. Next time I won't call you for breakfast. Psycho much?" He shakes his head and leaves my room.

I start shaking after he leaves, the feeling of terror still fresh. I don't want Mom to see me like this. I take another long minute or two, steadying my breathing, and try to look calm.

When I'm no longer shaking, I put on a fake smile and head downstairs for breakfast.

The kitchen smells amazing.

"Sorry for scaring you," JJ says as I walk into the kitchen. There is no sincerity in his tone, and I can tell Mom must have heard me scream and made him apologize.

I ignore him and turn to Mom. "Happy Thanksgiving." I give her my best fake smile.

She's pulling the pumpkin rolls out of the oven, so I grab the jug of freshly squeezed orange juice and a bowl of fruit salad off the counter and bring them to the table.

"Thank you, Emma." Mom sets the pan on the table and we both take our seats. "Happy Thanksgiving, kiddos."

"Looks great, Mom," JJ adds as he scoops a quarter of the pan onto his plate.

I take two pumpkin rolls and fill the rest of my plate with fruit as Mom pours us each a glass of juice.

"I'm just glad I could still find some canned pumpkin. I think everyone decided to go a little overboard with the holiday baking after the last few weeks. You wouldn't believe how bare the baking aisle has been."

The first bite melts in my mouth. Whoever invented the combination of pumpkin and chocolate chips is pure genius. Einstein has nothing on that person.

"These get better every year, Mom." I pick up a napkin, dabbing the sides of my mouth for excess frosting.

Chocolate is smeared all over JJ's face. I don't know how he even has time to taste anything with how fast he is inhaling his breakfast.

"Did you get any chocolate in your mouth?" I inquire.

He picks up a napkin and wipes off about half of the mess on his face. "It's just sooo delicious. I can't get them down fast enough."

"Well, I'm glad you're enjoying them, but let's try to eat a little slower at dinner. We are having company," Mom reminds us.

"What time is dinner?" I ask.

"At three," Mom answers. "JJ wants to eat while he watches the game."

I laugh. "Since when do you watch football?"

"Brent is coming over," JJ explains. "This is the first time his parents are letting him out of the house since he came home from the hospital. He always watches the game."

"Oh man, that's got to be tough, not being able to go anywhere. I didn't realize his parents had him on house arrest, but I guess there's not much to do right now anyway."

I feel like I've lost touch with our friends since I started seeing things no one else could. I still text some with Jenny and Izza, but we're not as close as we used to be. I don't even know what they are doing today.

When I finish eating, I wash the dishes and then decide it's time to remedy my friendships. It will take more than a day, but I send them each a text asking how they are doing and wishing them a fabulous holiday.

Then after puttering around my room for a bit, I decide to go downstairs and help Mom with the Thanksgiving food. It is too quiet up here, and I keep imagining Griffin appearing in the dark corners of my room.

Mom has Christmas music playing, which on any other day would annoy me. I don't think Christmas music should be played until after Thanksgiving ends, but the upbeat music helps to set my mind at ease given all that has transpired.

She's chopping away on a cutting board, the aroma of fresh herbs filling the kitchen.

"Can I help with anything?" I ask as I tie my hair back, working my fingers quickly through until a braid appears.

"Sure. Just give me a sec. I want to get the herb rub over the chicken before I pop it in."

Not having a culinary bone in my body—I've burned water before—Mom assigns me to peeling potatoes. She sets two bags of russet potatoes on the counter and hands me a peeler.

I can't imagine how we could eat this many potatoes, but I know better than to start a debate about food.

We work in silence, each focusing on our tasks. I catch my mom humming to the music every now and again. Before I know it, it's an hour until company is expected to arrive. I've peeled potatoes and carrots and made a fruit salad and a green bean casserole, although Mom saved me twice from adding a wrong ingredient.

"Now we just have to wait for everything to finish cooking." Mom looks around approvingly. "The rolls are just about proofed and I'll toss those in the oven soon."

Most houses have one oven, two if you're lucky. We have four. Two double ovens. Three are stuffed to the brim and the last one is preheating for the rolls.

"If you have everything in hand, I guess I'll go up and get ready."

Mom gives me a double thumbs up and I head to my room.

This is the first time I have advanced warning that Dante is coming over. I decide to put more of an effort into my appearance. It has just been the three of us since Dad died. Comfy clothes like sweats and a t-shirt is my go-to. But not today.

Instead, I take the time to straighten my thick, mousy hair. I have to do it in stages, pinning two thirds up to start with and then bit by bit letting more down. I put on mascara and laugh at myself. I heard somewhere that it's almost impossible to put the makeup on without opening your mouth, and of course I notice my mouth gaping open as I attempt to spread it on my lashes without clumping. Then I put on a pinkish brown lip gloss.

I examine myself in the mirror, twisting and turning, assuring all my hair is nice and straight. I don't look half bad. Nothing like Francesca. I am no model in the making, but I clean up nice.

Now for the harder part. My closet. I skip over my t-shirt section and my hoodie section. My dress section consists of three dresses. One is too small, the next is floral but I've never worn it because it's not my style, and the third is a cute black dress. It's knee length with a lace overlay. It has a sweetheart neck with cap sleeves and a fitted bodice with a sash around the waist that ties in the back. I love it. It looks fantastic on me. But my mom got it for me to wear to a funeral, and I can just see JJ bringing that up and ruining it for me, so I pass it by. Maybe if I ever get to go on a real date.

I settle for my super chic skinny jeans with a dark blue tunic that has tiny crocheted flowers around the neckline, hem, and sleeves. Hopefully Dante likes blue. I mean, it is his family color. Of course, maybe that makes him hate it. Oh well, it's one of the cuter shirts in my closet. I need to go out and do some more shopping.

Once I'm dressed, I peruse over my bottles of perfume, but they're all too obvious. Instead, I squeeze a little lavender hand lotion out and rub it on my hands and neck.

I feel like shoes would complete my ensemble, but they just feel wrong. I never wear shoes in my house. I pull out a pair of clean white socks and call it a day.

Just in time too because after I finish pulling them on over my toes, the doorbell rings.

Subtle is not a word I would use to describe JJ. I hear him practically fall down the stairs to answer the door. As excited as I am, I plan on not acting like a fool.

I can hear Brent greeting my mom and relax. It isn't even them yet. Still, Brent is my friend and I haven't seen or talked to him since I left him in that room with his leg broken. I should go see if he's even still talking to me.

Brent's sitting on one of the leather couches in the family room, which is now not freezing, thanks to Dante. His right leg is in an orange cast just up past his knee and it's propped up by a few pillows. A pair of crutches have taken up residency in the corner of the room.

"Hey Brent, looking good." I greet him with a warm genuine smile. I am glad he's going to be okay.

"Thanks to you and Jenny. And sorry to tell you this, but your belt…" he shrugs, "well, it's history. They had to cut it off me."

I wave my hand. "It's fine. I didn't expect to see it again."

"I'm glad you were wearing it. The doctors said it saved me. I'd have lost too much blood without it."

I come around the couch and sit in a chair kitty-corner to him.

"I still feel bad about just leaving you," I say.

He shakes his head and adjusts his leg. "Don't. None of us knew where JJ and Francesca were. You did what you could for us. Besides, we all made it, that's the main thing. I will forever be in your debt. You saved my life."

"Yeah, right." JJ laughs as he comes in from the kitchen carrying two cans of soda. "Emma saved your life."

Brent bristles at this. "Dude, your sister's a hero. Don't joke about this with me," he says, his tone more serious than I've ever heard him.

"Okay." JJ holds his hands up like he surrenders. "You just never told me what happened."

Not wanting to hear the story again and have the attention on me, I head into the kitchen. We'll be eating soon, but my mom has set out trays of appetizers on the counter. I've seen Brent eat, and he consumes as much as my brother. I load a plate up. There are pigs in a blanket, mini quiches, and three distinct types of canapés. I load two to three of each on the plate and set them on a side table where Brent can reach them.

"Look at that," Brent gestures with his hand, "double hero." He winks at me as JJ rolls his eyes.

I'm saved from any more praise by the doorbell ringing.

Mom has made her way back into the kitchen. She has changed into a pair of dark brown corduroy pants and a sweater covered in fall leaves.

I don't even contemplate moving. JJ would knock me over to get to the door first.

Francesca enters first, which doesn't surprise me at all, followed by Dante, who carries a pie in each hand.

He looks dashing in a fitted black turtleneck and jeans. The pies look exquisite also. They are deep dish pies. The pumpkin has swirls of white creating a unique pattern across the top while the pecan pie looks like golden perfection with petite leaves of crust scattered across its top.

I notice JJ staring intently at Dante's wings. I catch his eyes and try to give him a look that tells him to knock it off. He must understand because he shifts his attention to Francesca.

"Those look amazing," I compliment as I offer to help him carry one. "Where did you get these?" I ask as he follows me into the kitchen.

"Beautiful," Mom agrees as I set them on the counter. "You didn't need to bring anything, and not after fixing our window."

"It was my pleasure." Dante smiles, and I wonder if he knows I melt to pieces each time he does it. "I hope they taste okay; I've never made pies before."

If Mom hadn't been impressed before, then she is now. "These are your first pies ever? You've got talent, Dante. I can smell the flavors from here and the crust looks buttery and flaky. Everything you want in a good pie."

"To be honest," he adds as he brushes a strand of hair from his eyes, "these are my second and third. I misunderstood some of the directions and had to throw away the first pie."

I wondered what he misunderstood but don't want to press him in front of my mother. Mom has tried to teach me how to bake loads of times, and I either end up with brick-hard treats or raw dough in the center.

"Mom, kickoff's after the next commercial break," JJ calls from behind me. "Are we ready to eat?"

"Yes, I just need to pour the gravy into the tureen."

"Great, I'm starving," JJ adds, and I can hear him and Francesca moving towards us.

I can't imagine him being hungry after all the food he ate this morning. I turn back to Brent. "I'll make you a plate. Anything you don't want?"

"No, your mom can make even brussels sprouts taste amazing. Thanks for having me, Mrs. Harper."

"It's our pleasure, Brent." She offers him a warm smile as she hands me a plate for him.

Dante stands to the side and waits for me as I pile on food for Brent, letting JJ and Francesca go before him.

I hand Brent a plate, not as loaded as JJ's mounding pile, that I can scarcely believe isn't spilling. "Let me know if you want any more."

"Thanks Ems, this looks great."

I realize I've forgotten silverware and turn to get some but Dante is already by my side handing Brent a few napkins, along with a fork, spoon, and knife.

As we reenter the kitchen, my brother and Francesca bring their plates to sit beside Brent.

Mom looks at the table and then the couch. "It might be fun to eat on the couch for a change. Football is just so American on Thanksgiving. Shall we try something new?"

I laugh. "Go ahead Mom." She smiles and moves to the other couch.

"Do you want to sit with them?" I ask Dante as I scoop up some mashed potatoes.

He shakes his head. "I could never get into football. I prefer the conversation of beautiful women." He winks at me and flashes one of his brilliant smiles. "Unless of course you like football, then I'm happy to—"

"No," I interrupt. "Football lasts too long. I watch it on Super Bowl Sunday. But that's just because I like to see the commercials."

He raises an eyebrow as he places two slices of ham onto his plate. "Commercials?" he questions. "I thought that's why you stream everything nowadays. No one wants to see advertisements."

A smile tugs at my lips. "That's true for the most part. But the ad slots on Super Bowl Sunday are beyond expensive so companies get creative. They all try to have the favorite commercial. It's fun to watch."

He shrugs, and I can tell he doesn't quite get it.

We sit together at the kitchen table. I offer him the seat at the head and then sit beside him. It puts him closer to me than if we sat across from each other.

I have so much I want to tell him, but I worry with Francesca just a few feet from us that she'd overhear us. Plus, between all the cheering and jeering it's hard to have a real conversation. JJ and Brent are rooting for opposite teams which makes for some heated moments.

"What do you think of your first Thanksgiving?" I ask.

He stares into my eyes with such an intensity it makes me nervous and sends goosebumps up my arms. "I'm enjoying it immensely."

I nudge his plate. "I meant the food."

He straightens up as if awoken from a dream. "The food is excellent. I'm not sure about the stuffing though. Soggy bread." He moves his hands up and down like a scale. "Can't quite decide on that one."

"Stuffing is the best part!" I exclaim as I drizzle gravy over mine and then take a bite and savor it.

"If you say so." Then he leans over and lowers his voice.

I, in turn, lean closer, wondering what he's about to share.

"But if your mom comes back in here, you may have to repay the favor I did you with the rabbit."

He leans back into his seat, and we both start laughing.

"That's more than fair," I agree.

Once I finish my plate, Dante sweeps it up and washes our dishes.

JJ is filling his plate for a third time now, and he is having Francesca hold a plate for Brent.

"How long do football games tend to last?" Dante asks.

I roll my eyes. "Hours and hours."

"I know it's a little cold out, but would you like to bundle up and take a walk?"

"I'd love to." I motion for him to follow me upstairs while I add layers.

"Leave the door open," Mom calls.

I can feel my face redden and I can't tell if it's from embarrassment or anger. Because I have never once heard Mom tell my brother to leave his door open.

I pop into my closet and Dante politely waits by the door.

I throw a sweatshirt on over my blouse and slide into my snow boots. Then I grab my running gloves and a knit cap off my dresser.

As we start to head out the door, Mom notices that Dante doesn't have a jacket and insists on him wearing one of JJ's.

"Don't stay out too long or you'll freeze," Mom calls as I almost shove Dante out the door before she can do anything else to embarrass me.

The wind bites into my skin even through the sweatshirt. I pull on my gloves and cap and I'm grateful that Mom made Dante take JJ's jacket. As soon as we are off our street, he slides it off and I add the extra layer.

"Better?" he asks with a wry grin.

"Much."

"Emma—" he begins at the same time I start to speak.

We both stop.

"Go ahead," I offer.

"No, ladies first," he insists.

"I need to tell you about last night. Something happened."

His eyes shift to my arms in an instant. "The Tiger's Dream didn't work?" His voice is layered with concern, and I can see he is angry with himself. "Where do you need to be healed? Emma, we talked about this. I don't care what time it is. You don't need to suffer any longer than you have to."

I wait for him to finish and he realizes he may have gone a little overboard. "Sorry," he finishes. "Are you okay?"

"The plant worked great. But something happened. Something I don't understand."

"Tell me what happened."

I rehearse the entire ordeal for him, although I don't think I can describe the joy in Griffin's eyes when he thought he could torture me to his satisfaction.

"So, his hand just went through you?" Dante inquires.

I nod and he sweeps me up and kisses me. For a moment I get lost in his lips and his strong warm arms wrapped around me. But then I remember Griffin.

I pull away gently. "I haven't finished the story."

"Sorry, I'm just glad that it worked." He folds his hands behind his back and nods for me to continue.

I tell him how angry Griffin became and then how he shifted into almost hysterical laughing.

"His last words to me before disappearing were, 'Clever, you found help. This is going to make it too easy. Less fun, for sure, but way too easy.' It scared me. What does it mean?"

"It means I've been stupid. But I don't know what else I could have done. Instead of having to search the entire world, he knows you're in the vicinity of another fairy. It will still take time, but he will be able to find you."

I gasp, stopping mid-stride.

"I promise he can't get to you now. He is in my realm and no one, NO ONE," he says again, slowly, holding my gaze, "can leave or enter until the realm opens on the winter solstice."

"And when is that?" I ask before sighing with any relief.

"December 21st."

December 21st. I have about three safe weeks and then Griffin can come and hunt me down.

"We have a few weeks." Dante tries to sound reassuring. "And," he continues, "if he doesn't leave the realm, we'll have another six months until the summer solstice."

He cradles my face in his hands. "I'm not going to let anything happen to you." Dante leans in and kisses my forehead. "We will figure something out." He looks up at the sky. "We've been gone a while and your lips are starting to turn blue. We should get back, but let's get together tomorrow and talk more. I'll pick you up and we can spend the day together. If that's okay with you."

I nod and lean into him, trying to extract all the heat I can from him as we walk back.

"You're just in time for dessert," Mom notes as I shed some of my layers.

"Yay, fourth quarter is about to start. We'd better hurry and dish up," JJ agrees. "Brent, pumpkin, chocolate, pecan, apple or all of them?"

Brent rubs his hand over his stomach. "Dude, I'm so full. Just bring me one slice. Surprise me."

Francesca loads two oversized slices on her plate. "I have to try Dante's or he'll never forgive me," she explains as she notices me eyeing her plate.

Mom cuts a thin slice of each pie and dishes them up on her plate.

"What's your poison?" I ask Dante, handing him a paper bowl.

"I'll try your mom's pumpkin, then I can compare. Maybe get a couple of tips for next year."

"If your pies taste half as good as they look, then you don't need any tips." I cut a generous serving of my mom's pie for him and an equal-sized piece of Dante's pumpkin pie for myself.

We're still the only two at the table, which is fine by me. My fork cuts through the pie with ease, and I can see the flaky layers. A pop of cinnamon and cream cheese meet the pumpkin and melt in my mouth. He might rival my mom when it comes to cooking. "This is amazing," I manage before stuffing another bite in my mouth, not wanting to set my fork down.

"So," he says, twirling the fork in his fingers, "what do you want to do tomorrow?"

I think about his question for a moment and can't think of anything specific. Just getting to spend the day together sounds like the distraction I dearly need. And I think I'd even enjoy going to school if I were with Dante the entire time.

"Anything is fine with me."

"So, decisiveness is not your strong suit." He nods to himself. "Well, I have a few ideas." He reaches forward and takes my hand in his. "Let's make a deal. I know we have a lot to..." his eyes shift to his sister, "figure out," he says, careful to keep his words vague with company nearby. "But just for tomorrow, let's forget it all. I think you could use a carefree, normal, human day," he whispers the second-to-last word.

"Sounds like a plan." I smile, although looking at Dante and his not-human eyes, and the beautiful wings springing out of his back, I doubt I'd ever be able to shut all things Fey out of my mind.

The football game ends sooner than I'd have liked. Brent gets picked up by his mother. Dante, true to form, washes all the dishes, as Mom, JJ, and I clean up and put food away. Francesca gets up "to help," but she just moves around the kitchen attempting to look busy. I don't see her pick up a rag to wash a counter or assist in putting anything away.

By the time Dante finishes, Francesca is eager to leave. I think she's afraid we'll discover something else to clean.

"Thank you for another wonderful meal, Mrs. Harper," Dante says as they are leaving.

"Your desserts were the stars," Mom notes. "I'll be needing those recipes."

"You're being too kind," Dante answers. "But if you want them, I'll email them to Emma."

"It has been a lovely evening," Francesca chimes in. "But as Dante always reminds me, we don't want to overstay our welcome." She tugs on his shirt as she steps out the front door.

"I'll call you later," JJ says.

Despite the craziness going on in my life, I can't help but feel like I'd never top this year's Thanksgiving.

X
HAZY

Freezing water swirls around me. It takes me a minute to orient myself to which direction the surface is. I see the sword gleaming upstream and although I want to do everything in my power to reach it, my body won't let me. Instead, I kick to the surface. My lungs cry for air and I inhale a mouthful of water in my first breath. I cough and inhale again; this time it's all good ol' O2. I see rocks and trees on the ridges as the river sweeps me downstream. I cast my eyes upstream and see markings on the sides of the cliffs.

Instead of trying to swim against the current, I allow myself to be swept further downstream. As I drift, I make my way to the edge of the river. I smash my knee on a rock and wince as I grab for some roots overhanging into the water. As soon as I get a sturdy hold, I wake up.

I am cold and wet again. I turn on the hot water and relish in the warmth the shower brings. I'd love to stay here for an hour, but something in this vision caught my attention. When I can feel my fingers and toes again, I hop out and put on a pair of clean PJs. I have a vague memory of seeing the markings on the wall. But I can't remember where and I'm anxious to search for the location.

I pull a dusty photo book off my bookshelf. I haven't looked at these pictures since Dad died. I haven't wanted to remember. I don't remember when my birth father left, so there's not any pain. Maybe some emptiness and questions linger but it's not like the aching sadness I feel for JJ's dad. He was my real father.

Some hazy memory of me and Dad has something to do with the markings on the cliff. I see vague flashes, but nothing for certain. Dad and I used to take weekend painting trips. They were just day trips, but we'd be gone the entire day. Sometimes we'd just go a mile or two from home and other times we'd drive up to three or four hours.

I flip through each page, lingering on the images, letting the memories envelop me. These special times with dad. Enough time has passed that although there is still plenty of pain and sadness, I also have joy at the memories. Tears stream down my face as I turn page by page and remember.

I freeze halfway through the book. There I am with my easel; I'm waving to the camera and behind me, across the river, are drawings on the cliff.

I remember Dad telling me that no one knows who made the carvings. The best guess is an ancient American Indian tribe before this area became settled by immigrants.

This is the location in my dream. I am sure of it. I am also confident I remember this location as it was one of the last trips we took together.

I touch Dad's face, wishing he were still here, missing him desperately when I hear a small tap on my door.

It's just past seven. JJ can't be awake. Maybe Mom wants help in the kitchen.

I open the door, and Dante's standing there. He's dressed in a striped button-up long-sleeve shirt and dark slacks. He smiles one of his model grins. He's holding two cups and a white paper bag.

"Good morning."

I shut the door on him. Here I am with wet hair, PJs, and morning breath.

"Um, did I do something wrong?" he asks in a whisper. "I got your mother's permission, as long as we keep the door open. Which isn't happening right now."

"Yes," I hiss back. "You can't just show up with no warning, looking all hot while I look like a mess."

I can hear him stifling a laugh as I rush through my room. Clean my room or make myself presentable. It's not hard to guess which one wins.

I brush my teeth first and run the brush through my hair again. Then I change out of my floral flannel pajamas and into jeans and a t-shirt with a maroon cardigan.

"No judging my room," I warn him through the door before edging it open.

He takes one hesitant step as if waiting to see if I am going to slam the door closed on him again.

"For the record," he says as he hands me a Styrofoam cup, "I've never seen you look like a mess. You're beautiful."

I sniff at the contents of the cup.

"It's hot chocolate," he offers, then he opens the bag. "I've never thought to ask you what you eat in the morning." He shrugs. "I brought options."

I make my bed as he lays an assortment of breakfast items on my dresser.

"What's your poison?" he asks, chuckling, "That's such a weird expression." Dante shakes it off and points. "Breakfast burrito, blueberry muffin, a chocolate croissant, and a donut. Does anything look right?"

"I could eat them all," I answer, walking over.

His eyes widen, a little surprised. "By all means," he says, stepping back and offering a small bow.

"No." I laugh. "I didn't mean all at once. I meant any of these would be a fine breakfast choice." I hover my hand over them, not sure which one I should take and finally settle on the croissant. "This looks lovely." Then I turn to him. "What do you want to start with?"

"I'll go with the burrito. I like protein."

We sit on the edge of my bed and I tear off pieces of the flaky croissant, glad I picked something that I could eat that might make me appear daintier.

"When you say you want to spend the day with someone...well you don't waste any time," I note.

"Only because we have to be to our first stop by eight." He looks at his watch. "We have about ten minutes until we need to leave."

"Where are we going?" I inquire, curiosity taking hold.

He holds his finger up and shakes it at me. "Knowing is for the person who had to make actual plans. You gave me no ideas. Now you'll just have to be surprised."

I'm not big on surprises, but I feel confident any surprise from Dante couldn't be bad.

"Alright, you win." I pop the last bite of my breakfast in my mouth. "Let's go."

As we drive through town, I try to guess the destination in my head, but every time I think I've gotten it, we drive past.

"We're going to the HOE?" I ask as we pull into the empty parking lot.

"Beg your pardon?" He cocks his eyebrow up as he puts the car into park. "The HOE?"

"The History of Everything Museum. H. O. E. The HOE," I explain. "You've never heard it called that?"

"No." He chuckles. "Not once." He opens the center console and pulls out a badge.

"This is your mysterious job."

He opens his door and runs around to get mine.

He furrows his brow. "Job, yes. Mysterious?" He shakes his head. "I don't think you've ever asked where I work."

I think about that for a moment and then realize it's true. I tried envisioning jobs for him, which I would be sure to keep to myself, but I never came out and asked Dante where he worked.

"I thought a private tour might be nice. They don't open until ten and no workers will even be here until nine."

I take his hand as he helps me from the car.

"So why the museum? There must be a reason you work here. From your house and cars," I point to the black Porsche he's driving, "I don't think you're working for the money."

"Access." He winks at me. "There may not be much here in this dinky town museum, but its computers link up with museums all around the world. I get access to archives and inventory and all manner of information."

He places his card against a sensor by the door and it lights up green. Dante holds the door open. "Ladies first."

"I think I may have a good lead on a sword, but it's far from here. It may take a few days to travel there and back. I'll wait until after winter solstice."

"Shouldn't you go now? Won't another sword help your realm stay open longer?" I wonder.

He nods as he escorts me through a few back storerooms with crates and boxes piled high.

"But, for the moment, I'm not in any hurry to keep the barrier open longer. Plus, it's not from my family. I'll need to bring someone from another line with me. But enough of that. Today we are supposed to be leaving everything behind us and just having fun." He uses his badge again to let us into the main museum. "That was the promise, right?"

"Yes, I believe so," I agree as he hooks his arm through mine.

We tour the museum from top to bottom. Dante is the perfect tour guide. I haven't been here since I was in second grade on a field trip, and the mixed array of exhibits is unusual to say the least.

The first room Dante takes me through is full of taxidermied animals from around the world, although the most exotic looking one is a sickly-looking panther.

The next room we go through is filled with gems and diamonds. I learn about different cuts and clarity. It's funny though, I think my mom's quarter-carat diamond earrings are bigger than anything in this room.

I have a faint memory of the next room from a field trip in my youth. There is a hand-crank radio that kids can operate to see how manual power works. There is also an enormous ball that emits static electricity.

"I always wondered what this is called. Does it have a name?" I inquire, pointing to the silver globe.

"It's a Van de Graaf generator," Dante says as he sticks his hands on it. His eyes go wide as his hair sticks up along with his wings and all his feathers.

I laugh so hard I grab my stomach to try to stop myself from rolling over. I never thought Dante could look foolish or funny. But he proves me wrong.

The last room we go into has medieval weaponry mounted on the wall. Dante explains to me the differences in swords and their uses. I never realized there were various kinds. I just thought all swords were long and pointy.

"Well that about finishes this exciting tour at the HO... ho...ho." He scoffs. "I'm sorry, I can't call it that. I feel like Santa Clause. I much prefer The History of Everything Museum."

"Do you play tour guide often?" I ask.

He balks. "No, no way. I prefer to be a recluse." Dante tugs my elbow, still intertwined with his, and steers us back towards the way we came in. "I tag and catalog all the new items, and make sure the items we borrow get back to the correct museums."

"If you can borrow things, why not get a Monet? Or King Tut's mummy?"

"Um," I can tell he is trying not to laugh at me, "we can trade with museums of our caliber. Our security isn't quite up to snuff for a painting worth millions. And I'm not sure what the remains of Egyptian pharaohs run these days, but I'm guessing it's well above what the insurance policy covers here."

I elbow him none too lightly in the ribs. "That makes sense. Thanks for attempting not to laugh at me. Although you didn't do a perfect job since I can still see it in your eyes."

"My apologies, madame," he says through a grin the size of Texas.

"I'll let you know if I accept after I see where you're taking me next," I tease.

He heads the opposite direction from how we arrived, and I try to think of what else is out here. I can't think of much besides miles and miles of mountains and forests.

Maybe our next stop is a hike.

We drive for another half hour or so, and I introduce Dante to the music I love.

We pull off onto a little gravel road, and just when I think he might be lost I see a set of buildings off in the distance. As we approach the destination, I see a sign for horseback riding. The buildings I see are several barns and the homestead of the owners.

Once we park, a man comes out to greet us.

"Howdy folks, you must be Mr.—" the rough cowboy says. He is a little on the portly side, with a thick salt-and-pepper goatee. He has on black cowboy boots, bright red pants, and a red shirt with white sapphire stars running up both sleeves.

"Dante is fine."

"Alright, Dante. I have the horses ready to go, just as you requested, but we need to go over a couple of things. Also, I'd like you to reconsider taking a guide."

Dante glares at the man. "The deal has already been struck and payment has been accepted."

"Yes, sir." The man nods, looking a little nervous. "It's just that there's a bit of a difference riding a horse on the trail and just going off on one. The horses do all the work on the trail. They know what to do, but—"

"I assure you, I am a very experienced rider," Dante cuts the man off. "Show me to my horse, and if you have any doubt, I will allow you to accompany us."

"This way." The cowboy motions for us to follow, keeping his head low and his eyes to the ground.

Inside the biggest barn are two beautiful paint horses, saddled and ready to go.

Dante takes his time, inspecting each horse with great care. The first horse has a loose shoe, which Dante makes the cowboy fix. After inspecting both horses, Dante inspects the gear itself.

"It might be good for business if you upgraded these saddles once a century," Dante tells the cowboy as he readjusts both of our saddles and asks for a different kind of bit for my horse.

By the time Dante finishes, the cowboy is so ready for us to leave that he doesn't even hint at having a chaperone join us again.

"Have a great time," he says quickly. "I'll just be in my office if you need anything," he adds before scurrying away as fast as his legs can carry him.

"I think you scared him," I noted.

"Sorry about that, but I've learned you have to be a little gruff with folks like him. He doesn't think anyone that doesn't live on a ranch could know the front from the back of the horse. I've learned that sometimes playing the entitled brat like Chessy has its perks." He turns and helps me on my horse. "Have you ridden before?"

I nod. "But just on trail rides. I am not at all experienced."

"Don't worry. I came out here beforehand and met with another man. I picked these horses out myself and I'm right here."

"I trust you."

I wonder when he came. Was this already in the works before we made plans last night? Or had he come here last night or this morning?

I place a hand on the saddle horn and a foot in the stirrup and pull myself up. I don't look as graceful as Dante does mounting the horse, but I don't fall off.

I grab the reigns and wait as Dante and his horse saunter up next to me.

We ride side by side on a wide trail. Dante is patient and thorough, making sure I remember all the basics. Once he's confident I know how to stop, how to get my horse moving forward, and how to change directions he takes us off the trail and through the tall trees.

He stays in the lead going slowly, making sure I am keeping up. We're in the woods for a long time, weaving in and out between trees. Sometimes we take the horses up in elevation as we make our way deeper inside the forest. I spot three deer that dart away as soon as they hear us.

We cross a couple of shallow creeks and breach the forest. We enter a small clearing. It's a tiny field filled with wildflowers and I wonder if this might be our destination.

But we pass through the flowers and continue until we come to the opening of a dark cave.

Dante pulls to a stop and slides off his horse. I raise an eyebrow and look at him suspiciously.

"I'd have mentioned this before," I say, not getting off my mount, "but it never occurred to me that a cave was our destination." I shudder. "I am terrified of bats."

"Don't worry," he assures me, striding towards me, "this is a bat-free zone."

He reaches his hand towards me and helps me off my horse, then ties both horses to a nearby tree.

My rear is a little sore and I am glad for the excuse to stretch my legs. I've never done longer than an hour trail ride before, and although I don't pull my phone out to check the time, I sense we have been riding much longer.

I look back, puzzled by the cave. When I imagined a carefree, romantic day with Dante, I hadn't envisioned this.

He slides his hand into mine and I forget my worries. We're together.

It's dark and cool inside the cave as he leads me forward, but after a few minutes I can see light up ahead. Dante leads me around a curve and I stop, speechless. There is a large circular opening above us. Sunlight fills this little cavern. A small waterfall runs down from above filling a small pool with crystal clear water.

A large checkered quilt with a ginormous picnic basket is laid on the ground beside the pool.

"This is beautiful," I note as I make my way toward the blanket, relieved to see sunshine and not a single bat. He follows behind me, a grin on his face, obviously pleased I like what I'm seeing.

"How did you find this place?" I inquire, looking around in awe.

He tilts his head skyward. "Flying has its benefits. You'd be surprised at all the neat places nestled in the mountains. Places I doubt the humans ever set foot on."

His wings are shimmering in the sunlight, and I reach forward, my hand hesitant. "May I?" I ask.

"Of course." He turns around, his back facing me, so I can get a better reach.

They don't feel how I imagined them. They are soft, like velvet, but strong underneath. I move my finger around in a circle feeling them. Dante jumps.

"Sorry, that tickles." He turns back around.

"Your wings are amazing," I say as he pulls me into his arms. He pushes back the hair from my face and leans forward. I close my eyes as his lips touch mine.

I'm lost in a moment of pure delight until my stomach rumbles so loudly that it jars us both from this magical moment.

Dante pulls away. "Looks like I'd better feed you."

If I could kick my stomach, I would. He leads me to the quilt and I sit down.

"How did you ever set all this up?" I ask, looking at the basket that is almost half my size.

He brushes a lock of hair from his face and opens one end of the basket.

"A magician never reveals his secrets, milady, even to one as beautiful as you."

I feel my face go red. I'm not used to being called beautiful, not from anyone besides my mother.

Dante rubs his hands together. "So let's see what's on the menu today."

He pulls item after item out of the basket and I wonder if it will ever end. There are fruits and cheese, crackers, meats and more cheese, olives of diverse types, cold chicken, and chocolate truffles. Then on the other side of the blanket, he sets out sandwiches, chips and dips, chocolate chip cookies, and watermelon.

"Did you think you were bringing JJ on the picnic?" I tease.

"I thought I'd give you options," he says, pulling out a bottle and two champagne glasses.

"To the right is a typical picnic from where I'm from." He winks at me. "To the left is what I think is a more typical picnic from where you're from." He offers me a mischievous smile. "Take your pick." He opens the bottle, pours the reddish-purple liquid into a cup, and passes it to me.

I take it skeptically and he laughs. "It's just sparkling cider," he informs me as he reaches back in the basket and pulls out a can of Coke. "Or I have soda."

"The bubbly's fine," I answer, taking a sip.

He passes me a plate and I fill it with foods on the fairy side of the blanket.

"For the record, this is all amazing, but a PB&J sandwich would have sufficed. You don't need to go to this much trouble." I pop an olive in my mouth and can't help but think how much my mom would love this.

"I'll keep that in mind. For me, well, where I come from...this is considered a simple meal. Francesca would turn her nose up at it."

That was hard to believe. Not the Chesa part, but the part about this being simple.

After we eat, we take our shoes off and roll our pant legs up, then let our feet dangle in the cool pool. It's a surprisingly hot day, and the cold water feels nice. We peer up at the clouds and see what images we can make out of them. Dante mentions a few creatures that he sees up in the clouds that he has to explain to me, since I've never heard of them.

It's a wonderful afternoon, just leaning against him, his arm wrapped around me and my head resting on his shoulder. I don't want to move, but I can tell the afternoon is getting away from us, and I want to surprise him with something of my own.

At last, I get up the willpower to stand up, tearing myself out of his arms.

"I know you planned this amazing day, but do you mind if I take you somewhere now?"

He stretches his arms out as far as he can for a long moment before standing. I wonder if they were cramped from me leaning on one side for so long.

"I'm intrigued." He hops up, spreading his wings and then recoiling them back into their normal position. "If we are together the destination doesn't matter to me."

"What should we do with all this?" I ask, pointing to the basket and the remnants of our lunch.

"I'll come back for it later." We pack the remains into the basket and I grab one more chocolate chip cookie before we start the lengthy ride back.

It doesn't take us that long to return. When I question Dante about it, he admits we took a more scenic route the first time.

The cowboy is relieved when we make it back.

"Thank you for the use of the horses. You have lovely animals," I say as I get into the car.

The cowboy waves back. "Please come back anytime."

Dante hands the man something as he gets into the car. By the look on the cowboy's face, I imagine a generous tip passed between their hands.

The cowboy waves as we drive off, his grin spreading from ear to ear.

I give Dante directions on where to take us but I must doze off in the car because before I know it, I feel gentle hands shaking me awake.

"Emma, we are here."

I jerk up. "Sorry, I didn't mean to fall asleep." I yawn and look out the window. We have about a half hour before the sun dips below the horizon.

He smiles and helps me out of the car.

I take his hand and lead us down a dirt trail to an overlook. "My dad, JJ's father, took me here to paint once," I explain.

He gazes up at the sunset. "It's stunning here. I can see why he would like this spot."

"I've been dreaming about a river recently, a place where one of the swords is hidden," I say, but as I look at Dante, his eyes are fixed on the markings across the river. His expression is intense. "Dante, I saw those Indigenous drawings in my dream. This is the spot."

He shakes his head. "They're not American Indian. They are an ancient fairy language." He looks back at me. "Where did you see the sword?"

"It's hard to know for sure because I kept drifting downstream, but in the river, towards our side. Dante, it's your family's sword."

Spreading his wings, Dante takes to the sky, skimming the water up and down the riverbed. He stops, hovering in place. "I can see it," he exclaims. He stares at it intently for another long moment before he flies back and lands beside me.

"Why didn't you get it?" I ask him.

"It's safe there. Buried deep in the rock, it's not going to be swept away. I'll come retrieve it before the winter solstice. Only someone from my family line can touch it."

He sweeps me up in an embrace. "I can't believe you found it. I've been searching for a long time, and hadn't found any leads to its whereabouts, other than a clue that led me to this town. But the forests are massive and I've been searching without much hope of finding it."

As we walk back to the car, Dante stops me. "Do me a favor?" he asks.

"Anything," I say and mean it.

"Don't mention this to Chessy. Knowing her, she'll sweep in and take all the glory. I'm not sure how I want to let the Fey know it has been recovered, or what the best way to go about protecting you is, but I do want them to know that you found it."

I can feel a shift in him, a change in his demeanor since we found the sword. As we drive back into town I think back to when it changed. The markings on the wall. That's when Dante was caught off guard.

"What did they say?" I finally ask.

He sighs. "If I pretend to not know what you're talking about, will you let it go?" he requests, his eyes looking hopeful.

I straighten up in my seat and take his hand. "Nope." I smile. "Now you just made me more curious.

"It's a warning to leave the sword be," he says vaguely.

"Why, what kind of warning?" I press, although I know he'd rather I didn't.

"It says to leave the sword be, that humans and the Fey shouldn't mix. The road only leads to death." He says the last line in a whisper. Then he squeezes my hand. "I won't let anything happen to you. It's just someone trying to scare fairies away."

"But don't you wonder why the swords were moved in the first place?" I ask.

He shrugs. "Of course I wonder, but there's no record, no way to find out."

"Maybe I'll have a vision. I had one when the swords were handed out."

"Perhaps," he acknowledges.

The sun has long since passed out of sight. He looks at his watch.

"I know." I smile wryly. "You'd better get me home."

"I must be becoming too predictable." He chuckles as he holds the door open. Then he hurries around to his side.

"Let me at least run you through a drive-through somewhere and get you a high quality, nutritious, fast-food dinner."

"See, simple and yummy. You're learning." I nod. "Who needs caviar when you can have a greasy burger and fries."

I see a flash on his face and wonder if caviar had been on the menu prior to me hijacking our date. If so, then I am even more grateful that Dante took me up on our detour.

We pull into the drive through lane and both get cheeseburgers, fries, and Cokes. The food is hot and delicious. I almost never get fast food.

Mom finds it appalling, but I just don't think she has ever given it a chance. Burgers have come a long way since Mom's teen years.

Dante escorts me up to the door, and we share a brief kiss goodnight before I hear voices in the house approaching the door.

As I enter, Francesca is leaving. I smile politely to her and just like that my perfect day is over.

XI
DATE

The next few weeks pass by in a blur. I hang out with Dante as often as I can, but the closer we get to the winter solstice, the more he works at the HOE. He's determined to find the swords. If his family can claim the throne, he is hoping they will issue an edict protecting me, banishing any member of the Fey were they to harm me.

It's a long shot, since no issue of protection has ever been ordered over a human, but we don't have many options.

Dante pulls up in front of my house at six o'clock on the nose. He's taking me back to his house for dinner, where he says we can speak more freely. He has something he wants to talk to me about.

"You look divine," he says, and from the way he's staring I believe him, although it's a bit intimidating.

I'm wearing the black dress I have kept tucked away in my closet waiting for just an occasion. My hair is pulled up and braided, just leaving a couple of loose curls in the front to frame my face. The weather is cold again; we've had no more freak warm days like the perfect day we spent together. I pull on my black leather jacket.

"You don't look too shabby yourself." I smile, returning the compliment, which is a huge understatement. He's wearing a full suit tonight. Black jacket and pants, with a black-and-white swirled tie, complete with a white rose bud sticking through the button hole of his suit coat.

JJ has dragged Francesca to a back-to-back viewing of *The Lord of The Rings* trilogy. We should have complete privacy to discuss whatever Dante wishes.

He pulls out a bouquet of aromatic white roses from behind his back. I don't even have to lean forward to smell the wonderful fragrance.

"Thank you, these are beautiful." I take the flowers, careful to avoid the thorns. "Let me just run them inside."

I hurry inside and my mom eyes them. "Aren't you the pampered one," she notes.

"I tell him he doesn't need to do all this, but he insists," I explain as I pull a vase down from the cupboard. I fill the vase and place the flower bouquet inside.

"Remember, midnight," Mom calls, reminding me of my curfew for the thousandth time. Which I don't understand. I haven't been late once.

Dante has the car door open for me and is waiting patiently.

I hop in, and off we go.

The closer we get to winter solstice, the more questions bombard my mind. Questions I try not to think about. But I've begun to be hopeful about our future, hopeful that we find the swords and I get the protective order, and that everything works out. Hopeful and terrified.

It would be great if he could travel between realms whenever he likes. I know he misses things and family from his home. I also wonder but have been too afraid to ask about things like aging and immortality. Does he see a future for us? Or am I just as much of a distraction as Dante thinks JJ is to Francesca?

I'm deep in thought when we arrive at Dante's house. I don't even realize we've stopped.

"A penny for your thoughts?" he asks.

"It would take a lot more than that to let you inside my head." I laugh, but I see disappointment flash across his face, although he's quick to recover.

He opens my door and then leads me through the house. "I thought we could eat outside," he suggests as I realize we're headed back towards the strange door.

"You do remember I get cold?" I remind him as he pushes the door open.

I am greeted with warm air as we step outside.

"That's not a problem." He smiles. "The temperature stays the same year-round out here.

He helps me with my coat and leads me in a different direction than we walked last time I toured the gardens.

I spot a small round white wrought-iron table with two matching chairs under an opening in the canopy. Starlight shines down on our little table, which is adorned with two elegant silver candelabras donning white candles, along with five or six multicolored floating orbs, which shed plenty of light on our table.

There are two dishes on the table covered in fancy silver covers, the kind I've seen on television shows when people order room service.

"You know they say less is more," I tease. This is becoming our ongoing joke, though Dante doesn't seem to be listening.

He pulls my chair out for me and drapes my jacket over the back.

"What's the other common idiom...something about a tiger not changing its stripes," he counters.

I can imagine what's under these: lobster and crème brûlée. Or perhaps escargot and soufflés.

"After you." He gestures to my lid once he has taken his seat.

I lift my lid and start laughing.

"You see, I do listen."

On my plate is a PB&J sandwich and a handful of Doritos.

"Bon appétit," I say, lifting my sandwich. "It's perfect."

We talk of trivial things as we eat. I wonder what he really wants to discuss, but I let him take his time and work up to it.

When the dishes are cleared, he takes my arm and we walk through the gardens.

"I've been wondering a few things," I say when I gather up enough courage. "How does it work, the aging thing? Do you live forever?"

"I don't think anything can live forever, but we do age slower," he responds. "We start out growing at the same rate as humans but each day we age a little slower and a little slower. I don't know the exact numbers. I mean, if we were toddlers for too long, no one would ever have children. Imagine if the terrible twos lasted twenty years," he cringes, and then smiles. "But each year we slow down quite a bit."

"So how long have you been this age?" I ask.

"Just one year, but I will probably not look any older for another decade or two. But even then I won't have changed much. I still get older every year, just like you, even if you can't tell."

I am not ready to find out how old he is.

"So how long have you looked like this…not a kid anymore, and still like you're in high school?" I ask, my curiosity piqued.

"A couple of years at least. It's hard to tell when the changes are so subtle," he explains.

We peruse the gardens for a while, Dante pointing out the names of the varied species of plant life. Then he stops and takes my hand.

"I've been thinking about our predicament a lot lately," he says, and I'm glad I haven't been alone in contemplating our future. "I know I briefly described what it means to be claimed."

This conversation is moving in a different direction than I had imagined.

"Yes, but you didn't want to claim me."

He nods. "I know. I still don't, but I think it may be our safest bet. Especially now since Griffin knows you're out here. Once a claiming is announced, no one else can try to claim you." He shudders. "I'd hate to think what would happen if Griffin somehow found you and claimed you. I can't take that risk." He reaches up and runs his finger along the profile of my face and I tremble for a reason that has nothing to do with being cold.

Dante makes me weak in the knees, and all I can think about is feeling his lips pressed on mine.

"There are things you need to understand about being claimed," he continues.

"I know, slavery and no free will, but I trust you not to enact that part."

"Yes, but there are also parts I can't control. The bonding is very intimate." He pauses.

"What exactly do you mean?" I ask, remembering him mentioning that before but not expounding at all.

"We'd be tied to each other emotionally," Dante says, trying to find the right words.

That doesn't sound bad; I already feel tied to him.

"There's no privacy. I'd feel everything you feel, know every thought you have. I wouldn't know everything you have ever thought or felt. I wouldn't have your memories, but any present thought or feeling we would share. I, yours and you, mine. I imagine we would both feel a lot of vulnerability at first. It's not an easy thing to get used to, or so I'd imagine."

Every thought. I'd die of embarrassment. Every random thought, every feeling. What if Dante doesn't feel as intensely as I do? Now he'd know exactly how I feel. It would be humiliating. And he couldn't even exaggerate his feelings because I'd know the truth.

"Wow," I say. "That is a lot to think about. It's not like I harbor deep, dark secrets but..."

"Everyone likes to enjoy the privacy of their own thoughts, I get it." He cups my face in his hands. "Emma, I love you."

I have no words. I know I should say it back, but I'm too stunned to move.

"I know this would be hard for both of us. But after weeks of contemplation, I can't think of another way that offers you the same level of protection. Some may still come after you, but at least they couldn't claim you. It would be one less thing to worry about. I don't think I could handle the thought of you being bound to someone like Griffin."

I manage a nod. "When would this happen?" I ask after finding my words.

"The winter solstice is in two days. The barrier between our worlds will be open for about ninety-six hours. You would need to come with me. I'd announce it immediately upon entry, and then we'd have the ceremony a few hours later. It would take time to gather all the witnesses and the elder to perform the ceremony."

"So, I'd be able to return the same day?" I inquire, trying to figure out how I'd manage my mom.

"Not until early the next morning. You could say you were having a sleepover with Chessy?" he suggests.

I roll my eyes. "I don't even think my mother would fall for that. Or allow it with you in the same house. But I can say I'm staying at Jenny or Izza's."

"Sure, that works too. You can drive straight to my house and then we'll leave from here."

I hate lying to my mom, but I can't see any way around it. There's no way she'd believe me, even if I told her the truth. And if by some miracle she did, I'd be locked in my room until Griffin found me, Mom thinking the way to keep me safe would be by separating me from Dante's world.

"What time should I be at your house?" I ask.

"The barrier will come down at sunset. Let's say five-thirty. If you're to my house by sunset, there's no way anyone could get through and find you by then." He pulls me close, wrapping his arms around me. I feel safe in his arms, and don't want to move. He kisses the top of my head. "I will keep you safe," he vows.

"I know you will." I look up and slide my hand onto the back of his head, running my fingers through his silky hair as I bring him towards me.

I'm not sure how long we were kissing, but we're broken apart by a huff and the door to the backyard closing.

Francesca storms towards us. "Nine hours!" she exclaims hysterically. "Who can sit in a bloody theater for nine straight hours? Not me," she says, throwing her hair back dramatically over her shoulders. "And to make things worse, your brother was actually paying attention to the movie," she pouts.

I stifle a laugh as she continues.

"I don't even think he cares I left." She offers a dramatic sigh. "And he didn't even offer to come with me." She turns towards me. "Is there spinach stuck in my teeth?" she asks between clenched teeth, opening her lips wide. "Or is there some other reason my natural charms and beauty failed me?"

"It was *Lord of the Rings*." I laugh, but I'm cut short by her death stares. "The world ending wouldn't pull JJ from his seat," I explain. Although why I am trying to make Chesa feel better, I have no idea.

My comment helps some. She glances between me and Dante. "So, what are you two up to? Anything has got to be better than sitting in that theater for another moment."

"It's time for me to bring Emma home," Dante answers. "And no, you're not invited." He smirks.

As we walk away, I whisper, "I love that series. It's a great trilogy." I forget for a moment how excellent fairies' hearing is, and I hear Francesca moan in disgust.

"Just ignore her," Dante suggests as he leads me back towards the car.

I could strangle her for ending our night sooner than was necessary, until I get in the car and realize it's already eleven-thirty.

We drive back to my house, our fingers interlaced, and I try to take solace in the fact that I get to hold his hand at least, even if I'd rather be tasting his lips.

"I may not see you tomorrow," he mentions with some disappointment as we pull up to my house.

I'm glad he's not the only one disappointed. "There's a big shipment coming in at the museum tomorrow and I've got to catalog it all. If there weren't any pesky humans around, I'd be able to finish in no time."

I roll my eyes. "Why do you have a job again?" I tease.

"So you can learn how to miss me." He leans forward and gives me a peck on the cheek. "Now, I'd better get you inside and you can start working on it."

"Don't worry," I say as I reach into the car and grab my jacket, "I don't have any problems in that department."

The porch light turns on and I groan internally as the door opens. "You're home early," Mom notes. "I thought maybe an animal got into our trash. I didn't expect you home until midnight exactly."

"I'll say my goodnights then. Goodnight, Mrs. Harper." Dante turns to me and smiles, giving me a little nod. "Goodnight, Emma."

"Thanks for bringing her back on time." Mom waves as he drives off down the street.

"Well, I'm exhausted." I kiss Mom on the cheek. "See you in the morning."

"Night, Ems," Mom calls as I head up the stairs.

I'm in a small room. Dark red drapes line the three bay windows and an octagonal table sits in the center of the room. Eight fairies sit at the table. I am standing off to the side, but in such a tiny room, I'm very noticeable. And yet no one looks my way.

As I focus on the faces around the table, I realize that one member of each of the royal households is in attendance, each wearing their color.

"We've called this meeting to discuss Bregon's wild idea," the fairy in the purple tunic says.

"It's not wild. It's civilized, Loren," another fairy I assume to be Bregon responds. He is wearing a red tunic.

Loren, the purple fairy, leans forward, clearing his throat before waving his hand around, "Bregon wants us to show ourselves to humans." There are several gasps from the other fairies as Loren continues. "Wants us to share our secrets with them, our magic," he adds, speaking the last two words with more force.

"That's crazy!" the fairy in orange proclaims.

"Come now, Jem. Let's give Bregon a chance to explain," Dante's ancestor interjects, looking to the fairy in red.

"Thank you, Pip," Bregon says. "That's not exactly what I was saying. We live here in our own world, free to travel back and forth to the human realm. We are more advanced. We have magics unbeknownst to humankind. I suggest we share our knowledge. Think of how many humans die each day of diseases we eradicated centuries ago. Injuries that are fatal that we could cure with ease. Isn't it time that we reveal ourselves to the humans? Offer our friendship and more."

A female fairy donning a green tunic leans forward. "I'm not sure humankind is ready to be aware of our existence," she responds. I can see Bregon's face fall at her words. "Instead of all or nothing we can start by helping in the shadows. Sending healers in glamour to their clinics and hospitals. Offer assistance without revealing the real source and go from there."

"But why?" Loren asks, leaning lazily on one elbow. "Why should we even care about them? They're insignificant; their lives are but an instant in the long run."

"I agree with Loren," a female in white adds. "Why take any chance? Humans are weak, lowly, and brittle, with a desire to kill and destroy. Some of their weapons could pose a risk to us. Perhaps they'll think they can steal our magic."

"We need to squash this nonsense now," Jem, the orange fairy, agrees.

"Perhaps we should think on this for a decade or two and then revisit," suggests the yellow fairy.

"Or wipe them out now, and never have to worry about it." Loren yawns, bored, as I watch horrified that he has just suggested the murder of an entire world without a second glance.

"Yes, then we'd have two worlds to explore. The humans are poisoning it anyway. The earth would be better off without them," the white fairy adds.

"Estellia, that's barbaric. You can't believe that!" Bregon shouts.

"We can't be entertaining this idea," Pip yells.

"Of course we can. It makes more sense than Bregon's suggestion," Jem calls from the other side of the table. "I call for a vote!" he adds.

"Those in favor of human annihilation?" Loren calls.

I watch as the white, purple, and orange families raise their hands.

"Opposed," Pip calls, his voice full of anger as he raises his hand.

I watch as green and red join him.

"Come now, Armen," Loren says. looking at the fairy in the pink tunic. "You haven't said a word," he points out before turning to yellow. "And Savat, no abstaining, we are deciding this today and not in ten years' time."

"If I must choose today, then I oppose annihilation," Savat answers, "but let me be clear, that does not mean I am voting for us sharing our magic with humans."

I hold my breath as I wait for the last vote.

"You have my vote, Loren," Armen answers at last.

"Four to four. There must be a majority to pass a vote," Bregon reminds everyone.

"We shall see," Loren mutters.

"Come on," Pip says, pushing his chair out from the table. "There's no point in trying to discuss anything else today. He grabs Bregon, who looks like he is still in shock, and as they leave the room, I wake up in my bed.

How close it had come to the fairies just deciding on a whim to kill humankind. I wonder if they could, or if with our weapons we stand any kind of chance. Would we even be able to see them if they chose to attack, or could fairies glamour themselves completely, appearing invisible, and not just their ears and wings like Dante did?

I shudder at the thought of how little they valued our lives.

XII
SUBTERFUGE

I spend the next two days close to home. Guilt has been eating away at me ever since I told my mom the made-up excuse for me not coming home tonight. Okay, I lied. I lied to my mom. It's hard to even admit it. I want to spend time with her before I leave just in case something goes wrong. But I can't even stand to look at her. The guilt is overwhelming.

She doesn't hesitate for one second to believe me. She has complete trust in me, which almost makes it worse.

Dante assures me he is ready for tonight, that there's nothing to worry about. Other than laying bare my every thought for him to see. But at least it's a two-way street. I won't be the only one exposed and feeling vulnerable.

The nervous twinge in my stomach becomes worse the closer it gets to five-thirty. I pack a bag and sit on my bed waiting, just staring at the clock as if that will speed things up.

The doorbell rings at five, and a minute later Francesca enters my room.

She looks frantic.

"What are you doing here?" I ask.

"Something came up; I can't explain. But Dante sent me to get you. We're supposed to meet him at the barrier."

134

This isn't the plan at all.

"I'm supposed to be going to spend the night with Jenny and Izza," I say, feigning ignorance. Dante had no plans to tell Chesa he was claiming me.

"I know," she hisses. "That's why he sent me. He couldn't come get you and explain the change in plans, but he knew I could say I was spending the night and we could go together." She points to the clock.

"We need to leave now. Dante wants you by his side before the barrier opens. If we get there too late, there is a chance other fairies could come through."

I'm not sure what changed, but Dante must have told Francesca. How else would she know so much about our plan?

"Okay," I finally relent. I pick up my phone to see if I have a message from Dante but there is none.

"Hurry," Francesca says as she pulls on my arm.

"Bye, Mom," I call as I trip on one of the stairs, trying to keep up with Francesca's speed.

"Have fun girls." Mom waves, barely giving us a second glance.

Chesa speeds through the streets and I hang on to the hand hold above the passenger door.

"Where is the barrier?" I ask as she zooms in and out between cars and I wonder if we will even make it there in one piece.

"There are lots of places around the world it opens up, but the one closest to us is in the forest near McKay Falls."

We pull into the parking lot at five-thirty and my phone dings.

It's from Dante.

```
Where are you?
```

I send a quick text back.

```
Just parked.
```

He sends a second message.

```
I don't see you???
```

"Will you put that thing away? The barrier is opening; we need to hurry."

"I'm just letting Dante know we are here."

She grabs the phone from me and pulls on my arm hard.

"You'll see him in a minute."

I run and still can't keep up with her. I know the entrance when I see it. I don't have to be told. It's a door frame made up of flowers and vines. The door itself is translucent; it's almost like a shimmering piece of glass.

I jerk back my arm when we are just steps from the door. Something isn't right. Dante's not here.

"What's going on? Where's Dante?"

Francesca's eyes look frantic. She huffs. "He must have already gone through."

I shake my head, planting my feet. "He would never go through without me."

"Let's just go. I'll protect you and we can find Dante. Something must have happened."

"Give me my phone," I demand. "Let me try to reach him first."

Francesca tucks the phone behind her. "We don't have time for this," she exclaims, her impatience growing.

"I'm not going anywhere until I hear from Dante."

I shouldn't be here. This is all wrong. What did I do?

"Fine," Francesca relents. "Text Dante, but hurry. It's not safe out here in the open now that the barrier is accessible." She holds the phone out to me and I step closer reaching for it. Just as I realize my mistake, Chesa grabs me and jumps through the barrier.

I'm thrust into a room filled with fairies, and before I can get my bearings, Francesca shouts.

"I hereby announce my intention to claim her," she yells above the crowd, pointing to me as I shrink back, horrified. "Prepare for the claiming ceremony."

Francesca doesn't look at me, but two male fairies grab me by each arm and start dragging me away.

"Francesca!" I scream as I try to free myself from their grasps to no avail. "Please, don't do this!"

I'm dragged through exquisitely decorated hallways with polished marble flooring and golden walls that are decorated with shining gemstones. I'm tossed none too gently into a room as big as my house. Before I can even stand up I hear a lock click.

I bang on the door for five minutes to no avail and then begin searching for another way out. There are windows, but the walls are sheer and there is no ledge for me to try to escape on. I'd fall to my death. I'm up too high to jump.

The room I'm locked in appears to be a bedroom. I doubt I'll find anything useful, but I search the two oversized dressers and large trunk at the foot of a bed that's draped with a gossamer canopy.

Maybe I'll get lucky and find some sort of weapon I can use to defend myself. I come up-empty handed. There is nothing but ball gowns and an assortment of clothing in here. I glance around wishing for even a candlestick, but the mantle is empty, and there isn't even a book or lamp on any of the small tables.

Other than attempting to smother a fairy with a pillow, I have no options.

I wonder what Dante is thinking, or when he'll realize what has happened.

After watching how cold Chesa acted when my brother lay dying, nothing should surprise me, but it still stings. It still feels like a huge betrayal even if I wasn't her biggest fan. She is Dante's sister.

The door opens and I spin around, hoping it's Dante coming to rescue me. Perhaps he has convinced Francesca to let him claim me.

But it's worse than I can imagine. Griffin strides inside, a smug look on his face.

"I'm happy you made it. I knew I could count on Francesca. She always looks out for number one, even if it means betraying her family and bloodline."

I can't believe she worked with him. How did he even get to her with the barrier closed? Then I remember his gift. He can walk into dreams. Apparently, that didn't just apply to humans.

"What did you promise her?" I ask, wondering how much it costs to buy a fairy's soul.

He laughs. "Don't worry, she drives a hard bargain. You didn't come cheap. I just had to promise her myself," he shrugs, "after I collect the other six swords and become high king over all the Fey. Never having anyone question my rule. She will become high queen. The most powerful female fairy ever." He winks at me. "Not a bad reward, for delivering one little human."

"Dante—"

"Yes, Dante," he interrupts. "Dante has always been a champion for humans. To leave them be. It didn't even take me two seconds to figure out which fairy helped you. And now he's powerless to stop me."

"I won't tell you anything. I won't help a monster become ruler of the Fey."

"That's the thing, dearie," he says with a smile that turns my blood to ice, "you won't have a choice. And I'll get to have all the fun I want with you." He gives me a little wave before exiting through the door.

I shudder to think of the fun he has planned. But at the same time, I wonder if Francesca knows everything the bond entails. Dante said we'd be able to feel everything the other person feels. Did he just mean emotionally or physically as well?

If it were a physical connection as well, I'd almost relish the thought of Griffin hurting me, just so she could see what it feels like. Almost.

I feel like I've been here for hours when the door opens again. This time it is Dante.

"Emma," he calls, rushing towards me and scooping me up in his arms.

"Are you alright?" he asks, touching my face with a gentle stroke and scanning my body for any signs of injury.

"I'm sorry," I cry. "This is all my fault."

"What happened?" Dante asks.

I explain everything. Francesca showing up, her piecing together enough of the plan that I believed her. How I started to have suspicions but how she tricked me at the end, and then I tell him about her deal with Griffin.

"Francesca claimed you?" he exclaims angrily. I can see the pain and betrayal on his face. "I can't believe this." He falls to his knees. "To betray our entire house." He shakes his head.

"I thought you knew when you found me," I whisper.

"No, I entered and heard a human had been claimed. I demanded to know where you were taken and didn't press for details. I just assumed Griffin had taken you, even though I didn't know how it was possible."

He grabs me and gives me a quick kiss. "There is still time. The ceremony hasn't taken place. I must find Francesca and plead with her, make her see this is madness."

He starts to leave but I grab his wrist.

"In case you can't change her mind," I say.

"I have to." The look of desperation on his face pains me. I can see the guilt too, although it's my fault and not his.

"You said after the ceremony I'll share thoughts and feelings but not memories unless I think about them, right?" I verify.

He nods.

"If you can't talk Francesca out of it, go to my house and take my book. It has detailed sketches of every vision and dream I've had. Use it to help you find the other swords. There are six missing. If you find the majority then Griffin can't become high king. You know where one is, maybe two," I say, remembering the trip Dante planned. "That means you just need to find two more."

"Okay. I promise you, I will not give up. I love you," he says before rushing out the door too quickly for me to say it back.

Before I know it, I'm being escorted from the room for the claiming ceremony. Dante doesn't have to find me for me to know he has failed. He would have come to me had he succeeded.

My hope now is for Dante to find the swords first. I'm brought into a large room. There are eight thrones at the far end, and crowds of fairies, satyrs, pixies, and other members of the Fey line the sides of the room.

In each throne sits the ruling member of each house. I see Francesca kneeling in front of the steps leading up to the thrones. She has changed into a beautiful silver silk dress. Her hair is pulled up, wrapped with flowers, and she doesn't look at me as I am thrown unceremoniously down beside her.

An old fairy in multicolor robes comes forward. I think he may be the elder I saw in my vision, but he has aged even more now. He carries a bejeweled blade and a golden goblet encrusted in gems. My stomach sinks as I wonder what the knife is for.

Did Dante not know about this, or had he concealed it from me so I wouldn't worry about it?

The elder speaks in a tongue I don't recognize. After a moment, Francesca stretches forth her hand and he slices it, letting the blood drip into the goblet.

Then the elder gestures to me. I shake my head and grab my arm, holding it tight against my body.

The old fairy nods, and guards come forward, pulling my arm until it's stretched out. They slice my hand and I scream as blood drips into the mug. My hand throbs. I look at the deep cut in my hand and cradle it to my chest.

The elder says more that I can't explain as he waves his hand over the mug and color sparks from within. He then passes the cup to Francesca who drinks. They don't even attempt to hand it to me. I'm held down. I know it's pointless to fight, but I have to try. They force the goblet to my lips and pour some of its contents down my throat. I try to gag and spit it out, but a rough hand is placed over my mouth, and I am not released until I swallow.

More words are spoken that I can't understand and then the crowd gathered cheers and applauds. Francesca bows to the elder and then to the rulers and makes a hasty departure.

I feel weird. My head is light and fuzzy and I'm overwhelmed with a sense of confusion. I'm dragged from the room and tossed into a damp cell this time.

The bars are thick and the bed is hard. But I lie down, feeling strange. I feel guilt and fear, but I don't think they are coming from me. I see flashes of a room. A reflection in a mirror. It's not mine.

The effects of the claiming are already taking hold. I'm seeing flashes of what Francesca is seeing and feeling.

It's too much for my head. I need to find a way to sort through it.

I feel an overwhelming amount of fear and then I see Dante. But he's not here with me. He must be with Francesca.

He's screaming at her. He shoves her up against a wall, and I can feel the pressure. His body tenses and I see his hand form a fist.

"How could you do this to her? To me?" he yells, and I tremble, or Chesa trembles. I guess we both tremble.

His eyes are filled with hatred. "You're dead to me." He spits and punches into the wall just beside her face, leaving a fist-size opening.

I feel sorrow and sadness. I try to tell myself that Dante isn't saying this to me.

I also feel a tinge of regret, and Francesca tries to bury it.

When Dante leaves, Francesca collapses onto the bed. I feel her being overwhelmed too.

I close my eyes, willing it to stop. She must do the same. It's quiet for a moment and then I remember we are sharing everything.

I hate you. You think humans are low? I'd never betray my brother and my family as you have. You have no idea what loyalty and love are.

Shut up, she thinks back. *Dante will forgive me eventually. When I've restored all the magic to this world, my house will forgive me. I'll be a hero.*

Some may forgive you, I think, *but Dante never will and deep down, you know it.*

Sleep is fitful. It's hard to discern Francesca's dreams from my own. Her feelings intertwine with mine and I can't figure out where I end and she begins. I dream of my family. JJ and my mom. Imagining my mother's reaction when I don't come home. When she finds out I lied. When she's searching for me without any hope of ever finding me. I can't bear the pain I'm causing them even in a dream. I envision the damage this will do to JJ, too, just recovering from the loss of his dad. I hope Dante spares him the pain of finding out Francesca betrayed us. I don't want him to spend his days blaming himself for trusting her, caring for her, when she cares for nothing and no one. I wake up sweating and shaking, sensing Francesca is feeling the same.

As the day wears on, I sit in my cell. My only companion my and Francesca's thoughts. As the hours pass, I'm finally able to feel a sense of clarity. Little by little, I'm starting to be able to sort through her feelings and mine and tell them apart, the confusion fading.

I think of Dante, his strong arms, his beautiful smile, and then I shove those feelings down, trying to think of anything else. Those are private, personal thoughts and memories with Dante that I don't want to share.

I lose track of time in my cell. I'm brought meals so I have a rough idea, but although I'm regaining some clarity, seeing through another person's eyes is confusing.

I never realized we'd share everything, but our minds think everything we see. It's like a constant relay of Francesca that I've managed to push to one side of my head, while I see through my own eyes on the other.

Sometime in the evening or middle of the night, I'm not sure which, I hear my cell creak open.

I don't move. Francesca is still sleeping; I can see her dreams. If it were Dante, I'd already be in his arms. It's not mealtime. I cringe to think of the only other person who might be visiting me.

"Trouble sleeping?" I hear the voice I dread.

I sit up slow and cautious, concealing my fear as best I can, but I can feel my body tense. I know firsthand what he is capable of.

"I thought it was time we had a talk. I want to know where the swords are," Griffin says. He leans against the cell wall, relaxed and at ease, but his eyes let me know there is nothing casual about this visit. He's dressed in a purple tunic. So he's from the purple house. I guess now that I'm a prisoner, he doesn't feel the need to conceal anything from me.

"I don't know anything," I say, scooting back on the bed until my back is touching the cold stone.

He steps forward, determined, hatred in his eyes. "I know you're lying. It has been almost a day since you came here and already Dante has retrieved one sword."

I smile. "He has been looking for them for a long time." I shrug but can't contain my happiness.

"We've all been searching a long time. Perhaps you forgot the power of fairies. I mean, you can't even really count Dante as one of the Fey.

He's too tame," Griffin snarls at me, reaching forward. "If Dante finds another sword before me, what I do to you now will look like nothing compared to that."

He lunges for me. I try to dive out of the way but he's too fast. He gets a hand on my leg.

Searing pain shoots through me, and I feel like I'm on fire. I scream and writhe, but he pulls me closer and punches me in the stomach. I groan. I'm in so much pain it takes me a second to realize Francesca is screaming too. I feel fire running up my back and my arm, then my neck.

I try kicking away but he grabs my hair and yanks me to my feet, throwing me hard against the wall. I feel my head bounce as a new pain explodes in my head. He pulls a blade from his waistband and slices from my ear down to my chin.

I scream again, louder; actually, I'm not sure if I've ever stopped. Then he whispers in my ear, "If you don't help me, then you're of no use to me." He tightens his grip around my throat, and I can't breathe. For a moment I think this is the end, but then he releases the hold on me and I crumple to the floor as darkness surrounds me.

I hear my name; it's faint, just above a whisper. I can't tell if I'm dreaming.

"Emma, Emma." The voice becomes clearer in time, and I recognize it as Dante's.

But the pain is excruciating. He must be healing me because the agony in my jaw has lessened. Fire still flares all over my body.

It's too much. Too much for Dante to heal. I try to articulate this, but I succumb to darkness again.

I wake sometime later, opening my eyes, adjusting to new surroundings. It takes me a moment to remember I'm a slave bound to

Francesca until my human life expires. Which may be sooner than I can imagine if Griffin has anything to say about it.

My surroundings have been upgraded. I'm in a soft bed. I see Dante slumped over in a chair next to me.

I look over my arms and feel my face. I'm physically healed, although emotionally it will take longer to recover. This was too much for Dante to heal. I worry if he's okay.

"Dante." My voice is horse as I sit up in bed.

He jumps up from his seat. "Emma!" He sighs in relief.

"You're okay," I say and smile.

"Me?" he asks, surprised. "I'm fine, how are you?"

"I thought maybe it was too much for you to heal. Don't take risks with your life," I whisper.

He leans forward, clasping my hand in his. "My life is nothing without you in it. And you needn't worry about me. I healed your face and your head, but other healers came and aided with the...the rest."

"How's your sister?" I inquire, realizing she went through the same thing as me.

"Better than she deserves," he spits the words. "She healed as you were healed, and vice versa. At least it made your healing quicker." Then he goes on to explain my change in accommodations. "Your quarters have been moved. You will now be here in a guest room in Francesca's quarters. She won't let me move you to mine," he apologizes.

"But Griffin won't be touching you again. Francesca will see to that now. Self-preservation is her top priority." I shiver at the look of disdain on his face. I've never seen him this angry. "I won't leave your side again."

"Dante, you have to," I urge him. "Find the swords, check on my family. Try to make up an excuse. I don't know what." Tears stream down my face. "Tell them I died. Car accident, I don't know. Just don't let them wonder where I am for the rest of their lives."

"I can't leave you. Not after last night." Dante's voice cracks. "I can't lose you."

I squeeze his hand.

"You said so yourself, Francesca will protect me now, if only to protect herself. She's selfish and cruel but there is one thing she cares about...herself." He echoes the last word with me.

"If I leave, I may not be able to return for six months. I've given the blue sword to my cousin, the king of the blue house. It should help keep the barrier open longer, but we won't know how long until it closes." He leans forward and kisses me with such a need and hunger I've never felt from him before. "I'll check on your family, then I'll go with Calvin and see if my hunch is right about the other sword. Hopefully this will buy me more time to come and go."

"Dante, I should've said it sooner; you caught me off-guard and I still have a hard time believing it. I need you to know just in case anything happens."

"Tell me when I come back. Promise me you'll be here. Keep fighting. And you can tell me when I'm with you again."

"Okay," I relent.

He kisses me once more and is gone too soon.

I close my eyes. Francesca is still sleeping, but it's filled with nightmares of Griffin. I thought it would feel good to see this. Watch her get a taste of what she has done to me. But it makes me sick, even to watch Francesca suffer.

As she dreams, I see into her thoughts. I see some of her rationalizations. How Griffin wanted to claim me, but Francesca at least didn't allow that. How she thinks she will be the best high queen of the Fey. That her actions have all been in the interest of her people.

She's wrong, of course. Her thinking is tragically flawed. She has deluded herself into twisting her selfish choices into selfless ones. But there are not the evil intentions behind her choices as there are behind Griffin's.

XIII
CROWDED

Staying in a bedroom throws me off. I'm not sure how to act without bars on my door. I've been told I'm a slave now. Does that mean I'm confined to the bedroom? I'm certain that if I made a run for it the guards would stop me. Plus, the fact that Francesca would know what I'm thinking before I do it doesn't bode well for me.

You can leave the room, but stay confined to the quarters, Francesca thinks to me.

It's still a little eerie not being able to have any private thoughts. I feel suffocated. There isn't enough space in here for two.

Nice guy you partnered up with, I think back.

I didn't know he planned to do that.

But would you have cared if it just happened to me and not you? I ask her.

I don't know. I mean, before, I can't be certain. But yes, I can feel her shudder, *now that I know what that feels like. How brutal he is. I wouldn't wish that on someone. You may not believe this, Emma, but we have more in common than you might think.*

Yeah, sure.

I just mean being tied to your thoughts I realize I may not have given humans enough credit, she adds.

So does that mean you'll relinquish your claim on me? You've grown a conscience, I inquire.

I can't. I made a bargain. I must stick to it. Besides, believe it or not, it wouldn't be safe for me to release you now. Griffin would claim you and I don't think you'd want that.

I shudder. *Definitely not.*

That night I have another dream. An icy mountain range flashes before me, my eyes drawn momentarily to a cliff jutting out with a lone tree. I'm shivering and cold. Then I'm in some type of cavern. There's ice and snow everywhere I look. I wonder if I'm in Antarctica. I wrap my hands around myself and rub my arms trying to create some warmth. As I step towards the edge of an icy ledge, wind whips around me. I look down and see something shimmering in a stalagmite of ice. I can't be certain, but based on these dreams, I believe I am seeing the location of another sword.

I hear a loud screeching sound and look up just in time to see something flying towards me. This creature is not from my world. It's the size of a large lizard, blueish white with dragonfly wings. Sharp talons protrude in place of feet. I duck as it swoops down, reaching for me.

I look around, but there's nothing to defend myself with. Just snow. I reach down into the snow, my fingers burning from the cold, and form a ball in my hand. I throw it at the creature the next time it comes at me. The lizard screeches and retreats, but only for a moment. I make a few more snowballs, but my hands and feet have gotten so cold I can't feel them and I'm having difficulty moving them. The creature lunges for me again, stretching a spiked tongue in my direction and I wake up

"Wake up," Francesca is frantic. She's shaking me but stops once I sit up. We're both shivering. Her lips are blue. *I didn't think fairies felt the cold.*

"I don't," she responds vocally to my thought, "but I feel what you feel. If I were in the dream instead of you, we wouldn't be having this experience. Wow, is this what cold feels like?" She nods towards the door. "Come on, I'll have a servant get us some tea."

I follow her, wrapping the comforter around me. She rings a small bell. I don't hear any sound, but a moment later another fairy enters the chambers.

"Fetch us tea. Quick. Bring an entire pot."

"Please," I add. Chesa may not have manners, but I do.

The fairy bows and vanishes.

"Do you have to find fault in everything I do? Even in your world, I could always see you watching me, judging me. I got tea for you too. Not just myself."

"I'm sorry," I say. "You're right. It's hard. You've done so many selfish things. I can't help it when a thought pops into my mind. But thank you for waking me up."

I don't have the Tiger's Dream plant anymore. I wonder if other creatures can hurt me in my dreams or just fairies.

"Fairies have hurt you in your dreams?" Francesca asks.

"Just Griffin. Dante found that if I sleep with a plant called Tiger's Dream, I can't be hurt during my visions. But I don't know if that works on every creature. Although it did stop Griffin."

"What did he do?" she asks, and Chesa looks like she cares.

"A lesser version of what we both experienced," I say, not wanting to think about it.

We sit in silence, each wondering about the other when the fairy servant returns with the tea.

I take a sip. It's warm and sweet, reminding me of a blend of lemon and chamomile.

"Please send for Griffin," she tells the fairy.

"At this hour?" the servant asks, looking nervous.

Apparently, I'm not the only one who doesn't like him.

"Yes, tell him I request an audience with him."

"Why?" I wonder, but I hear her thoughts before she can say them aloud.

"No, you can't tell him where the sword is!" I exclaim.

"Once I am high queen, I can fix all this. Dante will forgive me. I will free you and proclaim a decree of protection over you. But we have to find the swords before Dante."

"If we tell Dante and he finds them, then he will forgive you. He will never forgive you if you mate with Griffin. No matter what you do with that power."

"I've struck a bargain. Fairies don't go back on their word."

Even if that deal is with a psychopath.

Chesa ignores me.

"Griffin's rooms are close. You don't have to be here when he comes."

I take my cue and head to my room, refilling my teacup before I go. I have no desire to see him. I'll know everything they say regardless of if I'm in the room or not.

"You called," I can hear Griffin's voice both through the door and in my head, which is weird.

"Isn't there anything you want to say first?" she demands.

He waves an idle hand. "Oh, that's right. My little chat with the human. You experienced that." He smiles, and I shudder. "How was it for you?"

"If you touch her again, our deal is void. I didn't sign up for this," Chesa hisses. "And there's no need for it. I have access to her visions. Emma doesn't have a choice. I see what she sees."

"You realize your brother already found one sword," Griffin retorts, his tone angry, almost accusatory.

"And now I have the location of another. And I will get the rest of them too."

"Tell me where it is," he says.

"First apologize to me," Francesca growls.

"I'm deeply sorry. Had I known the bond connects human and fairy physically as well, I would have, of course, never harmed my betrothed." He offers Francesca a small bow that eases her nerves.

"It's somewhere in the snozards' domain. In a cave at the bottom, encased in ice stalagmites. I'm not sure to which house it belongs."

"Then I'll just have to bring an assortment of fairies with us." Griffin gives her a smile that makes my toes curl.

"Us? That wasn't the deal," Francesca says.

"Those mountains and caves extend for miles. I'm not going to waste my time searching them all. You and the *human*," he says with disgust, "have seen the area. You may notice something familiar that will speed up the search."

"Both of us don't need to go," Chesa says.

"I don't trust anyone else to watch her, and I don't think she'll help me without any...incentive," Griffin says, rubbing his hands together and cocking an eyebrow in my direction.

"Fine," Chesa says. "We'll come, but only this one time. I have no plans to traipse around the world. This is your task."

After pulling open the door, Griffin motions to the hallway. "After you."

"We need to change first," she thinks to me. "Warm clothes."

I open and slam my wardrobe door, furious that Francesca is going to help Griffin. I wish I could get away. Warn Dante. Help him find the sword first...

Not a chance, I hear her voice in my head. But of course, I already knew that.

I tug on pants and two shirts. Then Francesca brings me a pair of boots and a leather jacket. I eye the jacket but before I can even form the thought she says.

"I have it for fashion, not warmth."

I put it on and follow her out into the hall.

We follow Griffin to a large stable. A dozen elves wearing his color have assembled themselves, along with a fairy from each of the other houses. There are horses already saddled and waiting for us.

I'm not trusted with my own horse. I have to ride with Francesca.

Where they think I'd go, I have no idea. It's not like I know how to get back to my world from here.

We ride towards a mountain range covered in a white blanket of snow and ice. The closer we get, the colder it becomes. I duck my head down to keep the wind off my face.

At the foot of the mountains, we pause.

"Anything look familiar?" Griffin calls.

"No," Chesa says.

I look up at the mountains and scan the area. The range covers a large area. As I marvel at its beauty, my eyes stop on a cliff. It juts out from the side of the mountain and has a single tree on it.

"There!" Francesca exclaims, pointing to the spot my eyes just fixed on.

I hate sharing thoughts. I should have kept my head down and never looked up.

By the time we make it up to the cliffs, I'm exhausted. I haven't slept much, and the cold is beginning to sink in despite my layers. I feel miserable. And to top it off, I'm pretty certain Griffin is about to claim a sword.

We enter the cave and Francesca directs Griffin and a few other fairies in the direction of the sword. It's easy for them to get to it. They're all male so they have the ability to fly. Francesca waits by the cave opening, impatient to get back to her bed.

I'm still hoping for a miracle. That something will stop them from retrieving the sword. I edge closer to the precipice.

I hear a loud screeching sound and look up just in time to see something flying towards me. It's just like in the dream. A large lizard, blueish white with dragonfly wings dives at me, just missing me with its sharp talons. I duck as it swoops down, reaching for me.

I look around, but there's nothing to defend myself with. Just snow. It's hard to focus; the sense of déjà vu is incredible. I reach down into the snow, my fingers burning from the cold, and make a ball. Just like in my dream, I throw it at the creature the next time it comes at me. The lizard screeches and retreats, but my reprieve lasts only a moment. I make a few more snowballs, but my hands and feet have gotten so cold I can't feel them and I'm having difficulty moving them. I wonder for a moment if I can alter the dream, but before I have time to think, the creature lunges for me again. It stretches a spiked tongue in my direction. I throw the snowballs, but the creature dives forward and a second one joins in.

I'm out of ammo and this is new territory. Francesca woke me up before I could see how this all played out. All I can do is duck and cover my face protectively with my arm, waiting for the painful talons to rip through my skin. But instead, I hear the animal's yelp.

Francesca stands in front of me. She has a stick in her hand and is swiping it at the creatures.

"Help us!" Chesa screams down to Griffin.

The creatures fly away for a moment but come back. Chesa swings at them again and the branch begins to break from the force. One of the lizards whimpers as the branch comes down hard on a wing, breaking the branch. It flies off, struggling to keep airborne. But the last lizard seems to sense that we are defenseless now, the branch now in two smaller pieces.

The creature seems enraged now and screeches in anger as it dives toward us. Francesca waves one small piece of the branch at the creature, when I notice the broken-off piece has a sharp end. I lunge forward and grab it as the lizard flies over me, talons outstretched towards Francesca. It knocks the branch away and I jab my stick upwards into its belly.

It cries out and manages to make it back over the edge of the cliff before falling to its death, but not before raking my hand with a talon.

By the time Griffin emerges with sword in hand, Francesca and I are both cradling a hand.

"You monster!" Francesca calls. "You just left me there. You didn't help at all."

"I got the sword," Griffin says, waving it in her face. "That's the priority. I knew the snozards wouldn't kill you. You're tough. Anything else can be healed."

Francesca huffs and storms out of the cave. I hurry after her, not wanting to be left alone with the psycho fairy.

She doesn't wait for the others. We both groan and strain to get on the horse but once we do, she kicks it hard and we bolt off into the night.

Chesa calls for a healer the moment we get back.

Once the healer leaves, I turn, furious.

"That's who you want to marry? Is power that important to you?" I ask.

"You don't understand anything. He's just ambitious," she says, but I can see her expression waver. "It will be fine once we get the swords. Then I'll be in charge." She spins toward her room but pauses and points to the counter. "I'm going to bed. I had the healer bring some of that Tiger's Dream."

I can't deny the peace I feel when I have it under my pillow. I don't understand Francesca. How can she be so uncaring one minute and then do something nice the next? And how she can't see the monster Griffin is. But I also sense that maybe she can and just won't admit it to herself.

I wait for a response, but she's silent.

My thoughts flash back to my house. To my mother. To JJ. I wonder who my brother misses more and I hope it's me.

Francesca hasn't even thought of him once. Dante was right; she just used him.

Maybe I just want someone to care for me the way my brother cares for you. She tries to push the thought away before I can hear it. But I do.

I wonder about Dante and Francesca's parents. Do they have them? Are they alive? Didn't anyone teach Chesa that loving someone is putting them first? Thinking about yourself last.

I think back to my mom. All the early mornings cooking for us before school. The late nights waiting up for us or attempting to. Mom did everything for us. I know that's where I first learned how to love, by seeing my mother's example.

She used to get up early just to watch Dad paint. Mom read books on chess so that JJ would have someone to practice with. A tear falls loose as I think about what she must be going through.

I see a quick flash of two elves and wonder if those are Francesca's parents. I see a boat and a huge monster pulling it down, killing everyone on board.

And as quick as the memory flashes, it's gone.

No wonder Dante never mentioned parents. I had never wanted to ask. I assumed he had his reasons for never bringing them up and that someday he might.

I wonder how old they were when it happened.

Twelve and fourteen.

I wonder if Francesca meant to tell me or if the ages just popped into her head. But she doesn't say.

How could one sibling learn to be selfless and the other...I stop myself. I am judgmental.

I see Francesca get up from her bed and slam the door shut. Closing the door. As if that could keep us apart.

I can't give her space but I try to think about something else. I open the window and look up at the clouds, remembering the day Dante and I laid out in the sun. I almost push the memory away, not wanting to share, but I stop. I need this. If I can't have Dante at least I can have this.

I don't come out of the room again until late afternoon. A new servant has brought trays of food and my stomach is growling. Francesca is sitting on the couch.

I make a plate and as I nibble meats and cheeses my mind floats back and forth between Dante and Griffin. I wonder where they are and who will be the first to retrieve the next sword.

I wish there were a way to pass information to Dante without Francesca knowing.

She snorts and glances at me.

That's why it's a wish, I respond snidely.

"Go get changed," Francesca orders. "Today we are going out. I'm tired of being cooped up. I'll show you my favorite places."

It grates on me to be ordered about, but my curiosity gets the better of me.

I open a wardrobe in my room and I'm relieved when I find more than just ostentatious dresses. I find pants and tunics and select a black one because it reminds me of Dante.

As I'm dressing, a thought occurs to me. If each fairy is blessed with one gift and Griffin can enter dreams, then how does he have the power to burn me? Is that something all fairies can do?

And what is Francesca's gift?

So, he didn't tell you? she thinks. *I thought that might have been one of the reasons you dislike me so.*

What gift could she have that would make me not like her?

I don't like you because you claimed me! I shout at her.

That's true, but it started before that. Before the day of the earthquake even, she adds when I flash back to JJ dying.

You acted like you wanted to be my friend, but you really wanted to get close to my brother. Even your brother warned me about you. I defended you, not wanting to believe it even as I was seeing it with my own eyes.

I can tell that statement surprises her.

I pull on a pair of boots. They are a little loose, but not unwearable.

As we step out of the chambers into the hallway, I notice purple everywhere. It's not loud and flashy, but it's hinted in the carpets and on the walls. We must be in a dwelling that is owned by the purple house. That's why Griffin arrived so fast. No wonder Dante hesitated to leave, why he was willing to risk him retrieving the swords rather than depart from my side.

I hadn't paid much attention last night. I was on the verge of developing hypothermia, but now that I think back, even the servant fairy wore purple.

As I follow Francesca through the winding corridors, servants and members of the house offer her a low bow as she passes.

They must know she is to wed Griffin. I wonder if he is the king of the purple house already. I'd think he'd have to be, to demand this kind of respect since he hasn't found the swords yet.

When we step outside, I glance behind me to take in the full building. It looks like a palace from a princess movie. It's all white with tall spires. The stone is polished and reflective and is blinding when the light hits at certain angles. There are stained glass windows scattered throughout the building, all of them etched in silver and purple.

Surrounding the palaces are large gardens as far as I can see, with white stone paths dancing through the greenery.

We stop on a wider path, and after a moment a large round carriage comes trotting towards us. It's white with golden swirls and designs decorating the outside.

Two pixies sit on a bench driving the team. A third rides standing on a step that leads into the carriage.

"I'll require your services for the day," Francesca states flatly as she slides something into the pixie's hand. A form of payment if I had to guess.

The pixie on the step opens the door and I follow Chesa inside.

The interior is plush and comfortable. The cushions are large and whiter than anything I've seen before. I wonder how they can keep them clean. The walls are white with the same golden design as the exterior. The windows are completely open; there is no glass.

"Our destination?" the pixie at the door inquires.

"The palace of blue," she instructs, and the pixie nods before shutting the door. Then she turns to me. "I thought you might like to see where Dante and I grew up. The gardens here are nothing compared to the blue house's."

I take in the scenery as we trot down the road. The carriage is a little bumpy, but then again, I'm used to traveling in cars with shocks and other technological advances.

I see towns off in the distance and we pass two other palaces on our journey, green and orange. I wonder how big this world is compared to mine. I am not sure what I pictured, but I didn't imagine it could be this big when I saw the entrance, just a normal-sized doorway.

"There it is," Francesca announces, pointing out the window. I turn to see blue flags waving in the wind. The palace looks like the others we passed. However, this one has luscious, green forests surrounding it and snow-capped mountains behind it. I can't be certain as we are still a fair distance, but it looks like it might even be carved into the mountain.

There are waterfalls on both sides of the palace forming a stream in front of it. A beautiful green bridge, full of blue and white flowers leads across to the palace.

As we get closer my eyes widen. The waterfall to the left of the palace looks typical, but the one on the right appears to be going upward against gravity.

"Is that water?"

"Yes, How else would the water circulate around the palace? One fall flows downward while the other flows upward. Above the palace, in the mountains, they form a beautiful pool. If there's time, we'll go there."

Does gravity not apply here? How can water flow up? We bump up and down as we cross the bridge. Then we come to a stop and a pixie opens the door for us.

Francesca steps out, head held high. She carries herself with grace and elegance, but also with an heir of entitlement.

I follow behind her and I'm overwhelmed by aromatic smells from all the flowers surrounding us.

Chesa strolls forward as if she owns the place. Gardeners and other servants scatter as she flows through the paths towards the palace. I rush to keep up. I can feel eyes watching me. I wonder what they think of a human being here. Am I the first one to be brought here?

"Good day, King Harlen." Francesca offers a small bow of her head to a satyr as he passes us on the path. His attire is elegant and expensive looking. He dons a golden jacket with lace fringe. My eyes widen as I notice large oval-cut emeralds are in the place of buttons on his coat. A silk dress shirt peeks through from under the jacket.

King? I thought the fairies were kings and queens here.

Other species have their own royalty and hierarchy. Under us, of course.

I'd never deem any creature above a fairy, I think back sarcastically.

"And to you, Francesca," he comments, offering a small bow with his head. "It has been quite a while since I've seen you grace these parts."

"I've been out of the realm for a few years," she explains, "but I intend to stick around longer this time."

We continue down the path and I see a few fairies murmuring so low I wouldn't know it if I didn't see their lips moving. Francesca can't hear them either despite her superior hearing, but she just doesn't care.

Chesa moves with a purpose and heads directly to what I assume are her chambers here.

The furniture is covered with sheets and I can tell she hasn't been here in a while. The rooms smell stuffy and I see a thin layer of dust on everything.

After digging through a drawer, Francesca pulls out a small silver bell. She shakes it and moments later a fairy donning a blue apron enters the room, eyes wide.

"Why are my rooms not ready?" Francesca huffs.

"We didn't think you'd be returning," the fairy says, her voice shaky.

"That's an inane idea. Why wouldn't I come home?" she asks but continues before the servant can answer. "Well, what are you waiting for? Get on with it."

The fairy jumps to work immediately, stripping away the sheets and opening windows to air out the residence.

As we wait, I hear running in the hallway.

"No," a man scoffs as he enters Francesca's quarters. "They said you were here but I can't believe you have the audacity to show your face here."

Francesca rolls her eyes. "What do you want Eldon? Shouldn't you be guarding something?"

"You have a lot of nerve showing up here." He crosses his arms and shakes his head.

"Nerve? Showing up at my own home?" She balks.

"You betrayed your brother." He steps forward. "Did you think we wouldn't hear?"

Francesca glares at him. "What goes on between my brother and me is nobody's business but ours."

Eldon shifts his belt. "Maybe so, but betraying your house is another story entirely."

"What?" she asks, confused.

"Don't play dumb. We all know the deal you made with King Griffin."

So he is the king.

Eldon goes on, "You chose to help him over your own house, all so you can be high queen? You'd better leave before King Levin hears you're here."

"I deserve to lead. It's in my blood," Francesca argues.

"You renounced—"

"Dante did that, I never did. He shouldn't get to decide for me. I'm taking back what's mine. I will be a good leader. And when I'm high queen, I'll do what's best for blue."

"Until then, don't expect to find much hospitality here." Eldon calls to the servant. "Farrah, if Chessy wants to stay here, let her clean up her own space. Don't answer her call again."

Farrah scurries out of the room as Francesca huffs.

"Enjoy your rooms," Eldon calls sarcastically before leaving.

Visibly upset, Francesca throws herself onto the couch.

I deserve this. Levin shouldn't even be king. How can this house think I'm in the wrong? Francesca thinks to herself.

"What did you mean when you said Dante made a choice for you?" I ask.

I feel like I already know the answer, but it doesn't make sense to me.

"Dante was in line to be the next king. Our father was the king of the blue house before Levin. But when he…"

I can sense how painful it is for Francesca to talk about. But she presses through.

"…when he passed, the throne went to Dante. But he didn't want to lead. He was young and for whatever reasons he renounced his claim to the throne. It should have then gone to me. But my brother renounced my claim too, making my cousin Levin king. It's my birthright to rule."

"But why would he choose for you?" I push. It doesn't feel like the Dante I know.

"Does any reason even matter? How would you feel if your family made decisions about your life without even discussing it with you?"

I don't even have to think. I know I'd hate it.

"Dante has plenty of secrets." Francesca shakes her head. "Did he ever even tell you that he should have been king? Or that he stole my birthright from me? And now when I try to get back what was stolen from me, I'm the villain."

Eldon bursts through the door.

"What do you want now?" Francesca asks, throwing her hands up in frustration.

"You need to leave. Now."

She waves her hand. "We already had this conversation."

"Griffin just retrieved the green sword, with help from their king, A sword you helped him find. I'm not telling you to leave for you. I'm doing this for Dante. The people here are mad. I don't know what they'll do."

She scoffs. "Dante doesn't care what happens to me. Don't pretend otherwise."

He spins, pointing at me. "He cares about her," he yells. "And if you ever have any hope of repairing your relationship, you'll get her out of here. Remember, whatever happens to her, happens to you. The easiest way to stop Griffin is to kill the human. I'm not sure what would happen to you, Chesa…either you'd be…" he doesn't say the word, "or perhaps it would just break the bond."

Francesca gets up hastily, her mind not believing that her house has turned on her, but also not willing to take the risk.

"I'll help you get to a carriage, for her sake." He nods to me.

Eldon leads us back to the front of the palace, pausing when other fairies are in the vicinity and motioning us forward once the corridors are clear.

Once we get into the carriage, Eldon leans forward, "Don't come back," he warns, then slams the door and orders the pixies to make haste.

I don't speak as we ride back to Griffin's palace. Francesca's thoughts are scattered, broken, and repetitive.

How could they turn on me?

I'm their true leader.

I'm of the bloodline.

I shouldn't have had to unite with Griffin.

I am the rightful leader.

I never gave it up.

I never renounced my claim.

It's mine by right.

I shove her thoughts to the back of my mind. I have concerns of my own. Griffin and Dante both have found one sword. That leaves four remaining swords. That means Dante needs to find three more. Whoever has found four swords first will be awarded the high king title for the Fey. Dante will pass it on to his cousin while there is no doubt in anyone's mind that Griffin will claim it for himself.

I can't help but feel sorry for Francesca, even though I still want to be mad. But her life is more complicated than I thought. I don't know why Dante did what he did. I get the feeling Francesca is holding something back, but I also can't think of a reason for making that kind of choice for someone else.

When we return to the purple palace, Francesca goes to her room. She lays there and her thoughts shift. I see her self-reflecting, and wondering if she will ever be able to fix things with Dante.

His words crushed her and as much as she tries to act carefree, Dante is the only one she genuinely loves. Her last living immediate family member.

Trays of food are brought to us as the evening progresses. I wish they had TV here. Anything to pass the time and drown out some of the noise.

I find some books on a shelf in the main room and pick one up. I skim through it and then put it back. I'm not in the mood to read about fairy history. There's a book about humans. I flip through it and find it comical.

Apparently, we don't feel things like fairies. We don't form long-term attachments. Also because of our short lifespan we are viewed as dumb creatures.

Funny how they need a dumb creature to help them find their magical swords. I replace the book and go back to my room.

The weather here is perfect, and I toss open my drapes and fling open a window. I bring the chair Dante once sat in over by the windowsill and sit and watch the stars.

They're different here. Brighter and bigger. They have more colors too. Shades of white, yellow, and orange dot the sky. I wonder if they have stories about their stars like we do. I spend the next while imagining shapes and creatures in the stars as my eyes become heavy.

XIV
FORGOTTEN

The room is dark, just a single candle lit. I recognize the fairy holding it. It's Bregon. He looks nervous and scared.

"We have to do something," he whispers. "We tied today. What happens if we get outvoted? Or if Loren finds a way around the vote?"

"I know," a female voice agrees, but she's in the shadows and I can't see her. "I still can't believe four houses were in favor of annihilating an entire species. Humans aren't equal but that doesn't mean they don't deserve a chance to live."

"As long as the barrier remains open, there is danger to the humans. We must remove our swords," a voice I recognize as Dante's relative, Pip, explains.

"But anyone from our families can replace them," another male voice reminds them. "We must hide them. Preferably in the human realm. It will weaken the barrier and keep it closed for longer amounts of time. The humans shouldn't mix with the Fey. It can only bring them death."

"Alright, we're all agreed?" Pip asks. "We take our swords and hide them."

"Agreed," answers Bregon. "We'll meet tomorrow. We hide them and never tell another soul where they are." Bregon blows on the candle and the room is covered in darkness.

I wake up and can see Francesca is awake too.

I never knew why our ancestors moved the swords. Two other houses must have moved theirs later. The swords that remained were from the houses of purple and white.

What if Griffin wants to get rid of the human species? Don't you see how dangerous it is to have just one family in power? One couple who answer to no one? I think at her.

I don't think anyone else knows this history. I've never heard it before. They kept it secret for a reason. Griffin just wants to rule our people.

But even if that's true, I think to her, *can't you see the horrific possibilities? Four fairies stopped this atrocity from happening. If the swords are restored there will be no one to stand in the way of history repeating itself, whether that's in a decade, a century, or a millennium. Absolute power is dangerous.*

Our internal dialogue stops and we both sit and wonder about different possibilities before I drift off to sleep again.

I'm standing on a metal railing or bridge. As I look down, I can see I am up hundreds of feet. I grab the edge of a piece of metal above my head. The ledge I am on is very narrow and not intended to be stood on. While the height itself doesn't bother me, the fact that I'm up so high with no way to get down does.

I look around, trying to figure out how I got here when I realize where I'm standing. I'm on the Eiffel Tower. I've never been to France before, but I've seen enough movies to know where I am. Above me, attached to the inside of the tower, I see another sword. A fairy with wings would had to have stashed this blade. I try to see the color of the stone but my angle is not good enough. I crane my neck and lean outward, hanging onto the metal with my right hand. I still can't see.

I stretch even further when suddenly my foot slips and I fall. The ground is fast approaching. This is it; I'm going to die.

"Wake up!" I hear Francesca scream and I bolt up, covered in sweat with my heart pounding.

She's shaking too. "Would that have killed us?" Chesa asks me.

I take a second to catch my breath. "I have no idea. Isn't dreaming fun?" I laugh, a little hysterical.

Neither of us are in much of a mood for sleep after that dream. Chesa tries to teach me a game, but it's not much fun when you know what the other player is planning. We both bore of it after a few rounds.

"I've been wondering. Do only male fairies have wings?" I ask, leaning back on a loveseat with my feet propped up on a coffee table.

"Yes, just the boys."

"Why?" I ask.

"Genetics?" She shrugs. "Why are men stronger and bigger than women for the most part? Why can females have children and males cannot?"

"Okay, I get it," I relent.

I have never felt less for being a girl or been jealous of a guy for anything. But if I were a fairy, I'd feel cheated as a girl.

Breads, cheese, fruit, and boiled eggs are brought to us for breakfast. Francesca is content digging into the various platters, but I miss my mom's food. Pancakes, sweet rolls, quiches. Foods made with love just for me and my brother.

Francesca sends for Griffin and I cringe, wishing there were a way for me to get word to Dante about the location of the next sword before Griffin finds out.

I take a piece of bread and spread a thick layer of butter on in. I'm about to take my first bite when there's a knock on the door.

"Emma," I hear the familiar voice call, and I almost knock half the trays off the table as I lunge for the door.

He cracks the door open just as I wrench it, open practically barreling into him.

"We found a sword. The one I'd been searching for these past years. At last, I found it. It's getting delivered now. It was from the pink house." He pulls me from off his neck and inspects me. "You're okay?" he asks.

"Yes, I'm fine, but tell me about my family," I insist, pulling him into the room. "How are they doing?"

He sits next to me on the couch, adjusting his back so that it's mostly facing his sister.

"JJ is upset. He wants to come, but I won't let him. He tried to follow me, as if a human could sneak up on me." Then he realizes his gaffe. "I didn't mean it like that. I just meant with my stellar hearing and sight."

"I know you don't look at us that way. How's my mom? What did you tell her?"

There's silence. I look at him, waiting for an answer, but he won't meet my gaze.

"Dante?" I press, grabbing his hand in mine.

"I couldn't tell her you were dead. Not when I have hope I'll find the swords. And I couldn't tell her what happened. I couldn't let her think you just disappeared...so I went with a different option."

I think over his choices in my head and I can't think of any other path.

"So, what did you do?"

"Please don't be mad. I didn't have time to consult with you, and by the time I saw your mother she was hysterical with worry. I made her tea and gave her a memory elixir. Right now she doesn't think she ever had a daughter. Just JJ."

My eyes tear up. My mother doesn't even know I exist. I pull away from him, confused and hurt. I'm forgotten, erased from her life in a swallow.

"I talked with the eldest of our kind. He assured me it's reversible."

I close my eyes and breathe. What would I have wanted Dante to do? Isn't it better for my mother to forget me for a while, rather than live in grief?

"I'm sorry," he says.

I open my eyes and wipe away the tears that are forming. "No, you did the right thing. It's just hard to hear."

The door bursts open and Griffin glares at me, then Dante and then Francesca.

"I see where your loyalty lies," he shouts.

"What?" Francesca asks, jumping up from her seat.

"Conveniently Dante has brought back his second sword. In almost as many days. And now I find him sitting in my house, with the woman who is supposed to become my wife."

"Dante has been searching for swords for years. I can't help it if he got lucky," Chesa yells back. "I sent for you because I know where another sword is. How dare you question my loyalty. I've taken all the risks. Lured Emma here away from her family. Gathered all the information. And now I'm about to put another blade in your hand.

Maybe I'm the one who should rethink this arrangement after how you treated me in the cave."

"Dante, it's—" I try to blurt out, but my mouth shuts beyond my control. Dante had been right about the bond being able to take away my free will.

Griffin's anger deflates. "You've found another one already? You're right, I have undervalued your importance. You are exquisite." He reaches forward and takes her hand, kissing it lightly on the top.

"Emma just dreamt it last night...or this morning. I'm not sure. But I sent for you and Dante has no idea where it is. Although that could change at any moment if you don't start treating me like the queen I am."

"I will. I won't fail you again," Griffin promises.

"Chessy, no!" her brother begs. "Please stop this. It's not too late."

"This is the way for me to get back what should have been mine."

"You know why I did that. It had to be done," he explains.

"It wasn't your choice to make," Francesca says, storming towards Griffin. She grabs his arm and leads him outside. "We have things to discuss, and Emma won't be able to tell him anything I don't want her to."

The door closes and my mouth loosens, but every time I try to tell Dante the location I can't.

"It's fine." Dante says. "We still have time. I'll keep searching."

"What is Francesca talking about? She said she has the right to be queen of the blue house and you took that from her."

He nods. "I did. I can't explain why. After our parents died, it wasn't safe for either of us to take the throne. I turned it down. It would have been even more dangerous for Francesca to take the throne. Our house has to have a ruler. I couldn't tell our people to hold the spot until I thought it safe. That's not done."

"Shouldn't she have had a say in it?" I ask.

"I did what I felt to be right. And I still believe it was the best course of action for all of us. But perhaps I should have discussed it with Francesca then. She didn't find out until last year. I waited to tell her because I didn't think she could handle anything else after the loss of our parents. Things would be different if I had explained it all to her then. I was fourteen. I did the best I knew how."

"I know you always try to do the right thing. But I can see where she's coming from. Having all her choices taken from her. She had no say in it. I can see why she feels justified in making the choices she is making now. She feels like she is the true queen and that she is best for the people."

He sighs, leaning back against the couch. I fold in next to him and he strokes my hair. "I never thought about what it must be like for her. Chessy never told me. Sure, she was upset. But I thought she got past it since she didn't mention it again."

"I wonder if I can tell you about my other dreams. The ones from the past." My mouth doesn't clench closed so I recount the visions about the meetings of the eight families and the reasons the swords were removed in the first place.

"Do you think Griffin could turn out like his ancestor?" I inquire. "I tried to show your sister the perils of having one leader, but she won't listen."

"She has been doing a lot of that lately, not listening. Honestly, I wouldn't put anything past Griffin. Now with four swords in place and a fifth on its way, the barrier should stay open for months I'd guess. Even if we don't find all the swords, as long as he finds the majority he will claim the position of high king and he'd have plenty of time to enter the human world and destroy it."

I shudder.

"But we don't know if he even cares enough to think about humans. He may be content to just rule over the Fey."

"Let's hope it never comes to that," I lean forward and meet him halfway for a kiss. It has barely begun by the time Francesca returns.

I can't hide my disappointment. I saw her tell Griffin. Just as she saw my conversation with Dante.

"I should go," Dante says, unwrapping himself from me and getting up. He pauses. "For my part, I am sorry Chessy," he says. "I didn't think about how my choice would affect you. I did what I thought best for you. I should have discussed it with you, or at the very least not kept it from you for that long." He leans forward and gives me a quick peck on the lips. "I need to research things." He winks at me. "I'll visit soon."

I can see that Dante's words affect her. I try to keep my thoughts blank to give her time to process them. But I keep thinking of Griffin on his way to retrieving his second sword.

I wonder if he and Francesca have ever even had a discussion on how they want to rule or their vision for their people. What if they have different plans for their world?

What if one wants to destroy us? Would she even care if JJ died? Probably not.

"Of course I'd care," she stammers. "I'm not a monster. I like your brother. He's nice and likes to be around me."

I remember her filing her nails and find it hard to believe.

"He was dying. I can't heal people. Dante shouldn't have healed him."

I scoff. "That doesn't sound like caring to me."

"You may not believe it, but after seeing my parents die, I couldn't watch that again. The one thing I had on me was a nail file, and I needed a distraction." She sighs, leaning towards me. "I never said I didn't want JJ healed, just that Dante shouldn't have done it. It's against the law. If our kind found out, he would be exiled. Banished from his world never to return. Maybe worse now that we know healing a human lifts the glamour. We aren't supposed to reveal ourselves to humans. The eight families decided that. Going against it..." she shakes her head, "you just don't do it."

I've burned my bridge with JJ anyway. There's no point in thinking about him. I hear her think to herself.

"If Dante or Griffin find enough swords to claim the high king position, will you release me from our bond?" I ask.

"Of course, I don't like this anymore than you do."

I find that hard to believe, me being the slave and all. Francesca being able to control what I say and do.

"Will you make sure I'm with your brother when you do it, that way he can claim me?" I exhort her.

She balks. "You want to be bound to someone else after this? After seeing what it's like?"

I stand up in frustration. "Of course not. I want to be free, but that's not an option. Privacy is not an option. As soon as you relinquish your claim the next fairy can just say 'hey, my turn.' I don't have a choice! I'd never treat someone the way your people view and treat humans. As least Dante is different. He won't try to control me. But if you think I'm happy that I'll never have another private thought again, you're crazy. And that I'm bringing this lifelong curse on your brother too. I hate it."

Francesca leans back and looks as if I've slapped her. "I didn't think about that. About someone else being able to claim you. Why would they once we get the swords?"

"Dante said even when the swords are found, fairies might want me because I can see. Even the future, although I don't think that's happened yet." Francesca's mind flashes to Griffin torturing me, and she knows just as I do that he would claim me if he had the opportunity. She thinks about her brother also. Chesa knows Dante would claim me in a heartbeat because he loves me. But that doesn't mean it would be easy. She has seen for herself what it's like to always have someone else in your head.

Maybe he'd get sick of me, I think. Or he might grow to resent me over time, having to sacrifice so much of himself to protect me.

Suddenly I'm in a dark place. The smell is musty and old. I hear yelling and metal clanking. I think I'm in a sewer. I make my way towards the sound. It takes time for my eyes to adjust to the dim lighting. Up ahead are grates in the ceiling, pouring more light down below. I creep forward, staying on the ledge, not wanting to fall on the tracks that I realize are below me. I see Dante. He runs past me, sword drawn, an intense expression on his face.

I hurry to catch up and see him clashing blades with none other than Griffin. "Marie, get the sword," Dante yells. And for the first time I notice another fairy. She's running to a ladder that's bolted into the wall leading to the ceiling. On the ceiling every few feet is a rectangular light fixture. They don't look like they've worked in years, but I see something shimmering above one of them. It must be a sword.

"Get the sword, you idiot," Griffin calls as he aims a blow towards Dante's head.

Dante flips backwards, narrowly avoiding the blade.

I watch as a fourth fairy takes flight, soaring towards the sword. I didn't see where he came from, but it's evident he's on Griffin's side.

Marie is at the top of the ladder now, and I notice writing on the wall. Owl's Head Park. It's not familiar to me and I ignore it for the time being.

Making sure the metal framing will support her weight, Marie tugs hard on the steel casing holding the light, and then latches on and starts swinging on it, like it's a set of monkey bars and she's a trapeze artist. She slides around the side of the light, and then swings to the next light. She's almost to the sword, but so is the other fairy.

"Edgamon, how can you be working with Griffin? Have you no pride?" Maria calls out, trying to distract him as she swings to the end of the final light.

"We'll see who gets remembered when a high king is named," the fairy retorts as he grabs hold of the other end of the light.

Dante feigns a hard blow to Griffin's right side, and when the silver-eyed fairy moves to block it, Dante lunges forward, giving him a hard kick in the gut. Griffin falls back onto the track, losing his balance, as Dante jumps up, flapping his wings. He flies towards the other two fairies.

Marie and Edgamon both reach for the sword, their fingers brushing against the hilt.

Dante reaches in his pocket and hurls something at the male fairy. It smacks him hard in the head, and he swings back, rubbing the back of his skull.

Only when the object falls and shatters do I realize it was Dante's phone. It delivers the desired effect, giving Marie the extra second she needs to slide forward and grab the sword, but the motion of the swinging causes the metal supports holding the light to start to break.

Edgamon's end rips away from the ceiling. He releases it, fluttering to the ground with a light thud.

Marie is suspended, dangling from the air, one hand on the metal brace and the other holding desperately to the sword. Her knuckles are white as she tries to hang on.

"Drop the sword and I might catch you," Edgamon calls. But his attention is too focused on her. He doesn't see Dante coming right for him. Dante tackles Edgamon to the ground and places the glimmering edge of his blade to the fairy's throat.

"Enough," Dante yells to Griffin as he is flying towards them. "Marie has the sword." He shoves Edgamon off the platform and down onto the tracks where I hear a thud and a moan. Then Dante jumps up, extending his wings, and grabs Marie before lowering her to the ground in a graceful glide.

"It's not over until the sword is back in our realm," Griffin hisses.

"Go," he tells Marie, who runs without hesitation. Then he turns back and squares his shoulders.

Edgamon pulls himself back onto the platform. His right wing is bent in an unnatural position, and there is a look of pure terror on his face.

"Even if she does make it back, you won't," Griffin sneers, raising his blade and motioning to the other fairy to do the same.

Dante pulls out a small dagger from his boot and his sword. "So, you're going to kill me because you're losing." He laughs. "Do your worst. Of course, I always knew you could never beat me on your own. Maybe even not now."

"Even you can't heal everything," Griffin taunts as he lunges forward.

They parry back and forth as Dante attempts to keep his eyes on Edgamon as well. The other fairy is making a wide circle behind Dante.

Griffin thrashes wildly at Dante, drawing his attention, as Edgamon rushes to attack.

When he's just about to strike, Dante throws his dagger behind him. It lodges in Edgamon's abdomen, causing him to drop his sword and stagger to the ground.

But as Dante twists back around, Griffin slices a wide cut in Dante's side.

I watch horrified, screaming, as Dante groans in pain. But no one can hear me.

"Stop!" Edgamon cries. "You can't kill him. He needs to heal me."

Griffin scoffs. "There are casualties in every war. Know that you die with honor, allowing me to finish this. Once Dante's gone, I will collect the remaining swords at my leisure."

Griffin attacks with a ferocity as Dante attempts to keep up, blocking hit after hit. But he's losing blood and fading fast. His movements become sluggish. Griffin's next blow sends the sword scattering out of Dante's hand, but before he can deliver the finishing blow, Griffin howls in pain.

Edgamon has used a knife of his own and plunged it deep into Griffin's calf. Blood leaks from the injury.

Dante uses the time to heal his wound, while Griffin turns on the other elf. He raises his sword to strike his companion but Dante blocks it with a second dagger he pulls from his other boot and pushes Griffin back, using his weight to send him stumbling a few feet.

Dante leaps for his sword, somersaulting towards it. He grabs it in time to parry a blow from Griffin who is staggering towards him. Dante launches to his feet, using his momentum to knock Griffin off balance, then delivers several quick blows, knocking the sword from Griffin's hand.

"Alright," he huffs, "You win this round. Heal us," Griffin demands.

Dante is already kneeling by Edgamon, using his gift on the wound.

"Find your own healer," Dante spits.

Griffin yells but limps away.

Then I'm back in the room with Francesca.

"Were you asleep?" she inquires, her face looking as surprised as mine.

"I don't think so."

"So that's a new development. It looks like Dante found another sword, or is going to find one." She shakes her head. "Griffin's not going to be happy."

"Did you miss the part where he tried to kill your brother?" I ask, stunned that's all she has to say. "Does it really matter if that's the present or future?"

"No," she answers simply.

Hours later, Griffin returns and this time summons Francesca to him.

I watch as he gloats about the ease in which he found the orange sword and presses Francesca to find the next one. I realize my vision is of the future because Griffin would not be gloating right now if Dante had beat him to a sword. If my vision is accurate, then Dante beats him to the next sword, and Marie gets away with it.

"I've been thinking," Chesa tells him. "We haven't discussed our plans. What happens once we succeed in reuniting all the swords? Once the barrier is open for good. For instance, what will we do with Emma? I'm ready to be rid of her. Having someone else in your head, isn't what it's cracked up to be. Do we just send her home with JJ and her mother?"

"JJ," Griffin asks, "is that her human boyfriend? See how disgusting humans are, they can't even be loyal."

"It's her brother," Francesca clarifies.

"Once the swords are found, release her if you wish, and then I'll have fun with her." He stares expectantly at Chesa. "Unless you object?"

"Why would I object? She's just a human. As long as I'm not linked to her, what do I care what happens?" she says, twirling her hair with her finger, looking bored.

"But will we still allow travel to the human world?" she adds.

"For as long as it's still their world."

"Oh," Francesca yawns, "is something going to change that? Do you have big plans I don't know about?"

"We can discuss this further when we are crowned high king and queen. Until then, go figure out where more swords are."

I'm fuming by the time Francesca gets back.

"My goodness, it was hard to not think about anything else until I got back," Francesca said, throwing herself into a chair with a sigh. "Keeping that vision out of my head...I don't think I'd have believed it if I hadn't seen it." She shook her head. "I can't believe I didn't see Griffin's true nature. Maybe I just didn't want to. I've been wrapped up in getting what 'I deserve.' I should have listened to you and Dante."

"So that was all an act?" I ask, unsure what to believe.

"I know I've done nothing to gain your trust, but know that regardless of how I feel about humans or my right to the throne, I'd never put my brother in harm's way. But it was hard to keep my mind blank and not think about everything he said. I feared if I did, your thoughts might distract me, and I needed to look like I didn't have a care in the world."

"So what now, we tell Dante and you set me free?" I ask, hope rising.

She doesn't look at me; instead, she tugs at her hem as she speaks.

"I will, I promise, but not yet. Griffin is dangerous. He'd just as soon kill you than let Dante get the swords. We must make him think I am still on his side. And we can't tell my brother. Griffin will know if Dante starts warming up to me."

"So, what's your plan?" I question her, curiosity piqued.

"We have to tell Griffin about the latest vision, but after we give Dante a head start. But how do we let my brother know, without him figuring out we are telling him?"

Silence surrounds us as we both contemplate different ideas, and then debate about why they won't work.

"I've got it. Maybe," I say.

She waits for me to explain.

"Before I came here, I drew pictures of the dreams I had. I could make another one and you could leave it out where he would find it or drop it as you clear stuff off the table."

"That might work," she agrees after thinking it over for a few minutes. "What do you need to draw?"

I shrug. "Just some pencils and paper."

It doesn't take long for Francesca to track down the supplies and I get to work sketching a scene from the vision. I take care to draw the other fairy and the words I saw written on the wall. That way he knows who to bring, since I never saw the color of the stone.

Once I'm finished, we arrange the paper on the coffee table sticking out of a book. We both agree to find an excuse to leave Dante alone in the room and then if the paper doesn't look moved, Francesca will pick up the book and let it fall out. Dante, being a gentleman, will pick it up and hand it back to Francesca.

"He simply needs to glance at it; we have excellent memories. This will work," she says and I am not certain if she is trying to reassure me or herself.

Then she catches me off guard. "You love him, my brother. I mean, you genuinely love him, don't you?"

"Yes, I know you can see that," I answer.

"Have you ever thought about how it will work? You know, with your lifespan being shorter than ours."

"Honestly, I try not to think of it too much. It's not like he can speed up his aging, right?" I ask, already knowing the answer.

"No." Francesca closes the book she's been flipping through. "There are stories though. Fictional of course, about humans falling in love with fairies and taking magical elixirs to slow their aging."

I roll my eyes. "Fiction doesn't help my problem."

"Perhaps," she agrees, "but in your world, books with fairies in it are considered fictional."

I lean forward, guessing where she's going.

"Sometimes there are kernels of truth hidden in fiction. It's worth looking into. If you both want to have a future together...someday."

"Chesa, can I ask you something? I've been racking my brain and haven't been able to figure it out," I say, changing the subject.

"Sure, why not?"

"How can Griffin burn people? Dante says each fairy has one gift, but Griffin can also enter dreams. Do all fairies have the power to burn someone they encounter?"

"No. We can't do that. And Griffin just has one gift. But as king of purple, he has access to other magics. Just like the swords were embedded with magic to preserve our land and keep the boundaries open, there have been other objects over time that are infused with power. Griffin wears a ring. That's what allows him that particular talent."

Talent is the last word I'd use to describe it, but at least it makes me feel better that not every fairy can do that.

XV
PLANS

I wonder if Dante will come. Or if he's even in this realm. Maybe he's searching or researching in my world. But I saw a vision of the future...he has to come. I think. Of course, I have no way of knowing if this vision is portraying events an hour from now or next year.

I lean towards thinking sooner rather than later. It's like the swords want to be found. The dreams are becoming more intense, even happening when I'm awake.

The day drags on. I hate waiting. And I can't get my mind off of Chesa's hypothesis. Something I haven't dared to dream of might be a possibility. But with the state of my life currently, I need to get my mind off it. I can't go there until I have more hope. A more solid chance at a future, one that looks so far away at the moment.

I take a bath, make my bed for the first time since I've been here, watch the clouds drift by, and I even give Chesa's history book another go. The book is too hard to follow, not knowing the towns, the landmarks, the bodies of water. There is nothing for me to reference to get an idea of where anything took place, not to mention the fact that I don't know what half the creatures or beings in the book are, so I end up tossing the book aside.

As the last rays of the sun fade, transforming the pinks and oranges of the sky into darkness, I give up hope of Dante coming. Perhaps tomorrow will be the day.

My stomach rumbles. I go out into the main room to see if anything remains. I didn't come out for supper. I hadn't been hungry at the time, a decision I now regret.

The trays have all been cleared away.

"I can ring for something," Francesca calls from her room. "I wouldn't be opposed to something sweet."

"If it's no trouble," I answer back. I look around the luxurious chambers and wonder why there isn't a kitchenette. Or a cupboard with snacks. But I guess when simply ringing a bell brings you anything your heart desires, it's not considered a necessity.

A few minutes later, there is a tap at the door. Francesca swings the door open as we await sustenance.

"Oh," she says, stepping aside.

"I'm sorry I couldn't get away sooner. I've been going through old scrolls written by the first set of kings and queens. I lost track of time and then had to grab something from your world." Dante's expression looks mischievous, and his hands are behind his back, concealing something from my view. He doesn't even look at Francesca. I can feel how much it hurts her.

I want to tell him to stop. That she realized her mistake and is helping us now. But even as the thought enters my mind, she issues a warning to keep silent.

So I do. Everything depends on this.

"You didn't," I exclaim. My stomach rumbles louder. I can smell the food from here. But as excited as I am for the food, I can't help but notice his tired demeanor and the dark circles under his eyes. Even his clothes look wrinkled. I wonder if he's getting any sleep.

He pulls the brown bag from behind his back. "Sorry, someone bumped into me and I dropped the Cokes."

I reach for the bag and open it. Inside are two cheeseburgers and golden, fried-to-perfection French fries.

"You're the best," I say, pulling mine out and handing him the bag. I don't want to burden him with my worries about him, especially when he's doing all this for me. I unwrap the burger and I'm about to pick it up when I realize that Dante didn't bring food for Francesca.

"Do you want to split it?" I offer.

Yes! I hear her immediate reaction, but her face is composed. "If you don't think you can eat it all." She feigns disinterest.

Dante watches me as I cut the burger with a plastic knife and give half of my fries to Francesca. I'm sure he doesn't understand why I'm being kind to her. And since I can't explain our plan to him, he'll just have to wonder.

My stomach rumbles again, and Dante laughs. "Here." He takes my half portions and switches them out with his. "It's easier for me to get more." He smiles as he takes a mouthful, by which I mean he eats almost the entire half burger in one bite.

I can't remember when I've tasted anything this mouthwatering. We've been eating a lot of cold meat trays since I've been here and I've just hoped none of it contained rabbit.

Francesca coughs and chokes on her bite.

I don't want to know, I think to her.

Dante looks between us. I'm sure he wonders what it's like and what's passing between us, but he just reaches in the bag and takes a few fries.

"This is delicious," I manage between bites, too hungry to stop.

I finish every morsel, and Dante passes me the rest of his fries, which I devour too.

"Next time I'll bring more," he promises.

Francesca finishes her burger and goes to her room, shutting the door. We're supposed to be giving her brother time in the room alone. And I suddenly remember the excuse I came up with. But it might be too obvious if I leave right after Chesa. I decide to wait a few minutes.

After cleaning up all the trash from the delicious dinner, Dante pulls me down on the couch next to him. I wrap my arms around him and lean my head on his shoulder.

"Let's just never move from this position," I suggest, half kidding.

"Perfect," he agrees.

I sit there relishing in these few moments of joy. Then I tilt my head up to kiss him and realize he's asleep.

Wake him up and let's get this over with, I can hear Francesca telling me.

No. Not yet, I think back. *Didn't you see him? He looks exhausted. And if he's going to be fighting Griffin, he needs his strength.*

We can't wait all night.

Fine, but can we just give him twenty minutes? A cat nap can do wonders. Or so I've read.

After the twenty minutes pass, I stand and Dante gives me a surprised look. "Sorry, I didn't mean to doze off," he apologizes. "Come back." He reaches for me. "I promise you'll have my full attention."

"I'll be right back," I promise. "I skimmed through a book earlier today and there was a picture of a... well, something. I wondered what it was." I go to my room and take my time.

It has only been a minute or two, but Dante calls to me. "Do you need any help?"

"Just a sec," I answer back. "I'm just trying to find the right page."

"Alright, but if you take too long, I can't promise I'll still be awake." I can hear him yawn.

When I don't think I can spend any more time in the room without arousing suspicion, I go back in with the book in hand.

My eyes dart to my drawing and my heart sinks. It looks to be in the same position. It hasn't been moved. He's either too exhausted or too polite to be nosy and do any snooping.

I sit beside Dante and he wraps his arm around me as I show him the small fluffy black pillow-looking animal. I lean my head on his shoulder and savor the moment, knowing that as soon as he does find the picture he'll leave.

"Ah," he notes. "That is a fluffnobber. They are very loving creatures. Like your cats. But they have simple vocal skills. They're our version of a pet, but you won't see one. Fluffnobbers are extremely shy and don't come out unless their owner is alone."

The door swings open and Francesca strolls to the table. She starts piling books in her arms, and as if by accident, my drawing floats to the floor as she turns to head back into her room.

Almost on cue, Dante catches it before it can hit the floor. "You dropped this," he announces as he looks intently at the drawing.

Francesca turns slowly, and then acts appalled that her brother is looking at the drawing. She snatches it from him.

"Thanks," she says and slams the door.

"One of your drawings," Dante notes, raising an eyebrow. "I know you can't say anything, but I need to go." He leans down and kisses me before hurrying out the door.

Once he's gone, Francesca comes back out and sits in a chair beside me.

"I wondered if he'd ever see it." She leans forward, setting the drawing on the table. "How was my acting?" Chesa inquires.

"Spot on." I laugh. "Hopefully he'll be okay."

"He will be," she says with confidence. "We already saw it. Everything is going to be fine."

"I know, but it's still nerve-racking. I've never seen the future before, what if that's one possibility, maybe there are more."

She taps her fingers idly on the arm rest. "Let's not go there. We just have to trust in the vision." She glances at a tall grandfather-looking clock in the corner of the room. "I'll give him five more minutes but then I have to tell Griffin. We can't risk him finding out before I tell him. Then he'd know Dante got the information from us."

"It's not a lot of time, but okay," I agree. It's not like I have any choice regardless.

True to her word, after five minutes pass, Francesca rings for Griffin.

He arrives in no time, as if he has just been sitting close by waiting for us to call him.

He strides into the room, wearing a purple jacket with gold embroidered on the lapels and cuffs. There is gold stitching around the buttonholes and shiny gold buttons. His pants are white and fitted and tuck into dark purple velvet boots. It looks quite striking, although it pains me to admit it.

"Do you know where a sword is?" he asks impatiently, sparing no time for small talk.

"You're dressed up," Francesca notes.

Griffin glances down at his clothing as if he can't be bothered to remember what he wore. "You interrupted a fitting. I need some new clothes." He waves his hand as if it's not important. "I'm not sure if I want to keep purple once I'm high king, or if we should have a new color. I don't want anyone to confuse things as being the same as they are at present. But purple does do me justice, right?"

This is the first time I notice his ring. It's not much to look at. Just a small silver band with tiny gems spaced evenly for as far as I can see. It's crazy that something this small and common can cause so much destruction.

Before Chesa can answer, he continues. "But that's not important. Did you find a sword?" he demands for the second time.

"Not exactly," Francesca says, pushing the drawing into his hands. "Emma had a vision. She sketched this afterwards. It is underground. Maybe New York or London. They have subways. Perhaps you can figure it out."

Griffin looks at the drawing for a long minute. "Well, at least I know which house I need to bring with me. Yellow." He smiles ingratiatingly at me. "You can draw, that's for sure. There's no doubt that this is Maria."

I curse myself under my breath. I should have made two sketches, one for Dante and another vaguer drawing for Griffin.

Without another word, Griffin departs, folding my drawing up and stuffing it into an inside pocket. As he's leaving, a servant comes in with a large silver tray laden with fruit and chocolate, along with two goblets and a vial of red liquid.

I can sense the relief in both of us once he's gone. But Francesca turns her attention back to the servant.

"You took your sweet time coming. I'd almost forgotten I rang for a snack."

"An accident in the kitchen caused the delay," the servant explains.

"It's fine, thank you," I say, intervening before Francesca can say anything rude.

Chesa rolls her eyes as the servant sets the tray down and hurries out.

"You might try being nice to the servants," I suggest.

"We pay them lavishly; shouldn't I expect excellent service?" she asks.

"Yes, but you can still be polite. Just because she isn't from the royal house doesn't mean you shouldn't treat her with respect." I can see I'm not making any headway. I try to change the subject.

"What happens if there is a tie? If Dante and Griffin both retrieve three swords? Is there still a high king named?" I ask, wondering how I couldn't have thought of this question before.

"Then they both have the right to claim the title. Either one can renounce their claim or they can fight to the death."

I think back to my vision of Griffin and Dante fighting. Dante fared well, until the odds were two to one.

"Who do you think would win?" I inquire.

"I'm sure my brother would," she answers. "He has always been the better swordsman. But it won't come to that." She pours herself a goblet of red liquid and takes a sip. "You'll see. After the next vision, we can let Dante know first again. Then Dante will have found four and will have won."

"I hope you're right." I want to have faith, but I have a sinking feeling in my stomach that things will not be as easy as that. When have they ever been?

I'm outside somewhere. I can feel a cool breeze on my skin. I peer around, trying to find my bearings. The stars are shining and I'm in an open field. Light catches my eye and I turn in its direction. It looks like a type of bonfire. The light is coming from some sort of outdoor cathedral-looking building. I make my way toward it. As I step through the doorway, my eyes lock on his. He's frightened and in pain. And the lone thought in my mind is that this is all my fault.

"Let him go," I demand.

Griffin sets a hand on my brother's arm and I can see it start to sizzle, blisters forming under his hand. "Make me," the evil fairy taunts.

"No!" I rush forward but Dante appears, grabbing me, holding me back.

JJ tries to scream but can't make much noise with the gag tied around his mouth.

"Francesca broke the deal." He tsks, shaking his finger like he's disciplining a two-year-old. Then he gestures up; hanging from a banister, spinning over the fire, is Francesca. She's up too high to burn, but she's being lowered down at a steady, albeit slow, pace.

I can't sense anything from her. She must be unconscious or maybe drugged.

"Bring me the last sword. Yield the throne to me and I'll end both your pets quickly. Can't promise the same for Chesa. But what can I say?" He shrugs. "She shouldn't have double-crossed me."

"Let's end this now," Dante counters. "Just you and me, a fight to the death." He touches the hilt of his sword.

Griffin tilts his head back and lets out a long laugh. "Why on earth would I ever risk that? I have the upper hand, the leverage." He draws his sword and drags it across JJ's leg. "I have everything lined up just how I planned it."

My brother screams and writhes, but he's tied to a cement column and can't move.

"By the end of this, the humans will be dead and you will be exiled from your own people. Wait until they see that you healed a human. And now he can see through glamour." He grabs JJ's face and squeezes it, shaking it up and down. "An unpleasant little twist to say the least. He startled me when I went to apprehend him. Even though he still didn't stand a chance to get away from me. I may even go back for dear old Mom when I'm through with you."

"You'll never get away with this," Dante yells. "I don't care if I'm exiled, I'll kill you first." He draws his sword from his sheath and dashes forward. But before he gets halfway there, strong arms wrap around me, holding a blade against my throat.

"Dante!"

He spins, sliding to a halt, and I see his face fall as he realizes we just played into Griffin's hands. We're exactly where he wants us to be. Dante caught in the middle between JJ and me.

I wake, shaking and sweating. I must get to JJ. Warn him, hide him. Francesca's out of her bed, throwing on clothes as fast as I do.

I look outside; the sun is up. It's well into the morning. I don't know what time Dante and Marie get the sword, but I do remember light filtering in from above.

There's still hope that we have time to get to my brother before Griffin does.

XVI
PANICKED

Francesca rings the bell and calls for a servant. "Fetch me a carriage," she orders, and the girl gives a small bow and leaves.

I'm sitting on the couch, pulling on some boots. "We need to hurry."

"I know," Francesca agrees, grabbing some coins off a counter. "Let's go."

I run after her. Francesca is faster than me; she has to slow several times for me to keep up.

A carriage is waiting when we reach the road. It's not as fine looking as the one we rode in earlier, but that doesn't bother me. Pixies are waiting and Francesca pays them and orders them to take us to a place I don't know. I assume it's an entrance to my world. Maybe even the one I came through to get here.

The drive drags on. I feel like I could walk faster than the carriage is moving, but I don't know the location of the door.

Francesca leans forward towards the door. We haven't stopped yet, but we must be close. I scoot to the edge of my seat, ready to spring out at a moment's notice.

The carriage slows before coming to a stop. Francesca swings open the door, knocking the pixie off the steps in the process.

He's angry, yelling and waving his hands, but I don't understand what he's saying.

"I'm sorry," I call as I jump down the steps and fly after Chesa. It's not far to the door, and I feel much more in control now that I'm running. It's action. I'm doing something.

Francesca doesn't hesitate as she thunders through the opening. I do the same. Once through there is no pausing. I recognize the woods. This is the same entrance we came through. I sprint down the hill, following Chesa to where her car is parked.

The car is already started and turned around by the time I make it to the parking lot. I throw myself into the seat and we're speeding away before I even have time to put on my seatbelt.

I'm glad she's driving. Her reflexes are quicker than mine, and we'll arrive much faster. I lose count of the number of cars that honk at us or have to slam on their brakes.

We hit a red light and Francesca merely pauses before weaving through the four lanes of traffic. We skid to a stop in front of my house and I run inside.

"JJ!" I scream, running up the stairs.

"What's wrong?" My mother comes running out of her bedroom. "Who are you? Are you a friend of my son's?"

I stop dead in my tracks. I turn back and look at my mother and my heart breaks as I see no recollection there.

"Um, yes, Emma. Friend of JJ's. Do you know where he is?"

"Well, miss, he's not home. But next time it would be nice if you'd knock. It's not polite to just barge into someone's house screaming." She places her hand over her heart. "You almost gave me a heart attack.

Then she notices Francesca in the doorway.

"Francesca, dear. How have you been? We've missed seeing you. Did you enjoy your trip?"

I feel like a knife has just entered my heart. My mother knows Chesa and not me.

"Mo—" I say but catch myself. I descend the stairs a few at a time. "Mrs. Harper," I say the awkward words and they feel foreign on my tongue. "Please, we need to find JJ. Can you tell us where he is?"

"What's so urgent? You teenagers are all drama," Mom answers.

"You're right. Emma is a drama queen," Francesca agrees, stepping forward. "She just helped me plan a surprise for JJ. I've missed him so much since I've been gone, and I wanted to do something for him."

"Well, I don't think he'll be long. He just left for lunch with a friend," Mom explains, waving us forward.

"You're welcome to come inside and wait on the couch." Her warm smile is inviting.

"Is he with Brent?" I ask.

Mom shakes her head. "You know Brent too. No, he's not with him. He's out with a new friend. What's his name again...Grant, Greg, G—"

"Griffin?" I pale as I say the name. My knees go weak and I brace myself on the couch to keep from falling.

"Yes, Griffin, that's it. He's such a polite young man."

Francesca grabs my arm. "We'll come back later. I just remembered part of the surprise I forgot to set up."

"Sure." Mom nods. "I won't ruin the surprise. I'll keep this little visit a secret."

"Thanks, Mrs. Harper. You're the best." Francesca waves as she drags me beside her.

"A pleasure meeting you too, Emma. Don't forget to knock next time."

It takes everything in me not to run to my mom and throw my arms around her. Tell her I love her. Apologize for what's happening to JJ. But I can't. She'd think I was some loon.

"What do we do now?" I say when we're back in the car.

Francesca's not driving fast anymore. "I'm not sure. Find Dante, make a plan."

I nod. Make a plan. One that doesn't involve us all dying. I can't get the images of my brother out of my head. Tied to the cement column. Griffin burning and cutting him. Francesca hanging lifelessly above the fire.

Since we know what is going to happen, we must be able to change it.

We drive back and Chesa parks in the same spot as before. We walk back to the barrier this time. There's no point in rushing. We don't know where Dante is or where Griffin has taken JJ. Francesca's right; we need to come up with a plan.

The forest is silent. I don't hear a single cricket, nor do I feel the slightest breeze. No squirrels scamper up and down the trunks of the trees, and I don't see a single bird in the branches. It increases the sense of dread I feel. As if even the insects are too frightened to be out.

"We're not going back to Griffin's palace, are we?" I ask.

"I don't know. Isn't that where Dante will look for us? We can't go back to the blue palace. No one will help me." She looks at me apologetically before stepping through the magical door that bridges our two worlds.

I follow behind her and we step out into a grassy field.

"This is the same door we came through the first time, right?" I inquire, a bit confused.

"Yes, it's the same one."

"But we entered a ballroom the first time and now we are in a field."

"That's just because we entered on the winter solstice. On the winter and summer solstice nights, all the barriers lead into the main ballroom. Those are the two biggest nights in the fairy year. All the houses get together and celebrate at the common palace."

The sun is shining down. The sky is blue and puffy white clouds float by. It's as if the world doesn't know my life is falling to pieces. I don't even know if we will all survive the night. It would be gray and raining if Mother Nature had any sense of what will happen to our world if Griffin wins.

I can't bear the thought that I might die tonight, and my mother won't even remember me.

"At least then she won't have to carry around the pain," Francesca notes. "I've heard it's worse when a parent loses a child, though I wouldn't know for certain."

She reaches down and picks a small red flower. "These were my mother's favorites."

"I'm sorry about the monster getting your mother. What kind of creature was it?" I ask.

She shakes her head. "That's just the story we told people," Francesca explains, flashing the image I saw before in her mind. "It's just what I picture when we tell the lie." She turns and holds my gaze. "A monster did kill them, just not that one."

I wonder if she'll say more, but that is to be the end of it.

Chesa shields her eyes as she looks up at the sky. "We'd better start walking. It's a long trek back. I was in too much of a hurry to leave; I should have asked the pixies to wait for us."

"Do you think they would have?" I wonder, remembering the furious pixie and how he looked after being knocked off the steps.

"No, probably not." She laughs, and then I laugh.

"Walking it is." I wait to see which direction we're headed and then fall into step beside Francesca.

It takes us several hours to walk back. The weather's pleasant but I long to do something. We decide the best course of action is to go back to our living quarters. Dante will go there and he has no idea that Griffin has JJ.

What if I have the visions to give me a chance to alter the course of the future? Before, I wanted them to be set in stone, but it's amazing how a day can change one's perspective. Now I'd give anything for that future not to be inevitable.

I keep going over the dream I saw. Griffin is standing too far away for me to throw a dagger at him. And even if I could hurl it that distance, it's not like I have a lot of practice throwing knives. I'd be just as likely to strike my own brother.

I move onto Francesca in the vision. Dante could fly to her and rescue her, sealing JJ's fate. The only way I can think of to keep Francesca's fate from happening is to stay at her side. If we are together, then we can change the outcome of the future one way or another.

Perhaps Chesa should just leave. Go back to my world until this is finished. At least that would lessen the number of pawns in Griffin's twisted game.

I won't abandon you. This is all my fault.

It's easy to blame Francesca. She put her trust in the wrong fairy. But somehow, I think Griffin would have just found another way to get what he wants had it not been through Dante's sister.

By the time we get back to the purple palace, we're exhausted and famished. We don't know what to expect. Will the rest of the purple house turn on us? Is Griffin waiting to ambush us?

It didn't feel like that in my vision, but I don't want to take any chances.

However, as we walk through the gardens, the servants show Chesa the same reverence and respect as before. My nerves ease slightly as we make our way back to the room.

Francesca orders food and drinks for us while I scribble out a message to Dante. Chesa says she can have a servant deliver it to the blue house. I don't know if it will make it there or if Griffin will intercept it, but I have to try something.

Dante—

I don't know if this will find you, but I had to try. Griffin has JJ. Come to our rooms. We have to figure out a way to get him back.

Emma

It's not fancy. I think about saying I love you. But if Griffin does intercept the note, I don't want him to read the words before I get a chance to say them to Dante.

Food arrives and we eat everything. As we're lounging on the couches, waiting to see if Dante comes, I have an idea.

"Do you know the location of that cathedral building in my dream?"

"Of course. It's the ruins of the first common palace. It's not an hour north of here."

"What if we go there? Now," I suggest, sitting up, leaning towards her. "We know the vision of the future happened at night, but what if we go now, while it's still light? Maybe we can spring a trap on him. At least stake the place out and hide until he arrives."

There's silence for a moment as I see Francesca looking for flaws in my plan.

"Agreed," she says at last. "But we need weapons. We can't approach Griffin unarmed." She stands up and finishes her glass of juice. "I'll go to the armory. It's not far, a few hallways from here."

I push a blanket off my feet. "Great," I say as I get up to accompany her.

"You should stay here," Francesca insists. "What if my brother comes and no one is here? We can't risk missing him."

"But we shouldn't separate either. We know the vision showed you captured and me free. To keep that from happening we need to stay together."

"I'll call for a servant to assist me."

"A servant who swears fealty to Griffin," I remind her.

"It will be fine. I can take care of myself." Her words are confident and she is almost cocky. "Besides, I'll be back in five minutes. I think it's worth the risk."

"Okay, if you're certain," I add hesitantly.

Francesca hurries out of the room. I watch as she goes down a long hallway and then passes two more corridors before taking a right. Then she pushes open the third door.

The armory was close. Francesca hadn't exaggerated. It's filled with rows of swords, daggers, and spears. Shields cover an entire wall. There are tables filled with arrows of various kinds and stacks of bows. I can't even see the entire room.

Francesca sticks some of the smaller daggers in her waistband. Then she hefts a couple of swords, feeling their weight. Chesa sets two to the side, presumably for us, and turns to look at the bows next. And then suddenly she's falling, and everything around her goes black.

"Chesa!" I cry. I whip around towards the door. I have no weapon, nothing but my mere human fists to attack with, but I can't sit here and do nothing. I run down the hallway, trying to remember which route Francesca took.

I find the door to the armory open. There are a few drops of blood scattered on the floor, but other than that, there is no sign of Chesa or her attacker.

I go back to the doorway, hoping to see some indication of which direction they went, but there is nothing.

Before returning to Francesca's quarters, I take four daggers. I slide one in each boot and two in my waistband.

I don't waste time on the bows. I've never shot one and I'm not sure I'd have the physical strength to pull it back anyway. I survey the swords and shields and arrive at a similar conclusion.

The shields look heavy and bulky. I don't know how to use one. The same is true with the swords. I've never taken fencing. Even if I could hold the bigger blade, a skilled swordsman would have no trouble disarming me.

So the daggers appear to be my best defense. They are light and I can at least jab with them. Stab Griffin like Edgamon did. No skill required.

I still think getting to the old palace before nightfall is my best plan. I jot a second note for Dante and leave it on my bed.

Dante—

Griffin has JJ and Francesca at the ruins of the old common palace. Come find me. I'm going to try to stop him. I can't just sit here and do nothing.

Emma

I wait as long as I can before I decide I need to leave, hoping in vain that Dante will come find me before I depart. I'm not sure how Griffin's burning technique works. But so far, he has burned me where he can touch my skin. I change into tight fitting pants that tuck into my boots, careful to conceal a dagger on each side. Then I change my shirt into a long-sleeved tunic I find in the armoire. I wish Francesca had turtlenecks in here, but I settle for the v-neck. At least my arms are covered.

I replace the two daggers I had in my waistband and secure them behind my back where they are less visible.

It will be dark in about two hours. Chesa told me that the ruins are about an hour north of here. Hopefully arriving an hour early will be enough time to give me the upper hand.

I slip out into the hallway. The last thing I need is some servant alerting Griffin to my whereabouts. I'm certain that I remember the way out of this palace. I creep softly through the corridors, halting at any sign of company.

Once outside I skirt the side of the palace, hiding in the shadows and behind marble statues and big shrubs when needed. Then once I run out of places to hide, I make a mad dash into the forest, hoping no one has spotted me.

With the trees offering me some camouflage, I make my way north. The forest is dense and at least where I'm at there are no signs of trails. I make my way as quick as I'm able, but it's much slower than I thought. I try to take a direct route, but as I make my way deeper into the forest, I come to a swift-moving river. The current looks too fast and strong for me to try to cross.

I try to take a mental picture of the trees on the other side, so that if I find a place to cross, I can make my way back to this point and continue. The last thing I need is to get lost.

All the trees look the same. I take out a dagger from behind my back and carve an X into a tree. But I worry about the mark getting lost in the surrounding trees. It's not very deep or wide. My last option is to tear the hem of my tunic. I rip off a strip and tie the bright purple material onto a branch.

It's much more noticeable. I feel confident I'll spot it if I can make my way back. The downside is that now my tunic is shorter and I worry that it could make it easier for Griffin to grab skin.

But I can't worry about that too much now. I start following the river to the east, hoping to find a bridge or a narrower section of water with a slower current.

As I make my way along the riverbank, I start to worry about Francesca. We have a bond, and I haven't heard a single thought or feeling since she disappeared. I hope she's okay. I wonder if she has been unconscious this long or if drugs are involved. Heck, I'm in the fairy realm, it could even be magic.

I see a felled tree over a narrow part of the river. But the river is still flowing faster than I like and the tree is not much more than a sapling. I keep looking.

After continuing for what I guess to be another fifteen minutes, I turn back. I'm wasting too much time; I'm going to have to try crossing over the small tree I passed.

Once I'm back at the fallen tree, I push on it. I tug on it from the sides and then push from the top. It's secure; it doesn't move much.

I think back to when I was five years old and doing gymnastics and the teacher said I had great balance. I sure hope that's still true today. I climb up on the trunk and find my center. Then I look straight ahead and take one careful step after another.

I can hear the current rushing by underneath me and I fight the urge to peer down. I wish I were in tennis shoes instead of these boots. I take another step and another, the other side getting closer. I'm about five to ten feet from my goal when I hear a crack.

This time I glance down and I see the wood beginning to split. It's getting thinner the closer I get to the other side. I take another hesitant step and the wood splits even more, lowering the section I'm on until it's touching the water.

I have no choice now but to jump. I take another step and launch myself towards the other bank. I hear cracking behind me, and I crash into a grassy patch, rolling roughly until I butt up to another tree.

When I glance back, the makeshift bridge I used is gone. My pants are now torn at the knees and my shirt has a slit in one of the sleeves but at least I'm on the right side of the river.

I hurry back downstream, searching for any sign of purple. It's starting to get darker and I know I'm running out of time.

At last, I see it, a splash of purple flailing in the breeze. I make my way towards it and then turn back in the direction I know to be north.

I hurry while I still have the light, but it's fading fast. In time my eyes adjust, but by the time I emerge from the forest, the light from the sun has completely vanished.

I keep moving forward. I'm in an open field now. The stars are out and I'm getting an eerie sense of déjà vu. There are some hills in the field and I head to the largest one to get a sense of my bearings. The forest is now just a shadow far behind me.

Light catches my eye and I turn in its direction. It looks like some type of bonfire. I can make out the outline of the palace ruins, the building I thought was once a cathedral, and a shudder runs through me. Despite all my planning, despite everything Chesa and I tried to think through, I've still ended up here. In the same spot of my premonition.

I square my shoulders and head for the doorway. I look around but don't see another entrance and the windows are too high for me to peek through. Even though I've seen this before, I'm still not prepared for it as I enter and my eyes lock on his. He's frightened and in pain. And the lingering thought in my mind is that this is all my fault.

What's the point of being able to see the future if I can't do anything about it?

"Let him go," I demand, my voice hard and strong.

Griffin sets a hand on my brother's arm and I can see it start to sizzle, blisters forming under his hand. "Make me," he taunts, just like in my dream.

It's as if my mind goes blank, forgetting everything I saw beforehand. "No!" I scream as I rush forward, but Dante appears out of nowhere, holding me back.

I watch petrified as JJ tries to scream, but little noise escapes through his gag.

All I can think about is how I can stop his pain.

"Francesca broke the deal." He tsks, shaking his finger, just as before, and I want to break it in two. How can anyone be so evil? Then he gestures up. Hanging from a banister, spinning over the fire, is Francesca.

I can't believe I didn't look for her. Her hands are tied above her head and her head is slumped forward. She must still be unconscious. She's up too high to burn but she's slowly being lowered down.

I glance up, willing her to wake up. I still get nothing from her. Although it shouldn't surprise me. She wasn't awake yet in the dream. But then I think If we are all going to die, maybe it's better that she does not feel it.

"Bring me the last sword. Yield the throne to me and I'll end both your pets quickly. Can't promise the same for Chesa. But what can I say?" He shrugs. "She shouldn't have double crossed me."

This is all happening too quickly. I need to do something, anything.

"Let's end this now," Dante counters. "Just you and me, a fight to the death."

I watch as he touches the hilt of his sword.

I turn and look around, remembering the vision. Someone else is here. If I can just spot them. But everything happens so fast.

Griffin tilts his head back and lets out a long horrific laugh that makes me shudder. "Why on earth would I ever risk that? I have the upper hand, the leverage." He draws his sword and drags it across JJ's leg. "I have everything lined up just how I planned it."

My brother screams and writhes, pulling my attention back to him as he tries to no avail to move underneath the heavy ropes tying him to a large cement column.

"By the end of this, the humans will be dead and you will be exiled from your own people. Wait until they see that you healed a human. And now he can see through glamour." He grabs JJ's face and squeezes it, shaking it up and down.

JJ never did anything to anyone. Why did Griffin have to bring him into this? Hatred like I've never known consumes me.

"That was an unpleasant little twist when I went to apprehend him. Even though he still didn't stand a chance of getting away from me. I may even go back for dear old Mom when I'm through with you."

"You'll never get away with this," Dante yells. I can see the guilt on his face. Dante blames himself for what's happening now. I want to tell him I don't blame him. If we are going to die, he should know that. But I can't seem to form any words.

"I don't care if I'm exiled, I'll kill you first." Dante draws his sword from his sheath and dashes forward.

I can't believe we're already here. I try to reach him, stop him, but my hands just grab air.

Before Dante gets halfway there, I feel a thump behind me and strong arms wrap around me, holding a blade against my throat.

Why didn't I look behind me? I saw this in my dream. But being here for real, watching Francesca slowly being lowered to her death and JJ being tortured, has left my mind a complete mess.

"Dante!"

This new fairy must have been up in the rafters, hiding in the shadows. Why couldn't it have been a wingless fairy, a female? Then maybe I'd have had a chance to spot her on the ground. A chance to change things in my favor.

Dante spins, sliding to a halt, and I see his face fall as he realizes we just played into Griffin's hands. We're exactly where he wants us to be. Dante caught in the middle between JJ and me. And I still have no idea what to do to get us out of this mess.

"Save my brother," I whisper. If one of us can get away, it should be him. It's my fault he's in this predicament. My fault for trying to fight what fate had already determined to be my destiny. I should have just let Griffin claim me from the start, should have told him my identity during our first dream encounter by the waterfall.

Then I'd be the one suffering. I'd be the only one dead at the end of this.

Francesca, Dante, JJ, and even my mother would all be safe. There would be no reason for Griffin to even notice them.

Colors flutter on the side of my mind. The part I've reserved for Chesa. I look up and see that she is stirring.

No! I think to her. *Don't wake up to see this. Just sleep for a few more minutes and it will all be over.*

I see her eyes adjusting to what's around her; I sense her fear when she realizes that there is an enormous bonfire below her feet.

"Let me go!" she screams.

I still have two blades in my waistband behind my back. The fairy holding me is gripping me hard. With my arms pinned behind my back, I can just brush the top of one dagger with my fingertips, but I can't move enough to find any purchase. If I can just cause enough of a distraction for Dante to rescue JJ, I don't care what happens to me. There is nothing I can do for Francesca; she is out of my reach.

I relax my body in hopes that the buff fairy will lighten his grip, but he doesn't.

Dante shifts his gaze between Francesca, JJ, and me.

"There's still time for you to walk away from all this," Dante tells Griffin. "You might be able to explain away killing two humans, and maybe even my death, if we were fighting for a sword. But Francesca."

He shakes his head. "Killing a fairy in cold blood. You know what they'll do to you." Dante tightens his grip on the sword. "And last I heard, changing your mind about marrying someone doesn't justify murder."

"Don't you worry your pretty little head about me," Griffin scoffs.

"Really, you think I'm pretty?" Dante asks, taking a tentative step closer.

Griffin motions to his goon, who pushes his blade deeper, just nicking my neck. "Not so fast."

Their conversation has caught my captor's attention though. I feel his grip loosen a little, and I carefully continue reaching for the blade. I feel my fingertips wrap around the handle, but I still don't have enough movement to do anything with it...yet.

"Last chance," Dante warns.

Griffin lets out a loud booming laugh. "Dante, really, who are you trying to fool with these pretenses? It's over. Just accept my deal and their deaths will be quick."

"Francesca," Dante calls. "Please," he begs.

Chessy looks down at him. "I can't."

I don't understand what Dante expects Francesca to do. She can't even move.

"If you don't, we all die," he says.

"I promised. Not ever again."

I see a young girl. She's beautiful and happy. She's on her way outside when two adult fairies step in front of her. The male is tall with dark hair and brilliant blue eyes, while the female is more petite, but still has a fierceness to her. She is elegant and resembles the young girl. I recognize them as Dante and Francesca's parents. It's then I realize that young girl is Chesa.

I'm not having another vision; this is different. Francesca is remembering something about her childhood.

"Chesa, we already told you, no riding today. We have to travel to the common palace. Today is a council meeting. You and your brother are getting older now. We want you to attend. Someday you're going to need to know how these things work."

"Council meetings sound boring. Just take Dante. I'm going to go riding. He'll be the next king anyway," the girl says matter-of-factly, and then tries to push past her parents.

"Chessy, stop." Her mom puts a hand on her shoulder.

"I'm not coming," she responds defiantly, shaking her mom's hand off. "And you can't make me."

"Chesa!" her father exclaims. "You will not talk to us that way. And you know better than to issue threats. You can't—"

"Yes, I can," she screams.

I watch as I see a spoiled brat who is used to getting her way.

Her father reaches for her, but his hand freezes in midair and then retracts.

"Stop this at once," her father orders.

"Chesa," her mother reprimands as she reaches for her daughter.

"I'm going riding!" Francesca insists, and she has worked herself into such a fit, I don't understand what happens next.

Both her parents step forward and Chesa screams again, and then suddenly both the king and queen fall lifeless to the ground.

I can feel the shame and horror as Francesca relives this memory.

Are they dead? I can't believe it, but the little girl seems to realize it just as I'm wondering it.

"Momma, Daddy?" She kneels by them and shakes each of them, first her father and then her mother.

"Dante!" she yells in a shrill voice. "Dante! Help!"

Out runs a younger version of the Dante I know. He's still recognizable, his dark hair, blue eyes, and chiseled face bones.

"Chessy, what did you do?" He slides on his knees to his parents.

"Fix them," Francesca cries.

Dante tries but nothing happens.

"Dante, fix them." Chesa is now hysterical. "I didn't mean to. I don't even know what I did. I just got so mad."

Dante takes his sister in his arms. "I'm sorry. I can't heal them. They're dead."

The memory fades away with Dante and Francesca huddled together, crying over the lifeless bodies of their parents.

I look at Chesa, horrified.

I was the monster, she thinks to me. *I am the monster.*

I don't know what to say to her. I'm horrified, not of Dante's sister, but of the fact that she had to witness and live through that. I can't imagine carrying that with her all these years.

Dante told me that their gifts immerge when they hit adolescence and they take time to develop. After seeing the memory, I can see it for what it was. A terrible accident. A young girl with too much power losing her temper, and in a split second her world changed.

It wasn't your fault, I think at her. *You're not a monster. You never were.*

It all makes sense now, why Dante took Chesa away. Gave up not only his right to the throne but hers as well. He worried about another accident. He wanted to give her time away from other fairies to learn how to control her powers.

Griffin is losing his patience, unaware of what's transpiring between me and Francesca.

"Give me your word now, or I finish the boy," Griffin hisses.

"Please, Chesa. You can do this. You know how to control it now," Dante begs. "Don't you owe it to them? They shouldn't be part of this."

I can feel the shame and hurt overwhelming Chesa. I know she doesn't want any of us to die. But she can't get past the monster she has seen herself as since the death of her parents. She can't bear the weight of taking more lives. I can sense that if she does it will break her.

"It's okay," I tell her. "You don't owe us anything. I understand it all now, Chesa. I forgive you."

I can sense the tears running down her face. I look back to Dante. "Don't hate her for this. Just save JJ. I love you." And then I wrench my arm forward with all my might, breaking my captor's grip, and spin towards him.

The fairy has become lax. I'm sure he's thinking he is just securing a delicate human. I can see his face full of surprise when I plunge my dagger into his heart. He collapses at once, grasping at his chest.

I spin back, seeing the look of fury on Griffin's face. He raises his blade as Dante lunges forward, but I know it's not soon enough. The distance between them is too great. Dante will never reach Griffin before the blade slices through JJ's neck.

It's as if everything is moving in slow motion. I run forward even though there is no hope for me to stop anything.

Dante flies forward with his sword extended. And Griffin's blade comes crashing down as he lets out an angry wail.

I know Dante can heal, but he can't raise people from the dead. I just witnessed that firsthand.

I'm about to close my eyes, terrified to see the life draw out of my brother's eyes. I'm too cowardly to have the blame he feels for me etched in my mind forever, even if it's deserved, but something happens. The blade halts midair, just a breath away from JJ's neck.

Before Griffin can figure out what has happened, Dante is at his side with his own blade at Griffin's throat. A moment later, the sword in Griffin's hand clatters to the floor.

"How?" I see Griffin's head spinning as he looks around the room at his perfect plan that has fallen to pieces.

I keep running to my brother. I slice through his cords and catch him as he starts to fall. Then I lower him to a sitting position.

I'm about to ask Dante to help JJ, who's bleeding, burned, and sobbing by my side, but then I feel intense heat burning the bottoms of my feet.

"Dante...Francesca."

He looks up to see her feet dangling just inches from the flames.

"Chesa, watch him," Dante orders as he soars up and grabs his sister with his right arm, swinging her to the side of the flame as he slices through the rope with his sword. Then they float down to the ground.

Griffin is frozen in place and now he realizes how he lost.

"She can control people. Get into their minds," he announces once he has figured it out. "How did you keep that hidden from everyone?" he asks, astonished.

"Because she doesn't use it. She's not a psycho like you," I spit the words.

Once Dante and Francesca are back on solid ground, he cuts the binds on her feet and hands, kisses her forehead, and whispers "thank you," before returning to JJ's side.

He works in order of severity, first healing the cut on JJ's leg that is still bleeding and then moving to burns and other injuries I hadn't noticed.

When he finishes, Dante slumps beside my brother to recover.

"I don't understand what happened," JJ says, when he has had time to breathe for a moment.

"How am I not decapitated?" he asks.

"Chesa saved you." I breathe deeply, feeling relief for the first time in too long.

I reach my hand out to her. "Get over here," I order. I know she's not certain where she fits after her part in the ordeal with Griffin, but I want her to know she fits with us.

She hesitantly makes her way towards us and I throw my arms around her neck, hugging her in a tight embrace.

"I even love you too," I say through tears, "but now that this is over, can I please get my mind back?"

She laughs through the tears. "The sooner the better."

JJ looks at us confused but doesn't ask any of us for an explanation. "Can we go home now?"

XVII
COUNCIL

Dante had found the note on my bed explaining where I had gone. Without waiting for reinforcements he had come running, just as I knew he would. But before doing so, he did take the time to send word to his friend Eldon, another member of the blue.

Not long after Dante had healed JJ, Eldon arrives with a dozen other fairies all donning blue. As we exit the building, I note that several horses with wings are waiting outside, along with a carriage pulled by more normal-looking horses.

"I thought you might be in a hurry to get back." Eldon nods to the winged horses.

Dante clasps his friend on the shoulder. "You did well, thank you. But before we go deal with the ramifications of all that has happened, I have another favor to ask."

"I'm at your service," he replies with a smile.

"This is JJ," Dante explains as he ushers my brother forward. "I'd take him home myself but I feel explanations will be needed and statements will have to be given. He needs to get home. The sooner the better."

"JJ, I'd be happy to assist you." He sticks his hand out but doesn't move it when my brother tries to shake it. "I'm Eldon." He grins.

Dante shrugs. "Eldon hasn't been out in the human world much. But he knows how to get through the barriers. And once you get through, I gather you can help direct him back to your address."

"Anything to get out of here," JJ agrees.

I see offended looks on the other fairies' faces.

"He hasn't had the most pleasant time; please excuse him," Dante explains.

Eldon pulls JJ up onto a brown horse behind himself and gallops off towards the south.

Griffin has been bound and gagged and is leaning against the outside walls of the ruins.

"Korbi, Davin," Dante calls. "Take Griffin to the palace. Do not let him speak to anyone and I want three guards on him at all times. I'll come for him as soon as I can convene the council."

"Yes, my lord," the blonde fairy says.

"Very good, my lord," says the dark-haired fairy.

I'm not sure who is who, as there is no further conversation between them. Each of the two fairies grabs Griffin unceremoniously under an arm and toss him into the backseat of the carriage. Once Davin and Korbi take their seats, the pixie on the step whistles to the others and the carriage pulls away.

I notice Francesca over to the side and I go stand by her, linking my arm in hers.

"Let's get out of here." I pull her forward towards the winged horses. Dante is already astride one.

Francesca stops in front of a white stallion and mounts.

Riding a horse on the ground is one thing, but I'm not about to take one of these flying stallions on my own.

Chesa turns and offers me her hand. I gratefully accept it and climb on behind her.

"Let's see if you can keep up," Dante challenges his sister.

"Bring it," she responds, but I can sense she's not into a race.

I sense a change in her. Like she's beginning to forgive herself for her parents' death and to think that maybe she's not a monster.

I try to keep my mind blank, allowing her the time to sort through her feelings.

After what I've been through these past weeks, I know monsters. Griffin is a monster. Francesca's not and has never been.

As much as I don't like the feeling of being bonded, I think it has changed Francesca's and my relationship forever. I feel like we're sisters now. We've shared so much. I'm quite sure she feels the same way.

We land near the stables at the palace, and Dante calls for two blue servants to attend to the horses.

"Thank you," he adds as we follow him inside.

Even through the confusing corridors and endless twisting hallways, I know that we are heading to the king's quarters, thanks to Francesca's thoughts.

A young fairy opens the door, and Dante offers a small bow. Francesca follows; I do the same.

"King Levin," Dante says.

"Dante." He nods and then barely glances at Francesca. "What can I do for you at this hour?"

"I apologize for the lateness, but I must request a meeting with the council. We have a traitor among us and there are crimes that must be answered for."

The king's eyes shift to Chesa for a moment, and I realize that the king thinks Dante is speaking about his sister.

"Are you certain this can't wait until morning?" The king yawns and looks back longingly towards his chambers.

"No, it can't wait," Dante insists. "Please call the council and we can meet at the common palace in an hour."

He nods. "Very well, but I expect this to be worthwhile." Then he turns and shuts the door.

"We have a little time if we want to clean up," Dante suggests.

He looks perfect...at first glance. Then I realize there's blood on his cuffs, and his pants have seen better days.

He takes my hand in his. "I hate to let you out of my sight, but my quarters are in the opposite direction of Chessy's. I can offer you a clean tunic that would be too big for you and that's about it."

"It's fine, I'll go with Francesca."

He takes my face in his hands and kisses me. I close my eyes and then it's over.

"I love you," he says before spinning on his heel.

I almost say it back. I did say it in the ruins when I thought we were all going to die. But we haven't talked since then, and I'd like to say it next in private, when it's just me and him.

"We should hurry. An hour to change and get to the common palace isn't much."

I look at Francesca for the first time since everything happened. I mean really look at her. She has soot all over her. Ash from the fire. Her wrists still have raw tears in them from hanging over the flames.

I was so preoccupied with Dante healing JJ that I didn't even think about Francesca's injuries.

"Sorry," I apologize as we walk to her rooms. We pass a few servants who glare in our direction.

"It's fine," she explains. "Really, I haven't even noticed them. You'd have known if I did. Besides," she adds, lifting the cuff of my sleeve, "you haven't complained either."

She was right. Francesca hadn't even thought of her injuries. And with all the adrenaline pumping through me, I hadn't even realized I had the same injury. Which of course made sense because we shared everything.

It's as if me noticing the raw marks brings the pain. They throb and I don't even want the light material of my shirt to touch them.

"How long do you think it will take my people to forgive me?" Francesca asks, interrupting my thoughts.

"Once they hear how you saved all of us, it will be no time."

Francesca gasps in horror. It's the first time she realizes that everyone will know what her power is. The gift she has kept hidden and concealed for all these years. It goes to follow that the story of her parents will come out too.

I feel for her. I hope her people will see Chesa as I see her.

Once we are back in her chambers, I let Francesca bathe first. I pick out some tan pants and a light blue tunic to borrow while I wait.

Francesca looks much like her old self once the dirt and filth from the day are washed off her.

I bathe quickly, not wanting to keep anyone waiting. The water and soap sting my wrists but I ignore the pain. Dante's already here. He's reassuring his sister that she made the right choice and that he will stand by her.

I use a fluffy towel that Francesca has set out for me and try to wring as much water from my hair as I can before tying it back into a neat ponytail.

I slip on soft pale blue boots that match my tunic and feel like my feet are wrapped in velvet.

The tunic I selected is short sleeved and Dante immediately spots my wrists.

"How? When?" he asks, but before stepping forward he lifts the cuff on his sister's arm and nods.

"I'm sorry," he says to both of us. "You should have said something." He heals Francesca's wrists one at a time and mine patch themselves together at the same time.

I move my wrists and even though I've had other healings, it doesn't cease to amaze me how the pain is suddenly gone.

Dante winks at me and reaches his hand out for mine. "We should go. I have a carriage waiting…" His look is far away and I wonder what he's not saying. "Griffin will be in our carriage. I want to keep my eyes on him, I don't trust him not to have another trick up his sleeve. I understand if you and Chessy want to take another carriage."

"It's fine. Chesa will protect us." I meant it to make her feel better, but I feel her inwardly cringe and worry I've said the wrong thing. But I can't help it; I do feel safer with her by my side. Francesca gives me an appreciative smile. "Together," I insist, looping my arm through Dante's and then Francesca's.

It's a little tight, the three of us moving together through the corridor, but I don't let Dante's sister pull away. We are in this together and I want her to feel that.

As we arrive in the courtyard, guards are manhandling Griffin into the carriage. He's fighting them with all his might and they are having a difficult time despite him being tied and gagged.

Dante drops my hand and rushes forward to aid them. When Griffin sees Francesca he stops and allows the men to get him into the carriage.

I assume he fears Chesa will just force him to do her will, but that's the furthest thing from her mind.

Dante sits beside Griffin in the carriage, allowing Francesca and me to sit together as far from the monster as possible in these confined spaces.

The carriage moves forward and Dante visibly relaxes, releasing a long sigh. He combs his hair from his face with his fingers and leans forward.

"When we arrive for the council meeting, let me do the speaking, unless they ask you a direct question. It will be simpler if just one of us explains. Plus, Griffin will tell them about JJ and I want to explain that too."

Even gagged I can see Griffin's smug smile.

"I'm going to be exiled. It's fairy law." He looks down, averting his eyes from mine when he says it and pauses for a minute. I can see by the slump of his shoulders and his entire demeanor that this is killing him. To know he will never be able to come home.

Another thing that is my fault. I can't regret my begging him to save JJ. I wouldn't take it back. The alternative is too painful to even contemplate. But I wonder if we can get past this or if he will grow to resent me.

I know what it's like to be taken from your home. The thought that you might never return gnawing at you like a constant companion. But I had a shred of hope to comfort me. Dante will have no such comfort.

He meets my gaze again. "The best I can do is try to set the record straight before it happens, and make sure justice is served when it comes to Griffin."

Francesca remains silent throughout the ride, her mind filled with panic over her secret being revealed, leaving room for nothing else.

I squeeze her hand lightly, letting her know I'm here.

The carriage comes to a halt just as the sun crests the horizon. Little rays of sunshine enter through the open carriage windows. And I hope the new day will bring better things for us.

As I step out of the carriage, I realize I've seen this palace before. Not counting the night I stepped into the ballroom through the barrier and was then taken to the dungeons. I have seen the outside of this palace.

Where the other house palaces are each a sparkling white, this one is gray. A flag for each of the eight houses waves from eight spires. All equal, as they should be. It takes me a moment to place it, but I saw the palace in my first vision. It seems like a lifetime ago.

I wonder if Levin will be a good high king. At least I assume he will be high king. Hopefully Griffin will either be imprisoned for all time or be out of the running to find the final sword. If that's the case, with one sword remaining, the blue house would have found the most swords. I never asked about the punishment for attempted murder, but Dante insinuated that it wasn't pleasant.

As soon as we depart the carriage, we are escorted through the palace to a large room with an oval table. Each house is represented, apart from purple. The seat belonging to the purple house remains vacant.

There are a dozen chairs lining the back wall behind the table and we are instructed to sit there.

King Levin scoots his chair back and stands. "I have called this council meeting on behalf of Dante of the blue house. I yield the floor to you, Dante."

My stomach flutters as he stands. I'm unsure what all this entails but I dread the fact that in the end, this loyal, noble, selfless fairy will be exiled from his home.

The room is so quiet I can hear every step Dante takes. Francesca grabs my hand, trying to comfort both of our nerves.

The purple chair has been removed and Dante stands where it once occupied, looking over at the kings and queens of the Fey.

"Your Majesties," he says, and offers a low bow. "I appreciate you convening at such an early hour. I ask that you hold your questions until the end. A lot has happened these past few months, and I feel that I must start at the beginning to give you a full picture."

He looks tall and regal as he addresses the council. Dante starts with our first encounter, then continues with my epic failure at stealth as I attempted to follow him and his threats against me.

He tells how he realized I had been gifted with second sight, and how he wanted to keep me from the fairy world because he knew it would bring dangers.

There are a few gasps when he explains to them how he fell in love with a human, but the biggest reaction comes when he tells them how I begged him to save my brother and he healed him.

"Enough, he broke fairy law," the yellow king exclaims.

"How dare you!" the red queen yells.

Levin's eyes are wide in shock but he composes himself and clears his throat. "I assure you," he addresses the council, "we will deal with this in due course, but we consented to let Dante finish, and unless I'm mistaken, this is not the end of his tale." He turns his gaze back to Dante for confirmation.

"Correct, your Majesty," Dante responds.

There are a few whispered complaints and grumbles but after a moment the room dies down and he goes on.

Dante is very thorough in making clear my willingness to help the fairies without being claimed. He tells how Griffin tortured me physically in my dreams, how Griffin and Francesca conspired to trick me into the Fey.

Francesca and I both cringe at this part, but I wrap my arm around her in a show of solidarity. A couple of the kings take notice, and I hope they can see I hold no ill will towards Chesa. What right do they have to judge her? I am the one most affected by her choices. If I can forgive her, that's all that should matter.

Dante reveals how Griffin left Edgamon to die. How the king was willing to do whatever it took to become the most powerful fairy—it didn't matter the collateral damage. He speaks with clarity and passion as he tells of Francesca's change of heart, how she realized what kind of monster she made a deal with, and the lengths she went through to try to stop him.

Finally he gets to the night in the ruins. I can see it pains him to reveal his sister's secrets, but I know once Griffin gets a chance to speak that he would have revealed it anyway. Dante doesn't share the story of their parents' death, but I watch Levin and he has a puzzled expression on his face. I don't doubt that he may piece it all together before the end.

The council is shocked by Griffin's behavior and his lack of moral conscience, having no regard for fairy life. But when Dante gets to the part where I stab the fairy who is restraining me, they look equally horrified and the dread in my stomach grows and a shiver runs down my spine.

When Dante wraps up his story, King Levin stands again.

"Of course we'll have to verify this as far as is possible," he says before turning to a servant. "Send for Edgamon."

"I understand," Dante agrees. "I just have one last thing I need to say."

King Levin sighs but waves him on.

"As is the right of the fairy who finds the most missing swords, and I think there is no question that I did," he pauses, giving his statement time to sink in before proclaiming, "I claim the title of high king, subject to no fairy's will but my own."

XVIII
HIGH KING

There are gasps all around, including my own and Francesca's. King Levin looks like he's been slapped in the face.

There is an explosion of discussion. I can't understand half of what's being said due to the commotion. Dante lets it go on for a moment, and then raising his voice in a loud boom, yells, "Silence."

The room is instantly quiet.

I shift my gaze to Griffin. He looks terrified by Dante's proclamation. It's about time.

"Does anyone object that the right to this and the law are on my side?" He waits a long couple of moments before continuing. "Then as my decree as high king of the Fey, I order the elder be summoned and the binding between Francesca and Emma be severed." Before he finishes his sentence, a servant departs, I assume to do as he's asked. "My second decree is to abolish this disgusting tradition. No Fey will ever be able to claim a human, whether they possess second sight or not. This is a new law that can only be undone by the high king. No council can ever revoke this law." He eyes each of the council members to make sure they are listening. "And my last decree as high king of the Fey…"

My ears perk up at the words last decree. Does he think in his long life that he will never have to make decisions or change laws again?

212

"...is that after I renounce my claim as high king in a moment, there will never be another high king again. Having one absolute ruler is insane. We cannot give that much power to one fairy. A council made up of rulers from each house is the best way to ensure that power doesn't corrupt our people." His eyes meet mine and he winks at me. "I think that's it," then he holds a finger up, "just give me a sec to make sure that I covered everything before I dissolve this power forever." I can see his face as he goes over a mental checklist. "Oh yes, one last, last decree. I can't believe I forgot. Emma is pardoned, absolved, however you want to word it," he waves his hand nonchalantly, "for killing the fairy in self-defense, and any other crime you might be able to think of against her." He nods, satisfied with his decrees. "I now renounce my claim and title as high king." He offers a small bow.

Some of the Fey look outraged by this. And the yellow king leans forward, slamming his hand on the table. "You may think yourself so clever, to end long traditions on a whim, without even seeing how the people feel—"

"It was wrong," Dante interrupts with disgust in his voice.

"Well," the king of the yellow house continues, "you forgot one thing."

Dante counts on his fingers and then shrugs, at peace with his decisions.

"You didn't pardon yourself." He smirks.

As much as I hate to agree, he's right. Dante never pardoned himself for healing a human. My heart aches for him, but as I meet eyes with Dante, he just gives me a small smile.

"I didn't overlook pardoning myself," Dante responds. "I broke the law. King, high king, fairy, pixie, satyr, or any member of the Fey should have to be held accountable. Using my power, for however temporary, to take that consequence from myself would be wrong. I leave my fate in your hands, and I'll accept the council's decision, whatever that may be."

The yellow king harrumphs and then returns to his seat.

"Thank you for your testimony. Now we shall hear from Griffin." King Levin waves to a guard to bring Griffin forward. "Untie him and ungag him so that he can present his defense, if he has any."

Griffin wrenches his hands forward as soon as they are free and rubs at his wrists. "This is treasonous. How dare I, the king of purple, be held against my will by a member of the blue house."

The pink queen leans forward on her elbow. "So do you deny these claims?"

"They are pure fabrication, made up by Dante to throw the attention off of him for breaking the law."

My jaw drops at these accusations.

Griffin points to Francesca and me. "And look at his so-called witnesses, his sister and girlfriend. How convenient. The truth is, I discovered that Dante broke the law, I confronted him, and gave him the chance to turn himself in."

I want to jump up and yell to the council "he's a liar!" but Dante is unfazed by the attacks, and Francesca touches my arm in warning.

"The truth is, I went to collect the boy in question, the other human who can now see through our glamour. My intention," he pauses, "was to bring him to the council and present him as proof, but Dante's little trio ambushed me. The human girl…"

It grates on my nerves that he referred to me as the human girl when he knows my name.

His eyes catch mine and he gives me the slightest grin.

"…that girl," he points at me in repulse, "murdered my subject…" he looks lost for a moment and I realize he doesn't even know the fairy's name.

"Greggon," Dante supplies graciously.

"Yes, yes," Griffins stutters, flustered. "She murders Greggon, and they take me into custody. Concocting this entire wild story on the ride back."

The purple king stands tall, looking smug, when a side door opens and Edgamon strolls through. Griffin's face pales and he grabs the table for balance.

I can't believe it. But it is as if the purple king forgot that King Levin had sent for him.

"Take a seat," King Levin tells Edgamon. "We shall hear your statement in a minute. Also, go out to the old palace ruins, Davin," the king orders one of his men. "Survey the area, see if there is evidence backing up Dante's story. Remnants of a bonfire, a human, blood, ropes, that sort of thing."

"Yes, my lord," Davin answers before exiting through the same door Edgamon just entered through.

The blonde one. That makes the dark-haired fairy Korbi. I make a mental note.

"Do you have anything else to add?" King Levin turns back, addressing Griffin.

"No." His voice cracks. He is escorted back to his chair by two blue soldiers who seem to have believed none of his lies. They watch him closely with their hands brushing against the hilts of their swords.

Next the council calls Edgamon to give testimony of the events in the subway. His story doesn't match up with Dante's version in every aspect. Edgamon paints himself as a more honorable fairy, but the main points about Griffin line up in perfect unison.

Francesca takes the stand next and tells her timeline of events, the parts she remained conscious for anyway. It's difficult for her when she tells how she had to go inside Griffin's mind to control him, to stop him from killing everyone.

But I don't see fear in the council's eyes. Instead, I see admiration. They can sense the truth as easily as I can feel it. Francesca didn't want to use her power. She loathes it. Forcing another person to do what you want is wrong, and only because the end outweighed the means did she use her power.

The council doesn't even take the time to hear my version of events. Apparently, I am not worth the effort, being a lowly human.

We are excused to wait in another room while the council deliberates.

Not even half an hour has passed before we are called back into the room. Edgamon has already been excused, but Griffin, Dante, Francesca, and I remain.

"The punishment for attempting to murder another fairy either is banishment and clipped wings, life imprisonment with clipped wings, or death," King Levin says.

"Banished to my world?" I whisper, looking from Dante to Francesca.

Dante nods at the same time that Francesca says "yes" in my head.

"However, since Griffin has already demonstrated such disdain for the humans, we don't feel unleashing him on them would be fair."

I breathe in a huge sigh of relief.

"So we are going to give you the choice, Griffin. Life imprisonment or a swift execution. Keep in mind that should you ever attempt to escape, there will be no choices; your beheading will be immediate."

I cringe at the thought.

Griffin is shaking; he looks terrified.

"Im-m-m-mpris-sonment," he stutters.

King Levin nods and then turns to two guards. "Bring the shears and commence with the clipping."

Griffin whimpers as two servants hold his wings out.

I feel sick in the pit of my stomach. "What are they going to do?" I ask.

"They are going to maim him. He will never fly again. It will also serve as a warning to others."

I bury my head into Dante's shoulder, too horrified to watch. I can hear the shears open and close as if they are being tested. I can't stand it.

"Stop!" I yell.

Everyone's eyes are upon me. Not all of them are pleasant to behold.

"I know you all think I'm just a lowly human," I explain, standing to address them. "But I'm begging you not to do this. Life imprisonment is enough. If anyone here has reason to hate him, I do, and I understand all about justice, but how about a little mercy. Let's be better than him. Please," I cry, then I turn and run for the door. I can't watch this.

Two guards block my exit, but someone from behind me must give me permission to leave because they each step to the side after just a moment.

I can sense Francesca following me, but I keep running. I'm not trying to get away from her, I just know if I hear Griffin screaming from getting maimed, I'll never get it out of my head. I run and run and run. I just want to get outside and away from here, but I'm hopelessly lost and I collapse on the floor when my legs give out.

I don't have the slightest idea how long I was running. Chesa catches up to me quickly.

"Is...this far...enough," I pant. I don't have to explain. She knows what I mean, and might have been able to guess even if we weren't bonded.

"Yes." She slides down on the ground next to me and we just sit and wait.

"You should have stayed," I say when my breaths are steady again. "What will happen to Dante? Now we won't know." Then I have a horrifying thought, but before I can even process it entirely, Francesca says, "No, no absolutely not. That's not even on the table. They will not maim Dante. The punishment is exile. The council can choose to be more merciful if they desire, but they can't add to the consequence. Not without making a new law first, and even then," she adds when I look up in despair, "it wouldn't apply to him because the law would have been enacted after his crime. It would be for future offenders."

"You're certain?" I ask, hesitant to hope. "Dante has been wrong about a lot of things."

"Yes, I promise. Dante made assumptions based on old journals and hearsay. I am remarkably familiar with our laws. I had thought I might rule one day."

"I'm sorry about that," I add.

She shrugs. "I'm not. Not anymore. I realize I wanted it to try to prove that I was good. To show my parents I was sorry. To try to make up for being a mon—"

"You're not a monster!" I exclaim forcefully.

"Keep telling me that," she says with tears in her eyes. "Someday I just might believe you." She gives me a small smile. "Besides, I have what matters," Francesca adds.

I lean my head back against the wall and tilt my face towards her. "What's that?"

"Family who loves me. A brother and a sister." She squeezes my hand and I can't stop a tear from rolling down my cheek.

Her face turns serious. "Ems, can you ever forgive me?"

I laugh. "Did you just ask me that? We're bonded. You know I already have."

"I've felt that, but I also know there were things you tried not to think about, feelings you tried to push down. Maybe only a part of you has forgiven me?"

"I don't know how to half forgive," I tease, nudging her with my elbow. "It's not a choice I would have made," I begin, wanting to be completely honest, "but I wouldn't go back and change it, even if it were possible."

Her eyes widen in surprise. "Really?"

"I understand you much better now, and I think you understand me too. It's not that I think this is the only way we could have achieved this. I believe we would have still gotten here in time." I laugh. "Years probably...at least...eventually. But we're here now and I can't imagine going back."

"Me neither." She beams, then throws her arms around me. "I love you."

I hug her back. "Right back at you."

XIX
FREE

Dante finds us in the hallway. "I have half a dozen servants combing the palace for you two. Do you think next time you could send up a flare?" he asks with one eyebrow cocked up.

"Francesca, that's your job," I delegate. "Make sure you're stocked with flares from now on."

She gives me a mock salute. "Aye."

Then I turn serious. "Dante, what happened?"

"We'll have time to discuss all that later. Right now, the elder is here. It's time to get you unclaimed."

Chesa and I both jump up, literally.

"What are we waiting for? Lead the way," she demands.

Dante reaches for my hand and laces his fingers in mine.

It takes us a couple of minutes to make our way back to the conference room. I must have zigzagged back and forth when I ran.

The room has mostly emptied. Dante's cousin and the pink queen remain, along with the elder.

The ceremony is the same to me. Perhaps the words are different, but I don't understand them so I can't tell. We both have our blood spilt again. This time no one has to force me to drink from the goblet.

When it's all over, the old fairy approaches me. "I hear you've shaken up our world, young lady," he notes, looking me up and down.

"I have?" I ask, confused.

"Keep up the excellent work. It's about time." He pats me on the shoulder and I watch him walk off, bewildered at his words.

I start to get dizzy and I take a seat. I didn't expect to feel any disorientation from being separated from Chesa, but it appears I am wrong once again. It's like half of my brain is turning into fog.

As I'm sitting there trying to find my equilibrium, the pink queen approaches me.

"Emma, is it?" she asks.

I offer an awkward seated bow. I'm afraid I'll fall if I stand.

"I'm Queen Eventide," she says. "I just wanted to thank you."

I look up, too shocked to answer. I didn't get the impression any of the kings and queens thought much of me. "Thank you for being brave. For standing up for what you believe to be right. I feel like when you live as long as we do, we become complacent and forget to fight for things. I do hope the unpleasantness of this trip won't stop you from visiting again. I think we can learn a lot from each other."

"Thank you. I'd be honored to visit again if I'm permitted," I respond, still shocked.

Once she leaves, my head feels fuzzy again. It's hard to explain, but I feel blind and empty inside. It's too quiet. I can't see Francesca anymore. I've become used to it. It's an odd sensation, but it's like I'm walking around with one eye closed.

I ache inside, missing the constant companionship, the comfort she gave me, knowing someone else understood what I went through and vice versa.

Tears stream down my face and I can't stop crying.

"Emma." I hear Dante's voice and I turn to see him hurrying towards me. "Are you okay?"

"I'm alone. I'm just empty."

He pulls me close. "I'm right here. You're not alone," he whispers. "Let's get out of here. You must be exhausted."

He pulls me into the hallway and we almost trip over Francesca, who's curled on the floor sobbing quietly.

"You too?" he exclaims, confused.

Chesa and I lock eyes, and I pull away from Dante as she tries to stand and get to me. We embrace and sob. Dante's at a complete loss. He just steps back and waits, not understanding.

I don't think anyone will understand. Ever. Eventually we pull ourselves together and grip hands. It feels like the one way we are still connected to one another. I never realized how deep our connection was, or how empty we'd feel once it dissipated.

We return to the blue palace, where we curl up on my bed and drift asleep.

In the morning, things feel a little more normal. There's still an emptiness inside, but it's not so overwhelming. Francesca is feeling better too.

"Are you alright?" Dante asks, then looks to his sister. "Both of you?"

She nods.

"I think we will be. I can't even put into words what it's like. We both hated the bond at first. Then we got used to it, and then we started to depend on it. Having it ripped away..."

"It'll just take some time," Chesa finishes. "But I don't feel so overwhelmed, like yesterday. Maybe our exhaustion played a part in it."

"Okay, well I have a little time. Are you both up to listening?" he asks.

I start to panic. "What do you mean 'a little time'? What's happening now? Are you okay?" Worry spills out of me, question after question.

"I'm fine. It's all going to be fine," he assures me as he sits us both down on the couch.

"After you both left yesterday, it was amazing. Some of the council listened to you. They stopped the maiming, had another discussion, and decided not to clip Griffin's wings. He actually wept when they announced it. Instead, the council just stripped him of his ring, put him in irons, and sent him to the dungeons to begin his lifelong sentence."

I feel a weight lift off me. And I think I might be able to start liking some of the council. I'm thrilled that they took the ring, although I wish they'd just destroy it. Who really needs the power to burn someone to a crisp like bacon?

"Then," Dante continues, "the council announced my sentence. The law is clear; I am to be banished. I have to be out of the Fey," he turns and looks at the clock in the corner, "in just over an hour." He shrugs.

"You don't seem too concerned," Francesca notes.

"They offered leniency due to my services to our world, and the fact that with your help we retrieved so many swords. The barrier should stay open for most of the year now."

I lean forward, wondering if Francesca had been wrong before. Are they going to clip Dante's wings? Is he going to be imprisoned instead of exiled?

"I don't understand. If you're still exiled, how have they shown you lenience?"

He grins. "First, they didn't force me to make an immediate departure. They permitted me to stay through the ceremony and make sure you were both alright."

"And second?" Francesca asks.

"I am banished for a year and a day."

Chesa jumps up and wraps her arms around him. "That's wonderful."

I lean back against the couch and smile, content to watch their happiness and feeling relieved that Dante won't grow to resent me for him being kept from his home indefinitely.

"So," he says, giving me a mischievous look, "any ideas on how I can spend my year and a day?"

I give him a lazy smile. "Maybe a few." I reach my arms out to him and he pulls me to my feet.

"You can start by bringing me home and restoring my mom's memories."

"I'm already ahead of you," he responds proudly, pulling a vial of blue liquid from his pants pocket. "We just need to add this to her tea."

I pull him in for a quick kiss that turns into a longer one.

I hear Chesa cough, and we pull away.

"We'd better get going. I don't think we should press our luck when the council has been this generous," Chesa reminds us.

"Excellent point." He leans forward and brushes his lips against my ear. "To be continued."

I smile, ready to go home. Ready to find my new normal. Ready to see my mom and have her actually see me.

We take a carriage to the barrier.

"Are pixies forced to be carriage drivers?" I ask, hoping they aren't some type of Fey slave.

Chesa bursts into laughter and Dante chuckles.

"What?" I ask.

"Pixies aren't forced to do anything," she explains. "They have a monopoly on the transportation business. Satyrs tried to start their own business once, but never cross a pixie. They are fiercer than they look. Their fares are exuberant, and pixies are the wealthiest creatures in the Fey."

"It's true," Dante agrees. "One day I'll take you to a pixie city. You won't believe the extravagance."

"Hmm, who'd have thought," I respond, leaning back into Dante's arms.

Thunderstorm clouds are forming overhead. The sky is growing darker. It looks as though it is late in the afternoon even though it's just midmorning. Lightning flashes as a giant clap of thunder roars overhead. Despite the grayness and bleakness, I still think it's the most beautiful day ever.

Francesca's car is still waiting for us in the parking lot when we pass through the mystical door. We barely make it inside before the heavens open and a torrential downpour is upon us. Chesa drives much slower than she did on our previous visit, causing no skid marks in front of my house.

Dante and Francesca go up to my door and explain the situation to JJ as I wait in the car.

I see Dante pass the vial to JJ who disappears into the house. A few minutes later, my mom comes running out, shouting my name.

Tears explode from my eyes and I can't get out of the car fast enough. I run into her arms as we both sob.

The rain is drenching us but neither one of us minds.

"Where have you been?" she asks, wiping tears from her eyes. "And I don't understand why I didn't notice until now? What kind of horrible mother am I?"

I can't lie to my mom anymore. I won't do it.

"It's not your fault," I insist. "Let's go inside and I'll try to explain."

XX
ADJUSTING

We sit around the kitchen table and Mom's drumming her fingers on the wood. JJ brings us both a towel and I wrap mine around my shoulders.

"Ems, what is going on?' Mom demands.

"Do you think I'm a liar?" I ask, feeling guilty for playing this card, because in fact I am.

"Of course not."

"Do you think JJ's a liar?"

"Emma, you know I don't think that," Mom answers in frustration.

"Well, remember that. Because what I'm about to tell you will be hard for you to believe." Mom nods and I continue. "There's more to the world than we've been led to believe. Some of the things in fairy tales actually exist."

Mom huffs, and I hold up my hand.

"Difficult to believe, remember." I wait to see if she's going to protest, but she doesn't so I continue. "There is another world, I don't know if it's parallel to or inside ours and I don't understand the specifics of how it works, but inside there are fairies along with other fantastic creatures. Not the Tinker Bell kind of fairy, but beings that look like us. They have some distinctive features that would stand out to us if we could see them, but there is a magic called glamour—"

"I've read the books JJ reads; I like to know what you all put into your heads. I know all about glamour. Emma, this is ridiculous."

"Mom, I'm being serious."

"She's telling the truth," JJ chimes in.

Mom gets up from the table and walks over to the wall calendar.

"What are you doing?" I ask.

"I must have the date wrong because it has to be April 1st."

"I'm not pulling a prank. Dante and Francesca are fairies. You can't see it, but their ears are pointy and Dante has beautiful translucent wings."

Dante pushes his chair back and moves towards my mother. "Would you do anything for your daughter?" he asks.

"Of course," my mom answers. "But I can't believe this nonsense."

"What if I can prove it to you? Give me sixty seconds."

I give Dante an uncertain glance.

"Fine," Mom agrees, throwing up her arms.

"My apologies, but I don't know another way to do this."

He pulls out a small switchblade from his pocket and before I can stop him, he opens it and cuts a small slice in my mom's hand.

She screams, horrified. "Get out!"

He drops the knife and holds his hands up. "I'll leave after my sixty seconds are up. Just let me see your hand."

"No," she barks, cradling her hand to her chest.

Dante shrugs and puts his hand over my mother's for a few seconds. She struggles against him. "Get away from me and my children, you lunatic."

Dante steps back, releasing her. "Look at your—" Before he can finish his sentence, my mom's mouth drops open.

"How did...? Are those wings?"

He stretches them out and my mother gasps, covering her mouth, then she looks back at her hand.

"The cut...it's gone."

"Dante!" Chesa gasps.

In less than twenty-four hours from his sentencing, Dante has broken the highest fairy law again. He is never going to see his home.

"I healed it. I apologize for the cut, but when I heal, I transfer some of my magic and that allows you to see through the glamour."

Mom is quicker to accept it all than JJ and I were. Dante lets her feel his ears and his wings. She verifies Chesa's ears are pointy as well, and then returns to her seat.

"Okay, finish your story," she instructs me.

It takes a while to tell her everything. But Mom accepts it all. She looks disapprovingly at Dante and Francesca a few times but holds her tongue until I finish.

"So you took away my memories, hid things from me, lied to me?" She looks hurt.

"Mom, I just proved it to you; you wouldn't have believed me," I try rationalizing.

"And Dante, you were just banished for healing JJ. If they find out, they'll never let you go home."

"Don't worry about me, Mrs. Harper."

"I want you both to leave," she orders. "I need time to process all this. And I know you think everything is hunky dory now, but I feel betrayed and you put both my children's lives at risk."

"And saved them!" I exclaim.

"I need some time; I don't think that's unreasonable."

"Of course," Dante agrees. He motions to Francesca and they head for the door.

"I'm coming with you," I say, jumping to my feet. I can't imagine being separated from both Dante and Francesca after all we've been through.

"Absolutely not," Mom says. "You're still a minor and you're not leaving."

"It's alright. Your mom's right, we need to give her time." He leans in and whispers, "Just try. I'll come for you if you need me."

"Ems needs a new phone." Chesa reminds Dante. Mine was taken from me and it's still in her quarters in the purple palace.

"I'll leave one on the front porch. Check in an hour," he promises.

I check the porch every five minutes, even though Dante told me an hour.

Mom has locked herself in her room and JJ's just staring at me. I know I look frantic, like a deer in the headlights, but he doesn't understand.

Once the phone is in my hands, I FaceTime Dante and Francesca, and finally feel like I can breathe again.

"I think it's just going to take us time to trust things are going to be alright," Chesa tells me, almost reading my mind.

"I know...it's just hard. It's easier with you all."

"You should talk to JJ. He has been through something traumatic too. And he hasn't had anyone to talk about it with," Dante suggests.

I know he's right. I also know he's trying to get me off the phone. He wants me to be normal again.

"Alright, I'll try. But you'll answer if I call?" I ask in desperation. Something's broken inside me. Dante said no fairy would ever unclaim someone. I'm not sure if it has ever been done before, but this is why. I wonder if I'll ever feel whole again.

"On the first ring," he promises.

I find JJ has moved up into his room.

"Worst sister award." I raise my hand. I've earned it for many reasons. The last of which being I haven't even checked to see how he's doing. "How are you?"

He shrugs, and I sit down on the edge of the bed.

"We need to talk about this. The stuff that has happened. I hear it helps; talk therapy is all the rage." I give him a small smile.

"It's too hard," he says. "Besides, look at me. I'm fine. Dante healed me."

"Physically, but in case you hadn't noticed, I'm a little bit of a mess emotionally. It's okay if you are, too," I say.

"What happened to you? I know you didn't tell Mom everything, sparing her from the worst parts."

I sigh and lean back on his bed. "Torture, slavery, having your mind melded with someone else's and then ripped away."

"What? Ems, tell me what happened. All of it," he pleads. "I want to understand all of this. I'm confused. Dante told me Francesca betrayed you, but then you both seem...I don't know, a little Stepford-ish. Like you have Stockholm syndrome or something."

"I think maybe I do. But not in a bad way. I just understand her better."

"But that's wrong. You need help. You bonded with your captor, and what she did was horrible. She betrayed you, me, and her brother."

I can see his anger rising.

"I know," I agree, and my answer calms him. "But she has changed. Chesa realized her mistakes and tried to fix it. She saved us all."

"But we wouldn't have needed saving if she hadn't taken you in the first place."

I don't think that's exactly true, but I don't argue. He needs more time. Maybe he'll never forgive Francesca. He wasn't forced to get to know her as I have.

"All I can say is, I saw inside her mind. I know she's sincere. We grew to love each other. She's my sister now. It may be weird to you, and it might take time to get used to, but even though she is partially to blame, I also know I wouldn't have made it through this without her."

"Have the nightmares started yet? I mean, do you get them? I don't know if I can go to sleep again. When I close my eyes, I'm afraid sleep will bring horrible, terrible dreams, like the one I had last night."

I hadn't dreamed at all last night, the first time since I can remember.

"I've had my share," I reply. "Time will help," I add reassuringly, although I have no idea. The idea of going asleep tonight, alone, terrifies me.

That night I feel hollow and empty. I know I'll have to get used to being alone again, but I'm not ready yet.

I FaceTime with Dante and Francesca on my laptop. Chesa is feeling much the same way I am.

"I never thought unbinding you two would be so difficult, that it would have such an effect on both of you," Dante apologizes.

"How could you have known?" Francesca asks. "No one has ever broken it off once a claiming ceremony took place. Also there was never any record of a relationship between the two. We already shared a connection. Knew each other. I don't think anyone could have expected this."

"I just hate that this morning I felt better, and now, being separated again, I feel worse. I don't know that I can sleep here alone."

"I know what you mean," Francesca agrees. "Perhaps we can leave our computers on. That way at least we're not alone."

That idea did make me feel better.

"Alright, let's try it."

It still took a long time to fall asleep. I hated closing my eyes and feeling nothing but myself.

I know I'm dreaming. I'm back in the fairy realm. I see the ruins of the palace where so much horror took place. I stay far from it, having no desire to relive it. I hear a sound behind me and I spin on my heel.

I jump back, looking for any weapon.

"Stay away from me!" I yell. I can't believe I didn't think about this. Griffin may be imprisoned for life, but he still can travel through dreams.

He holds his hands up and doesn't move towards me. "I just wanted to ask you why you helped me." He looks completely fathomed at the thought.

But I can't trust that it's not a trick. I shake all over, terrified of what he could do to me. I don't have Tiger's Dream anymore. I didn't think I needed it.

I stagger back. "Leave me alone."

"Please just answer me," he says in frustration. He takes a step towards me and I jerk away from him and run.

I run like I've never run before. My feet are bloody and raw, but I won't stop. I can't.

"Emma, wake up!"

I bolt up in bed, shaking and crying. My bedroom is full. JJ and my mom are standing by the doorway and Francesca and Dante are at my side.

"Are you okay? You were shaking and moaning," Dante explains.

"Griffin," I murmur.

"Dreams," Chesa exclaims.

"I didn't think about that." Dante shakes his head. "I'll get more Tiger's Dream. I'm sorry."

"Is that blood?" JJ asks, pointing towards the foot of the bed.

Red is seeping through the comforter. Dante and Francesca jump off the bed and Dante throws the covers off.

The bottoms of my feet are torn up, and before I can even look at them Dante is leaning over them, healing them.

"What is going on?" my mom demands. "How did this happen in her sleep? And how did you know?"

Dante escorts my mom downstairs. I'm not sure if he tells her everything, or how much he shares. JJ puts new sheets on my bed and Francesca brings me into the bathroom to clean up the blood on my feet.

"I can't believe he's still torturing you," Francesca says. "I never should have left you."

"He didn't do that to me," I say, correcting her. "I did that to myself. I got scared and ran. I ran so hard that I tore up my own feet. Griffin didn't touch me. He said he just wanted to know why I helped him. But I can't trust anything he says. I felt helpless and weak." I turn my head, ashamed of how much I let him get to me.

"Anyone would have the same reaction if they'd gone through what you did. I'll let the council know. They will punish him if he bothers you again."

I nod.

"I'm not leaving you tonight. I don't care what your mother says." I squeeze her hand, appreciating her loyalty.

Dante returns and asks us to come downstairs. Apparently, my mom wants to speak to all of us.

JJ, Francesca, and I sit on the couch, while Dante stands behind it, resting a hand on my shoulder. Mom's pacing in front of us, muttering.

"Okay," she says. "I still don't understand all of this, but I'm not going to keep you from seeing Dante and Francesca. Not after tonight. Not after I've seen what can happen to you," she looks at me with tears in her eyes, "when you sleep." She dabs her tears with the hem of her shirt. "But we are going to have rules. Starting with no leaving this world without permission."

I try not to laugh at her first request.

"Second," she continues, "no more lies. Now that I know, I want to be kept in the loop. No hiding things to spare my feelings or leaving things out that you don't think I can handle. I'm the parent. I protect you, not vice versa. There may be more rules to follow as I have more time to think. But for now, the last rule is Francesca can sleep over, but Dante stays on the couch. And only until we get this dream stuff worked out. After that, we have to get back to normal. Even if it's gradual."

She looks to me. "Agreed?"

"I can live with that," I respond.

"JJ?"

"Fine with me," he answers.

"If you'll excuse me, I need to go get some more of that plant I told you about," Dante says.

"Of course," my mom answers. "And thank you. For this, for the healing, and even though I'm still peeved at you for some of this, I do appreciate what you did, telling me or showing me," she amends, "the truth."

The next few weeks I start to feel like I can breathe again. Francesca sleeps in my room with me for the first few nights, then downstairs for several nights, and finally back in her home. The gradual separation makes it easier. It gives me time to trust that I am safe now. And for the emptiness of us basically sharing a conscience to heal.

Dante brings Tiger's Dream for my room, but also plants it in our backyard. Now I'll always have access. I still have vivid dreams, of the past for the most part, but they are mine. Griffin hasn't entered them again.

Mom is becoming more relaxed, and the icy wall she built between her and Dante has begun to thaw.

I don't think she'll ever fully believe that my gift of second sight has nothing to do with him. He didn't force it upon me or trigger it. I think it was just fate.

Now that I'm feeling human again, I have a date with Dante tonight.

He picks me up just before sunset, and we walk to the cliff I met him at once. By the time we arrive, the gorge and surrounding landscape is painted in pinks and oranges.

"Dante," I say as he reaches for my hand, "I want to thank you for being patient with me. I know I haven't quite been myself. Maybe I'll never be. My experience with the Fey changed me."

He starts to open his mouth, but I hold up a finger to his lips.

"But you have to stop risking so much for me."

Dante tilts his head in question.

"Healing my brother was one thing—his life hung in the balance. And as much as I appreciate what you did for my mom, you can't do that anymore. I mean, I love being able to be open and honest with her. If anyone finds out, you'll be banished forever."

The wind blows, and a piece of hair gets stuck in my mouth. Dante reaches forward and carefully moves it back behind my ear, and then caresses my cheek in his hand.

"You don't have to worry about me. I made a deal with the council. I knew it would be too hard to keep all of this from your mother, and I convinced them we owed it to you for all your assistance. So, I got a one-time free pass."

I throw my arms around his neck, relieved he didn't risk losing his home.

He leans forward and whispers in my ear. "You asked me once to go flying at night. Are you still interested?" He kisses me soft and slow down my jawline.

I'm barely able to murmur the word yes, as I'm overwhelmed by the blissful sensation I feel when he's near me.

He kisses my lips once, and then pulls me tight against him, wrapping his arms around my waist. I loop my arms around his neck, feeling his heart beating against my chest.

The stars peek out as Dante lifts us into the air.

There are no words to describe how beautiful it is. I feel safe in his arms, a feeling I don't think I'll ever take for granted again. I hold on to his neck with one hand, while I pull the other one down, touching his cheek. "I've been waiting for the perfect time," I say. "I actually said it once before, right before I thought we were all going to die, but I want you to know, I love you, Dante." It's hard to hold his intense gaze, his eyes glowing yellow in the moonlight, but I do. "I can't imagine my life without you. You are my reason for breathing." I know I sound sappy. I wish I had more poetic-sounding words. But I've never been one for love sonnets.

"I love you too, Emma Harper." He starts to kiss me and then I lose myself in the passion I feel, pulling him closer and kissing him hungrily. Suddenly we're falling.

I gasp, but Dante recovers and we soar back towards land. "Maybe we should finish this with our feet planted on solid earth." He laughs as his cheeks turn pink from embarrassment. "You're a little distracting," he adds. "Just in case you couldn't tell."

Then he kisses me again as our feet find firmer surroundings. And I allow myself to revel in my happiness. Life isn't perfect. I have no idea what the future will hold, if his world will ever truly accept me. If I'll age and he won't or if there's some magic solution out there. I push everything else away. I can figure it out tomorrow. Today I just choose to be happy.

EPILOGUE

Sometimes a curse is not what you think, or rather, something you deem a curse turns out to be an altogether unexpected blessing.

I couldn't imagine anything worse than going blind, and then my eyes were opened. I entered a strange new world. It was scary, terrifying, and painful at times, but I also found love, friendship, and family. Suffering through the darkness brought me a world far richer and more expansive than I ever dreamed.

I'm not sure what the future holds for me. I still have unanswered questions. But I have time to figure things out. I just needed to open my eyes and see what was out there. Tomorrow just might surprise me.

ACKNOWLEDGEMENTS

There are always so many people to thank when you finish a book. First off, I'd like to thank my readers. This is my first time writing a stand-alone novel. It's a little bit different fitting a story into one book instead of multiple books. Hopefully, you enjoyed *Opened.* I may try this again. It was fun.

Thank you to my beta readers, Emma Robbins, Dawn Potter, Casey Bell, and Lynndel Laherty.

Always many thanks to my editor, Courtney Johansson, who polishes my manuscript and saves me from looking like a fool. My grammar is atrocious. For this fact, I never thought I could become a writer. But finding a talented, patient editor changed everything. So if you're lost like me and can't place a comma to save your life or you have no idea what to do with a semicolon, don't give up. Everyone has unique talents. Team up with someone who has strengths where you have weaknesses.

As always, thank you for taking the time to read one of my novels. If you enjoyed it, please go leave a review. Check out my other series and look me up on social media.

I love to hear from readers.

Connect with me at:

www.thepamperedcatpress.net

authorstsanchez@hotmail.com.

Blog: www.authorstsanchez.blogspot.com.

 Don't forget to sign up for my newsletter while you're there!

Twitter: @authorstsanchez

Facebook: facebook.com/authors.t.sanchez/

Goodreads:

goodreads.com/author/show/16847543.S_T_Sanchez

Instagram: @thekeeperarchives/

About the Author

Sarah Sanchez has always been a fantasy fan. There are no limits to fantasy beyond one's own imagination. She was born and raised in Texas, where she continues to live with her husband, Armando, three kids, a cat, and a dog. When she's not coming up with her next story idea, she loves baking, spending time outdoors, and trying out new restaurants. She is also a huge movie buff and enjoys anything from Harry Potter to Pride and Prejudice. Be sure to check out her other books!

Coming Soon

Shadow Locked

Winter 2023